DARK HOUR

DARK HOUR

SERPENT MOON TRILOGY

BOOK ONE

GINGER GARRETT

NAVPRESS®

BRINGING TRUTH TO LIFE

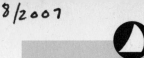

J
Gar.

C. 1

8/2007

NavPress
P.O. Box 35001
Colorado Springs, Colorado 80935

ISBN 1-57683-869-2

Cover design by Kirk DouPonce, dogeareddesign.com
Cover photo by Stephen Gardner, shootpw.com
Author photo by donsparksphotography.com
Creative Team: Terry Behimer, Erin Healy, Jeff Gerke, Arvid Wallen, Darla Hightower,
    Pat Reinheimer

Unless otherwise identified, all Scripture quotations in this publication are taken from the HOLY BIBLE: NEW INTERNATIONAL VERSION® (NIV®). Copyright © 1973, 1978, 1984 by International Bible Society. Used by permission of Zondervan Publishing House. All rights reserved. Other versions include: the *New American Standard Bible* (NASB), © The Lockman Foundation 1960, 1962, 1963, 1968, 1971, 1972, 1973, 1975, 1977, 1995.

Published in association with the literary agency of Alive Communications, Inc., 7680 Goddard Street, Suite 200, Colorado Springs, CO 80920 (www.alivecommunications.com).

Library of Congress Cataloging-in-Publication Data

Garrett, Ginger, 1968-
  Dark hour / by Ginger Garrett.
    p. cm. -- (Serpent moon trilogy ; bk. 1)
  ISBN 1-57683-869-2
1. Jezebel, Queen, consort of Ahab, King of Israel--Fiction. 2.
Bible. O.T.--History of Biblical events--Fiction. 3. Israel--Kings and
rulers--Fiction. 4. Religious fiction. I. Title. II. Series: Garrett,
Ginger, 1968- Serpent moon trilogy ; bk 1.
  PS3607.A769D37 2006
  813'.6--dc22

                        2006009603

Printed in the United States of America

1 2 3 4 5 6 7 8 9 10 / 10 09 08 07 06

FOR A FREE CATALOG OF NAVPRESS BOOKS & BIBLE STUDIES,
CALL 1-800-366-7788 (USA) OR 1-800-839-4769 (CANADA)

Based on the story told in
2 Chronicles 21–23.

Royal Families in DARK HOUR

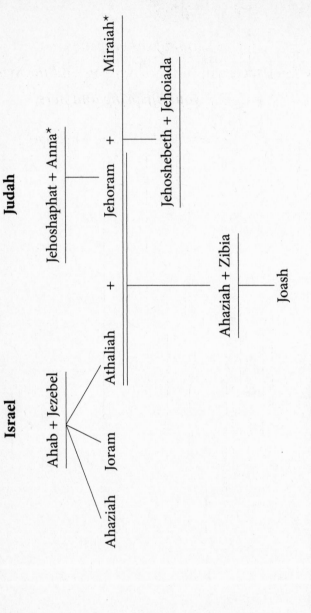

Israel

Judah

Ahab + Jezebel

Ahaziah   Joram   Athaliah   +   Jehoshaphat + Anna*

Jehoram   +   Miraiah*

Ahaziah + Zibia   Jehoshebeth + Jehoiada

Joash

*Note that the Scriptures do not give the names of these two women.

GOD told the serpent . . .
"I'm declaring war between you and the Woman,
between your offspring and hers."

Genesis 3:14-15, The Message

LONG AGO, in the days of King David, the tribes of Israel were united as one nation. David's son Solomon ascended the throne and built a temple for God and a palace for himself, both in Jerusalem. The tribes remained at peace with each other. But Solomon's son Rehoboam had none of his father's wisdom and vision. When he took the throne, the kingdom was immediately and bitterly divided. Ten tribes tore away to create the nation of Israel in the north. The tribes of Judah and Benjamin remained in the south. They became known as the House of David in the kingdom of Judah.

Over the years, war broke out many times between the kingdoms. The house of David had the prized temple, the focal point of the nations' shared religion. The wealthy northern tribes of Israel built trade relations with the mighty Phoenicians by their King Ahab's marriage to the Phoenician princess Jezebel. Both nations were surrounded by hostile armies, however, and at times rose up together in battle.

But the real war between all nations was an ideological

one, for when the tribes of Israel had first taken the Promised Land, they were commanded by God to expunge all those who worshiped other gods. This they did not do, although they clung to their own religion, strange and new to other nations, a religion that claimed there was but one God who chose to remain unseen, who was angered by any representation of Himself in clay or gold. Like the hundreds of other gods in the land, He demanded sacrifices and worship. Unlike the others, He would share none of His power or glory, not even with gods and kings. He could install and remove rulers as He pleased, and to this end, He had promised the people that in Judah, a light from the house of David would always shine. The promise meant that a king descended from David would always reign. Future generations would understand this as a promise of the Messiah, a descendant of David who would save the people for eternity.

This God who made such extravagant promises was to be called *Yahweh*, the great "I Am." He would let no one see His face, but He demanded all of their hearts. And yet He was a loving God, caring for anyone who sought refuge with Him. But as the house of David fell into complacency, assured by the promise of a covenant with this God who was like no other, a foreign woman slipped quietly onto the stage. She loved the old gods best and was bent on reclaiming glory for herself alone.

Palace of Judah, 868 BC

HER DARK robe swept the floor behind her as the servants clung to the wall to avoid touching her. A pile of rejected amulets and broken clay goddesses lay outside a thick linen curtain.

"How long has she labored?" Athaliah demanded of a servant girl who would not look up. The wife of the future king noticed the girl trembling and felt a glow of satisfaction. The men in her husband's court did not tremble — yet.

An older servant stepped between Athaliah and the girl.

"My Royal One, I heard her first cry in the darkness of morning, in the third watch. She begs for a midwife who worships Yahweh. She refuses your healers."

Athaliah stared at each servant and narrowed her eyes. "Leave us. If she refuses a healer, she shall not be healed. The people of Yahweh have despised my line; I will not suffer a new generation taught to bite and snap."

The servants fled down the hall. Athaliah smiled to see their haste, then she swept back the heavy linens sheltering her enemy.

Miraiah was standing, grasping onto the edge of the window for support. Her pale face glistened and she grimaced as a contraction took her breath. A servant was motioning for her to be seated on the stone birthing stool. A plain, framed bed and a little table swept clean were the only furniture in the room. All the items brought by Athaliah's priests had been tossed outside by Miraiah.

The servant pressed her hands together as if she were praying, then shook them at Miraiah. "You cannot stop the labor! This child is coming! You will not be attended by a midwife from your people! It is too late! Athaliah has won!"

"That snake! Would a man crush her like one!" Miraiah spat. She opened her mouth to take another great ragged breath and saw Athaliah. Athaliah watched fear seize Miraiah's muscles as her mouth opened. The servant's back, which was to Athaliah, stiffened, but she did not turn around.

"Athaliah is the wife who will be queen!" the servant said too loudly. "You are a lesser wife who will never rule. You've been at her throat since she got here!" The servant turned and feigned surprise. She bowed and scurried from the room. "Please call if you need anything, my Royal One."

Athaliah let the servant pass and then approached Miraiah. Miraiah pressed her back against the wall.

"How naive men are," Athaliah crooned, edging closer still, "thinking their many wives are content to live as sisters. Our secret lives would surely shock their gentle hearts, and yet you cry out for such a man to save you. What man has ever saved a woman who deserved to live, Miraiah? Show me your strength, my sister. Make me tremble at your fierce will to see this child born."

Wailing incantations of an ashipu healer rose beyond the

curtains. He pleaded with the underworld to cease the struggle and permit the child to be born.

"I would rather die alone in the sight of my God than submit to your sorceries," Miraiah said.

"How strange you Hebrews are, giving such allegiance to an invisible God and refusing the assistance I offer." Athaliah shook her head and settled herself on the edge of the bed. Miraiah exhaled and tried to move back to the support of the window ledge, but a contraction hit and she groaned.

"Be reasonable, my sister, and we will make our peace. For too long you have smeared my name among the other wives and poisoned my husband against me when you were in his bed. Now I have favor only in my son's eyes. Let us make our peace in this room and perhaps, if your words find me in a forgiving mood, I will call a Hebrew midwife for you. We could even send for your mother, if she's done in the market."

Miraiah curled her hands into fists and lunged toward Athaliah, but a contraction caught her midstep. Falling to her knees, she pressed one hand beneath her belly and moaned.

Athaliah grinned. "I'll wait for your answer."

An hour stretched on as Athaliah made herself comfortable on the bed, sampling the grapes left on a tray with a watery wine. She had never liked this birthing room and was thankful she had been here only one other time. The room was too plain, and old blood that could not be cleansed from the wood floorboards produced a musty smell. And in this room, the wives gave birth. No sound pierced her ears so terribly as that of a newborn male.

She took pleasure in seeing the pains break over Miraiah's body in unrelenting waves. The Hebrew crawled a few feet in between contractions, trying to get to the stone birthing stool in the center of the room. A fever came upon her, slowing her progress, and she sprawled on the floor, gasping. Athaliah watched as her face grew hot and red and her head lolled from side to side between contractions. Blood came, but no child.

"When the child is born, I will withdraw my offer of peace," Athaliah said as she examined her hands. Riddled with veins, they were the only feature she was not proud of. Her hair was thick and black like the midnight sea, her skin as clear and smooth as a river stone. She was a woman crafted by moon and tide; her body's curves called out and receded in perfect proportion, and she followed the rise and fall of her flesh with admiring eyes. An air of perpetual dampness clung to her, as if she was never free from the waters that birthed her, as if they returned every hour to draw her back into the depths. Her eyes, however, were a perfect shade of green, the green of earth, not sea, the green that promises a lush spring bloom to those who were patient enough to see her secrets pried open.

She licked a ring on her finger and rubbed it vigorously against her robes, then held it to the light and examined it once more. "If it is a boy, I will call down curses on you both. I will depart and send no one in for you. We will see whose god is stronger then."

Miraiah spoke a soft rush of words Athaliah could not understand. She swung herself off the bed and leaned closer to Miraiah, who was clinging to the birthing stool, her wet red face resting on the cool stone.

"Yes, speak once more," Athaliah urged. "I may yet forgive."

"My mothers, the mothers of Israel!" Miraiah strained. "Rachel, Sarah! You are beautiful. I will . . . I will cross to you. But no . . . I must do this. Do not go! Wait for me!"

Athaliah frowned and jerked her head back. She glanced at

the door. Seeing no one, she wished now she had not sent all the servants away.

Miraiah's outstretched hand tried to touch her vision, but with a cry she pulled her hand back and turned her face away, moving to all fours and roaring with each push.

"The child will be born in this world, not the next!" she gasped. Tears ran down her face, mixing with the spittle running from her mouth. The child came forth in a sudden rush of blood and fluid as Miraiah screamed. It took its first breath and let out a rattling cry.

Miraiah collapsed, laughing, turning onto her back and trying to pull the infant to her breast. Rivers of blood ran in all directions. Miraiah's eyes fluttered as she lost her hold on the baby.

The Hebrew was going to die.

Athaliah realized her own body was trembling. She tried to steady herself and call a servant, but a living Presence moved into the room and silenced her. She watched as the hairs along her arms stood straight up, and the hairs unseen everywhere on her body raised as well. Her breath stopped and terror overwhelmed her; perhaps, if she looked out of the corner of her eye, she would see the God Miraiah had called. She bit her lip until blood flowed and forced herself to look, but there was nothing.

When she turned her head back, she screamed. Miraiah was standing, though there was no blood left in her body. Her arms were outstretched and she wore a strange smile. She seemed to see what stood next to Athaliah. She moved like a puppet, her lifeless body animated only a moment longer by her spirit, which was breaking free.

Miraiah's head snapped to look at Athaliah, and Athaliah could see there was no life in the eyes any longer, yet something there saw her. She screamed again and stumbled backward. Something brushed against her arm as if to steady her and she screamed once more, swatting the air, climbing onto the bed.

"This child will be your doom." Athaliah heard Miraiah's voice, though her mouth did not move. "He is near." The body collapsed into a pile. In that moment Athaliah thought she heard the sound of laughter, of distant sisters speaking a tongue she did not know.

The Presence was gone.

Athaliah shook and began to heave, vomiting over the side of the bed. The silence of the room was marked only by her ragged breath. She wiped her mouth and forced herself to look at Miraiah's corpse.

"You died from the birth," Athaliah said. "I did not cause this."

She could see the infant shaking, lying on its back in the cooling pool of blood. Miraiah's hand had come to rest low on its stomach. No one would know it had been born alive. Athaliah reached for it, her hands just like her mother's. She saw her mother's thick-veined hands, recalled the thousand nights her mother had reached for an infant just before its death at Asherah's temple.

"I cannot." She moaned and turned her face away.

It began to cry, and Athaliah heard a footstep outside the hall. Someone was creeping near. She looked from the entrance to the child, whose cries were growing louder and more indignant.

In a panic, she scooped up the child. Its cord was still attached, smeared with birthwax and blood. The placenta was stuck under Miraiah's body. Athaliah lowered herself to the floor, trying not to touch Miraiah's body, kicking at it with one foot as she held the squirming infant.

"I need a servant! Quickly! Help us!" she screamed.

The linens swept aside at once and Miraiah's loyal servant entered. She looked at her mistress lying dead and Athaliah clutching the infant.

"The stupid woman refused all offers of assistance," Athaliah said. "I stayed with her but could be of no help. She lost too much blood. Call a nursemaid for the child."

The servant ran from the room and Athaliah could hear her shouting to the other servants for help.

Her mind raced but could find no way that Miraiah's death would harm her claim to the throne. If Athaliah told the tale well, would she not be the heroine of the story? Could she not benefit from this turn of events? This wet infant, its tiny eyes now squeezed shut and hands curled into the weakest of fists, was no threat. Not now. It could be dealt with later.

A nursemaid entered, followed by two of Miraiah's servants peering over the nursemaid's shoulder to see if their beloved mistress was really dead. Athaliah looked at the three faces, then handed the baby to the nurse, wanting them all to see how grateful she was to wipe the sad tears from her eyes at last. The nursemaid took the baby and scooped up its placenta, turning her back to Athaliah. She dipped a cloth in the basin of water in the room and she began wiping the blood and yellow waxen coating from the child. She tended to the cord and then removed a bag of salt and rubbed the baby with it as it cried.

"We both knew she was dying, but she didn't want any help. She said she was ready for death, glad to be free of a husband she despised. I swore then to love this child as my own. In this way we two women at last made our peace," Athaliah said.

The servants' chins trembled, and Athaliah had to swallow back her smile as tears welled in their eyes. They had all loved

Miraiah. The nursemaid turned back now, uncovering her breast to let the child nurse.

In this calm moment, Athaliah understood it was a girl. She laughed; she couldn't help it. She covered her mouth with her hands and tried to keep her shoulders from shaking as she willed herself to stop.

She knew Miraiah's maids were staring at her, condemnation in their expressions overcoming their shock. She swallowed hard and spoke.

"I'm sorry. The grief was simply too much for me for a moment and I lost myself. It hit me, all at once, that Miraiah is dead and I have another child I must raise."

The servant girls nodded, looking at each other once and then away from her, and they began to move, calling for men to carry the corpse away and arguing under their breath about which one would clean the blood. The nursemaid watched them all but did not speak.

Athaliah held up her hand. "Do not clean the blood yet. Call Jagur to me."

No one moved.

"Do not be afraid," Athaliah said. The servant closest to the door called the hated name down the dark passageway. Each remained still, even when they heard the weight of his feet pound the cedar planks of the hall and the terrible sound of iron against iron as his dagger swept against his sword, both worn over his back in a leather brace.

His hair was black, slicked back across his head but ending in long curls down his back. Swollen veins ran between taut rises of muscle and sinew. His eyes were rimmed with black kohl, a thick long line stretching out to the hairline, so that his darting eyes looked like rats scurrying in an unlit room.

He walked past them and bowed before Athaliah. He did not raise himself until she spoke.

She pointed to the two servant girls.

"Kill them both."

Athaliah pushed the nursemaid from the room and let the linens fall behind her as she heard the first sweep of the sword.

She shoved the nursemaid along the hall until they were near the children's quarters.

"You may nurse this child, but it will never be said again that she was Miraiah's, or I will kill you too. I will blot her name from this place forever."

The nursemaid held the child and tried to reply, but she was breathing too hard. Athaliah saw her ribs heaving under her robes, and the woman's fear pleased her immensely.

"There is nothing to fear if you obey," Athaliah said, stroking her cheek. "I am as generous as I am vengeful and will repay you many times over for your loyalty. Yes, I will repay anyone many times over for what they do."

"But Prince Jehoram," the nursemaid whimpered. "He will always know."

"The truth is, Miraiah never loved him. I entered as she died and saw her servants stealing from her warm body, ripping the rings from her fingers and the gold from her neck. They watched as she died, refusing to call a healer, circling like jackals as she weakened. Jagur killed them in their dishonor, and it would be this child's heartbreak to know her mother was so despised and so full of hate for her father. For the child's sake, her name must never be spoken again."

"Yes," the nursemaid replied, her voice more steady. "Yes, her mother was despised."

Athaliah walked away.

"My Royal One?" the nurse called.

Athaliah turned and raised an eyebrow.

"What shall we call her? In our land, the mothers name the child."

Athaliah paused, then a name came to her, flashing in her mind from some forgotten conversation.

"She will be called Jehoshebeth, daughter of Jehoram, the future king."

The nursemaid nodded and retreated into her unlit room.

Athaliah walked back to her chambers, a sigh working its way through her.

"A girl." She laughed once more.

CHAPTER ONE

Fifteen Years Later

HER BARU, the priest of divination, opened the goatskin bag and spread the wet liver along the floor, leaving a path of blood as he worked. Retrieving a wooden board and pegs from his other satchel, the satchel that held the knives and charms, he placed pegs in the board according to where the liver was marked by fat and disease. He turned the black liver over, revealing a ragged abscess.

Athaliah covered her mouth and nose with her hands to ward off the smell but would not turn away.

"Worms," her sorcerer said, not looking up. He placed more pegs in the board before he stopped, and his breath caught.

A freezing wind touched them, though they were in the heart of the palace in the heat of the afternoon. Athaliah cursed this cold thing that had found her again and watched the sorcerer search for the source of the chill before he returned to the divination. There was no source of wind here; in her chamber there was a bed, the table where her servants applied her cosmetics from ornate and lovely jars shaped like animals, a limestone toilet, and in the farthest corner so that no one at the chamber door would see it, her shrine. Statues of Baal, the storm god, and the great goddess Asherah, who called all life into being, stood among the panting lions carved from ivory and the oil lamps that burned at all hours. Here she placed her offerings of incense and oil, and here she whispered to the icy thing as it worshiped alongside her.

The baru watched as the flames in the shrine swayed, the chill moving among the gods. The flames stayed at an angle until one began to burn the face of Asherah. Her painted face began to melt, first her eyes running black and then her mouth flowing red. He gasped and stood.

"I must return to the city."

Athaliah stood, blocking him from his satchel.

"What does the liver say?"

"It is not good that I have come. We will work another day."

She did not move. He glanced at the door. Guards with sharp swords were posted outside.

"A dead king still rules here. You set yourself against him and are damned."

Athaliah sighed. "You speak of David."

The baru nodded and bent closer so no other thing would hear his whisper. "There is a prophecy about him, that one from the house of David will always reign in Judah. His light will never die."

"I fear no man, dead or living."

The baru continued to whisper, fear pushing into his eyes, making them wide. "It is not the man you must fear. It is his God."

Athaliah bit her lip and considered his words. She wished he didn't tremble. It was such a burden to comfort a man.

"Yes, this God. It is this God who troubles us. Perhaps I can make an offering to Him. You must instruct me. Stay, my friend, stay." She patted him on the arm, detesting his clammy flesh. "I have dreamed," she confessed. "I have a message from this God, and I must know how to answer Him."

The baru took a step back, shaking his head. "What is this dream?"

"A man," Athaliah said.

"Tell me."

"At night, when I sleep and the moon blankets my chamber, I see a man. He is not as we are: he is coarse and wild. He wears skins hewn from savage beasts, run round his waist with careless thought, and in his mind he is always running, ax in hand, running. I feel his thoughts, his mind churning with unrest, and he knows mine completely. I hear a burning whisper from heaven and shut up my ears, but he turns to the sound. A great hand touches him, sealing him for what lies ahead, and speaks a name I cannot hear, a calling to one yet to be. I try to strike this man, but all goes red, blankets of red washing down."

She licked her lips and waited, breathing hard. The baru nodded.

"You see the prophet of Yahweh, Elijah, who plagues your mother."

The baru began to reach for his goatskin sack. He picked up the liver and put it in the sack, keeping an eye on the door as he wiped his bloody hand on his robes. She knew he was measuring his steps in his mind, thinking only of freedom from here, and from her.

Athaliah grabbed his arm. "I let those who worship Yahweh live in peace. They mean nothing to me; what is one God in a land of so many? Why would this God send a man to make war on my mother and then claim me also?"

The baru narrowed his eyes. "This God is not like the others."

"How can we be free of Him?"

The baru thought for a moment then reached into his satchel. He pulled out a handful of teeth and tossed them on the ground at her feet. She did not move.

He squatted and read them, probing them with a shaking finger. She watched as the hair along his neck rose, and goose bumps popped all along his skin. The cold thing had wrapped itself tightly around him. She could see his breath.

"There is a child," he said. "The eye of Yahweh is upon this child, always. I must counsel you to find this child and kill it, for when it is gone, Yahweh would trouble you no more."

Athaliah murmured and ran her teeth over her lips, biting and dragging the skin as her thoughts worked back in time. "It is my daughter you speak of. Only a girl. But even so, I cannot kill her yet. I would lose my rights as the most favored wife. I will not risk my crown for so small a prize. No, I will find another way to get rid of her, and I will deal with this threat from Yahweh as I must."

Athaliah walked to her shrine and cleaned the face of Asherah. She could hear the baru scooping the teeth back into the bag. She turned with a sly smile, pleased that her mind worked so quickly even with the cold thing so near.

"My mother has already angered this God. We will let her have our problem. She has a talent for these things."

He had finished putting everything back into his two sacks and edged toward the door. She wondered if he would return. He was the best she had at divining dreams and saw in the liver so many answers. She sighed and tried to think of a word to reassure him.

"A farmer may own the field," she began, "but much work is done before a harvest is even planted. Stones are removed, weeds are torn free. We must break loose the soil and uproot our enemies so the field will be ready. On that day I will sow richly."

He managed a weak smile.

"Let your appetite grow, my friend," she coaxed. "The harvest is coming."

He fled so quickly she knew her words had been wasted, as all words were on frightened men. He would never return.

PRINCE JEHORAM nursed a silver bowl of dark wine and wished the business of inheriting a kingdom did not involve so much listening. He rubbed his beard, its thick clinging brown curls now flecked with gray. His beard was weathering his age better than the hair on his head, he realized, which had already surrendered to the assault of time, great gray streaks overtaking the brown. He knew his face was kind, though, not hardened or roughened by his years, but retaining a boyish appeal in his wry mouth and a small scar just under his left eye. Any woman could look upon him and see the child of mischief he once was. All women looked upon him and still thought to correct him.

He dined in a dim, private room with his advisers. The room was adjacent to the throne room, where he would one day rule, and was bare, save for an oil lamp on a low table. Cedar beams topped the limestone walls, giving the palace a sweet, smoky scent under the afternoon sun. The men sat around the table, scattered with maps, sharing a lunch of grapes, bread, wine, and cheese. Normally they would eat more, and in the dining hall, but the kitchen servants were busy preparing for the great send-off feast and it was easier to be served here.

Tomorrow, his father, King Jehoshaphat, would lead Judah's army north toward Israel and King Ahab. Together, the two kingdoms would fight their inconstant friend Ben-Hadad to end his trade monopolies. Ben-Hadad fought alongside them against the cruel Assyrians but turned often and claimed the richest of trade cities for himself.

"There are implications, my prince," Ethan said. Ethan was the tallest, and his skin turned red when he was angry, which was often. His temper had plagued him since he and the prince were boys, but now Jehoram no longer found pleasure in goading his friend. "If the kings succeed at Ramoth-Gilead against Ben-Hadad," Ethan continued, "and the proposed alliance is accepted, your father will have obligations both to the north and south. In this way, Ahab's kingdom will be strengthened by this victory, and your own kingdom will be compromised. Judah may weaken and fall at last to a king of Israel."

"I have married the daughter of Ahab," Jehoram replied. "I have given their daughter an heir and promised her the crown. I have curried the favor of the north well enough. They will not turn on me, for their own daughter is at my side." He tried to entertain himself with the food and wine while his advisers prattled on. He wondered what would be served at the feast tonight. If the servants' exhausted expressions were any indication, the spread would be remarkable.

"That is true, my friend," Ethan said. "But you are wrong to think this is Ahab's war. It is a woman who is shaping this new world. Think on this: What does the powerful Jezebel desire more than to bring glory to her own name? She wants the north and south reunited so that she may one day rule them both, a queen equal in power to Solomon."

Ethan smirked as he continued. "Everyone knows Ahab wears the crown but Jezebel rules. With Ahab and Jehoshaphat together in battle, their voices silenced for a time, Jezebel will be listening for yours. Let her know a lion roars in Judah. We will never be ruled by a woman, especially one who hides behind her husband's crown."

Jehoram listened, running his tongue across his lips, catching a spot of wine resting just above his lip. Ethan was his truest friend, if a man about to wear the crown had one, but he was always ready for a fight. Jehoram preferred to suffer a blow and stay with his women and wine. He sighed. "Ethan, you look into darkness and see monsters, but I see only shadows. It has always been this way."

Ethan frowned. "We are no longer children hunting with our fathers at night. Listen to me, for I am the voice of God in your ear."

Jehoram turned his face away and crossed his arms. Then he sighed and reached for a bowl of grapes and began to eat. He did not like an empty stomach.

Another adviser bit into some cheese and leaned in. "Mighty Ethan is right. Jezebel wants to see you on the throne because of your union with her daughter Athaliah, but she is no ally. Listen to what I tell you: Something evil here stirs the water and watches."

"These voices of doom!" Jehoram yelled, slapping his bowl down on the table so that it spilled. "These voices and whispers, will they not cease?" He gripped his head and glared at the men. Each had but one wife and thought to advise him on his many? "You warn me against women, even my own wife, but they are women and nothing more!"

Ethan scooted closer to him. "Do not play the fool. Athaliah practices her strange magic and you slip under her spell little by little. There is still time to save yourself, and the kingdom, if you are indeed a man and king."

Jehoram rose and adjusted his robe around his shoulders, staring down at Ethan.

"Do even my friends turn against me now?" he asked.

"I have always been like a brother to you. I desire nothing but your good," Ethan said, rising. Jehoram held his temper and the two men glared at each other, breathing hard.

The adviser Ornat spoke. "May I address the future king of Judah?"

Jehoram nodded and sat, returning to his grapes. He glanced at Ethan and shook his head.

Ornat was new to his inner circle, an adviser Athaliah had recommended for his influence among the people who did not worship the God of Judah. She promised his voice would balance the harsh messages the others always gave. He had long, straight gray hair that always hung as if he had just come in from the rain. A magnificent bump crowned his nose, but it was the only remarkable feature about the man, a man who looked as if he were melting before their eyes.

"Good Jehoram," Ornat began, "the king knows you are a son who is not like the father. King Jehoshaphat has conspired with your brothers to ensure you never take the throne. They plot behind closed doors, taking their meals without you. I have heard the plans from my spies among the servants."

Jehoram felt his stomach churn at the accusation. He would not allow such ridiculous talk and raised his hand to dismiss the man at once.

The arrival of Athaliah interrupted them, and all bowed as she entered.

"Jehoram, I seek your face with a burden on my heart. Hear

me and help me, my lord and husband," she said.

Jehoram looked at her a moment, his eyes having trouble adjusting to the light that streamed in when the door had opened. She stirred something in him, as she had from her first night in the palace, rain-soaked and announced by thunder, her sheer robes clinging to her tiny frame. She came bearing boxes of shrines and gods, like the dolls of a child, and she clung to them even in their bedchamber. She was the only wife who did not submit to his will, and he had found her exotic. Now she had grown, but his exotic pet was still wild, shaking off the customs and manners he tried to teach her. He knew she hungered, but not for him. His face burned with shame.

"Speak, Athaliah," he said.

"Your daughter has grown quite pale of late. I have seen this sickness before."

Jehoram sat up straight. Sickness in the palace would spread rapidly, a threat as swift and fierce as any Assyrian.

"What sickness?" he demanded.

Athaliah smiled at him, then at the men reclining.

"Of course you do not understand," she said. "You are men. You have tended your kingdom well but neglected to see that your daughter has come of age."

Jehoram exhaled and sat back, an indulgent smile on his lips.

"And what remedy does this sickness crave?" he asked.

Athaliah bowed before Jehoram. "She must marry, my lord."

Jehoram waved his hand, a broad gesture. Here he could be master.

"I command, then, that she be married. If there is a commander well thought of, it would be an honor to give a daughter in marriage just before a battle."

Athaliah nodded, just once. He felt his victory slipping away.

"I have sent word to the north," Athaliah said, "to my mother's house, that a nobleman from my own home who serves in the ivory palace of my mother be given her. King Ahab has sent you his favorite daughter." She smiled. "Now let us send ours to him. It will be good for Jehoshebeth to hold your name ever before my father, Ahab. And Jezebel would relish a grand-daughter so near."

Jehoram stopped and frowned. "It is Jehoshebeth you speak of? She is a special child to me. I would not have her sent north."

"But you have given the order that she be married. There is no one else worthy of her," Athaliah said.

Jehoram rubbed his chin and pretended to study a map. Finally, he shook his head. "I must think on this."

Athaliah bowed low, her eyes closed. "May the God you serve bless all your decisions, good Jehoram," she said. She straightened and looked at the advisers. Jehoram could not bear to see their eyes upon his bride, the only territory he owned and could not rule. He detected secrets moving between her and Ornat like a sudden spring bubbling up from a dark source. Only a few found it distasteful and turned away. Ethan was the first to scowl and return his glance to the prince.

"I will see you all at the feast tonight," Athaliah said as she left. She wagged a finger at Ornat. "Take care of my good husband."

Jehoram slouched in his seat and returned to his grapes.

CHAPTER TWO

JEHOSHEBETH WAS still in bed late in the morning, sleep having taunted her but stayed at arm's length all night, again. Nights such as these had been too many of late. The noises she once loved had turned sour and her imagination did her no favors. The palace sat at the far end of the city, with the city walls running behind it to separate it from invaders. Last night she had dreamed of these walls in that half-hearted way when eyes will not open but sleep will not descend. She could hear the wind screaming, raising itself against them, and dreamed it was the sound of the dead armies who had once fought King David. His son Solomon once slept in a room not far from her own. What had he dreamed of when those winds cried out?

And the wolves, the wolves had howled too on this night, mourning the walls that barred them from empty streets and butchered lambs hanging low and unguarded in dwellings. She wondered what else they spoke of in that unsearchable tongue, the voice of the wild. She rolled over and tried to shut her ears, but still they called.

Even in the latest hours of the night, noises rippled through the palace, noises she heard but did not dwell on: the voices of servants, of council arguments (doused well with beer by this hour and never resolved), of fires beaten out and embers combed in preparation for baking breakfast cakes. She had loved these noises as a child and allowed them to comfort her, wrapping herself tighter in her bedclothes as she drifted into sweet, unsilent sleep.

Yet last night the noises grated on her. Fights that had nothing to do with beer, curses and cries from those who stole down the halls, paces of the old ones who checked on the sun's arrival and prayed too loudly.

When she rose at last, her maids brought her the polished bronze mirror and began combing her hair. Her face looked tired, her eyes swollen as if she had wept. She sighed as they lifted the pitcher of heated water and waited. She rose and allowed them to remove her linen robe, then stood in the center of a large shallow basin. They poured the water over her weary limbs, scrubbing her with a soap made from ashes, and rinsed again. They applied oil to her face and body, rubbing it in and scenting her with perfume along her neck and hairline.

When they began dressing her at last, she wondered why they took such pains to curl her hair and set it with jewels.

JEHOSHEBETH EMERGED hours later from her chambers in a blue robe that fell gracefully around her and a fringed black shawl draped over one shoulder. It set off the brown hair that hung in thick curls, pinned back behind each ear by a jeweled comb. The blue of the robe softened her brown eyes and invited those near her to let their gazes linger a moment longer. It is true her servants said she was lovely, but what servant would not say this to her mistress? Jehoshebeth knew only this: she was neither tall nor short, too full or too thin. She had never seen herself through anyone's eyes but her own, and to herself she seemed unremarkable.

Her servants had chosen a necklace made from turquoise beads and fat hammered-gold circles, with long gold earrings that brushed her shoulders. They had taken care to paint her face, mixing fat into the precious pigments imported from the Egyptian cosmetics dealers, deep reds for her full lips and brilliant greens for her eyelids. She wondered if her father would be pleased when he saw her. She knew her mother would not. Athaliah hated seeing her in jewels and cosmetics and made sure she was rarely invited to the feasts that called for these accessories.

Jehoshebeth did not begrudge her mother this discourtesy. She understood. Her mother had always been protective. She cherished her daughter too dearly, although she never had the words for it. That was why Jehoshebeth was rarely allowed into the city, even with many escorts, and why Athaliah did not like putting her on display before the men of the palace. Athaliah had told her many times a jewel's value increased when it was withheld, and one day she would be thankful her mother had taken such pains to protect her.

Jehoshebeth had been schooled in several arts as a daughter of the future king, but it was in this subject, the study of her mother, that she excelled. No one understood Athaliah like she did. She saw that her mother worshiped many gods and was rebuked by those who insisted there was but One. Her mother loved one man but shared him with many, the other wives and advisers and nobles who claimed his time and affection. The numbers were never in Athaliah's favor. If Athaliah was lacking in the extravagance of maternal affection that the other mothers showed their daughters, it was only because she suffered such injustice and was made numb at times. She truly had no choice but to spend such energy on Ahaziah, Jehoshebeth's brother, for one day Ahaziah would rule.

Jehoshebeth emerged from her chamber for the feast and was not surprised to see her guard, Midian, on the evening watch outside her room, although he had been there throughout the previous night and into the morning hours as well. She knew he loved to escort her to the feasts when she wore her jewels and had been freshly adorned by the servants. He was her servant, yet she always felt as if he kept her for his amusement, considering the way he smiled at her and laughed when she scolded a servant for following too close and tripping on her robe. But at night, when she sensed her maids drifting to sleep and at last none watched her, on the best nights she dreamed of Midian.

He had been with her since she was a child, and even then she adored his perfect black hair, which curled around his neck, and his dark eyes, which said so many things to her. He was not so much older than she but had always seemed so immovable and certain, as the landscape beyond her window. He was her north, and she found each day that she measured her steps until she could return to him.

He bowed low, keeping a hand on his sword. He led her and her servants down the hall and to the banquet but did not enter the hall, instead taking his post outside the entry. He would be fed with the other servants later, after all inside had eaten the best portions and picked through the food.

Low tables, hundreds of them, filled the hall. Each was crowded with spiced wines, fruits, and sticks of cinnamon floating in the tops of the bowls. Marbled slices of nutmeg sent their pungent sweetness across the room, making everyone tilt their chins upward as if to inhale more of the smell. Ornamental rugs woven with precious gold threads and tied off with tassels surrounded every table for the men to recline on.

Smiles began to play across all the faces at the sight of such foods. Servants emerged from the kitchens carrying meats still smoking from the fires, their crusts blackened in places, the fat sizzling and popping. Breads, hoisted up into browned globes by the sour yeast kept bubbling in the kitchen, were laid in clusters on every table. Plates were filled with cheeses, and pots of bubbling juices to seep the breads in were set alongside them. On every table, small rosebuds sprang to life, unraveling and blossoming before their eyes. All who saw them clapped and praised the cooks. It was a small trick they had learned from Damascus, this presentation of rosebuds that could be forced to bloom by the warmth of a fresh meal.

Jehoshebeth moved to the table set aside for her brother and herself, as children of the highest wife, Athaliah. Her brother Ahaziah would join the feast but she did not know when. Ahaziah was likely drinking with the cooks below or matching his archery skills against a guard's in the courtyard. He had won his sister many trinkets this way, though she always discreetly returned these by hanging them on a post outside her chamber, so that the soldier could anonymously reclaim them and his honor.

The hall was filling with royals, nobles, and the commanders of the armies, who made their way in from the House of the Forest of Lebanon, a reception hall Solomon had built of sixty towering cedar posts. Guests claimed to feel lost in a forest until a royal guard escorted them through to the wonderland of Solomon's palace.

She watched the nobles and commanders survey the unmarried daughters from across the room and nod to each other with appraising eyes. She knew her mother wished the children of the lesser wives gone, for every child gave that mother claim on her husband. Ordinarily, only a great man could take the daughter of a king, but perhaps now a daughter could be had for a lesser price. Bargains could be made in this palace tonight if a man knew how to approach Athaliah. Jehoshebeth looked at her half sisters seated nearby, giggling and stealing bites of food before the feast began, and she felt sorry for them. Their birth condemned them to a smaller life, with fewer jewels, less honor, and her mother's displeasure. They probably did not even realize Athaliah would use this evening to get rid of as many of them as possible. It was just as well, Jehoshebeth realized. Some of them were pretty, and it would be best to have them gone before she was of the age to marry.

The trumpets sounded and all turned as King Jehoshaphat entered. Jehoram, his firstborn, entered next, followed by Athaliah, then her son and his heir, Ahaziah. Ahaziah would stand for the ceremony behind King Jehoshaphat and Jehoram. Jehoshebeth caught Ahaziah's eye, and he returned her glance with a funny, pompous expression as he adjusted his royal mantle around his neck. Jehoshebeth giggled and bowed her head. A large couch was at the head of the hall, flanked by gold chairs. Jehoshaphat reclined on the couch with some assistance. Jehoram and Ahaziah took the closest chairs, then they were joined by Jehoshaphat's other sons. Jehoshebeth grinned at the men. Ever since she was a child, she believed no men could be as valiant and handsome as these. They all had Jehoshaphat's eyes, kind eyes, with wrinkles that rose like rivers when they laughed. The brothers had been close, always, but the arguments she heard between them some nights made her uneasy. Someone was stirring the brothers against her father. Poor Athaliah, she thought, another battle she must confront for her husband. Jehoram relied on her judgment so often; she would no doubt protect him from their petty complaints.

The commanders of the armies banged their bowls on the wood tables, making a low thunder in the hall. They chanted "Hail, Jehoshaphat, the conquering king!"

King Jehoshaphat enjoyed their display for a few minutes, then raised his hands to silence them. It took a few moments to bring everyone back to silent attention. Clearly, a few commanders had begun their feasting and drinking hours ago.

"Queen Anna sends her greetings and love to the people tonight. She is unwell and begs your prayers and your pardon that she cannot bid you good evening herself."

The people nodded gravely to each other. Jehoshebeth frowned at the news; many credited Jehoshaphat's good reign to Queen Anna's quiet and gentle wisdom. But these days she seemed to grow sick more often, and the servants' whispers grew more urgent.

"We have much business tonight," the king said. "Tomorrow we go to war."

The commanders shouted and a few banged on the tables again, but the bowls had been quickly filled with wine, and not many men would risk spilling any. King Jehoshaphat motioned for the royals near him to sit, and they did.

"I am growing older," King Jehoshaphat continued, "and these feasts make it hard for me to be heard throughout the room. My second son, Zechariah, who rides with me into battle tomorrow, will address you first."

Zechariah rose. "Tomorrow my brothers and I ride with the

good men of Judah, and with our father, to reclaim Ramoth-Gilead. My father requests that our oldest brother, Jehoram, come forth and bow before the throne."

Jehoram stood. His newest adviser, Ornat, gave him his arm for support and whispered to him with a sour expression.

"Jehoram, you are charged by the crown to give hear and receive your father's will. Let all who bear arms for Judah witness what is about to be done."

Everyone in the hall fell silent, even the drunk ones, as Jehoram bowed, his face at his father's feet.

"In my son," King Jehoshaphat said, rising to be heard more plainly, "I have found a good and constant man. He was willing to go to war, but I asked him to stay. He would never allow Judah to fall into dishonor, yet he himself is willing to be humbled before us today. Because he trusts in my commands, I can trust this son to rule. I give him my blessing as the co-regent king of Judah. All hail Jehoram, and swear allegiance to the man who will rule alone when I am gone!"

Everyone in the hall cried out blessings of goodwill, and Jehoshaphat motioned Jehoram to rise. Jehoshebeth saw her father's face was red, and she wanted to go to him to ask what troubled him, what thing Ornat had whispered. She knew she had inherited this much from her mother, if not her pale skin: She loved her father too much at times and often forgot protocol when it was most needed. She wished to run to him, to see what she might do to soften his wrinkled brow. But tonight he was not her father. Tonight he belonged to Judah.

A heavy gold chair with roaring lions at the base of each leg was carried out by four servants and placed next to the king's couch for Jehoram. He caught Jehoshebeth's eye as he sat, and both smiled broadly at the other. She thought he looked every bit of a king and was relieved that he had smiled. She began to relax, feeling the tension draining from her neck and shoulders, and knew this feast would be a good one. She never tasted food when she was nervous; it all was the same bland, sticking stuff. But now she could eat, and it was a fine night for that. The cooks had surpassed every feast in memory. She reached for a dip of curds and shallots and spied a bowl of fresh flatbread to begin with.

The king motioned for Zechariah to continue.

"We are honored tonight by the arrival of a noble of the house of Ahab, a Greek known for his wisdom in trade and commerce. He is so valued in the house of Ahab that the king has given him royal quarters there, and he is regarded as one with that great house. He was sent to us to teach us how we may exploit the trade routes with Ramoth-Gilead, but we were surprised and delighted to learn he seeks a wife."

Athaliah clapped her hands and rose uninvited.

"Surely one of our own daughters will catch the eye of the great merchant Philosar and live a life of spoiled courtesies in the palace of Ahab and Jezebel!" Athaliah said.

Athaliah caught Jehoshebeth's eye, and both smiled. Jehoshebeth nodded. *Well done.*

The catcalls from the commanders were deafening, and the younger daughters elbowed each other playfully.

Jehoshebeth saw Athaliah looking at her again, making a small motion with her fingers to the man from Ahab's house. Following Athaliah's gaze, he saw her, his eyes appraising her quickly, assessing the value of her frame and features. This man had spent his life measuring worth and counting coins. His eyes were narrow and his nose blunted, perhaps pressed too close to his writings for too many nights. He hunched over his wine as if to guard it. His chin dipped in a curt nod, and Jehoshebeth watched as the man gave Athaliah several gold coins, clasping her hands to mark the exchange. She felt the blood drain from her arms and dropped the bowl of flatbread she held.

The deal had been struck before anyone even finished their first bowl of wine. She gasped for air, coughing. A maid tried to offer her wine. Jehoshebeth pushed it away, trying to inhale between coughs. A maid slapped her on the back, and Jehoshebeth got her first full breath.

When the man turned to speak with Athaliah, Jehoshebeth excused herself from the table, holding out her hands to prevent her maids from following. "I am only going to the window for air," she said. "You can watch me from here." The maids and the guards standing near her, seeing she was restored, shrugged, unwilling to miss any more announcements if she had no need of them.

As soon as Jehoshebeth reached the window, she ran. She ran out, down the stairs, through the cedar forest of Solomon's hall, and out into the garden of the courtyard, not pausing for breath until she reached the main palace gate. The soldiers posted near it struggled to hide their bowls of wine and resume their positions as she ran to them. She eyed their drinks and the abandoned posts, then held her finger to her lips. They agreed to the bargain with a sigh of relief and turned away.

The main road that led down into the City of David from the palace would be well traveled tonight, so she chose another path, a narrow route west of the palace that she once had spied the guards using. It was rocky, with limestones jutting up here and there from the ground. She picked her way through them as fast as she could, cursing the thin leather of her sandals. Her breath came in hard gasps as her legs took long strides, and she stumbled a few times over the stones until she reached a cluster of trees. Her throat burned, both from the running and her tears. Her feet stung.

She began to climb. The branches scratched her skin and snagged her robes, but she didn't shield herself as she went higher and higher. Each of the branches was a little pair of claws trying to force her back, and she was strengthened to hear them break and give way to her will. A few limbs from the top, she rested and began to cry.

The tree shook with the weight of another person. As she looked down through the branches, she saw him following her, climbing more gracefully and avoiding the little limbs that had fought her.

"Midian!" she gasped.

Midian hoisted himself near her. "I saw you run. I knew you wouldn't be fast, you wore such heavy robes tonight."

She gripped the branch she sat on. It was strange to have him so near, and all to herself. She felt the flush of stinging nerves, her body betraying her romantic, childish thoughts by making her tremble and turn red.

He seated himself on a nearby branch and looked at her.

"My mother promised me to a noble from Ahab's house." She did not know what reaction she hoped for.

Midian nodded, not meeting her eyes. "The servants talk. Some knew it was coming, though no one knew much."

"You knew?" she said, her voice higher and louder, "You said nothing to me?"

He waved for her to be quiet, looking around to be sure they were undetected.

"Jehoshebeth," he chided, "what could I say? You are a royal."

"Is that why you followed me?" she asked. "Because I am a royal?"

He turned away. They sat in silence. He had betrayed her by keeping this secret, but she began to feel she was the guilty one, making them both suffer with her open accusation.

She tried to laugh.

"I will not go. Did you see him? Every coil of his hair is dressed with oil, and his robe is more elaborate than mine!"

"He's from Greece."

"He's odd. Imagine me, married to that fussy old man, who probably smells of garlic and stinks up the bed."

Midian laughed and nearly slipped from the tree. Jehoshebeth steadied him, her hand shooting out and catching his arm. It was the first time she had ever touched him. His skin was different from her own, which was bathed and oiled every morning. It was coarse, and warm, and she could feel the muscles under her palm. She looked at him, handsome in the fading light, green leaves and budding boughs highlighting the tanned planes of his skin. He watched her as she studied him.

She blushed and turned away to the scene beyond them. His eyes followed hers, taking in the view. When he saw, he exhaled and grabbed her hand to drag her down from her perch. "Get down from there or we'll both be killed! Now!"

She bumped and scraped too fast down the tree and frowned at him when she righted herself next to him on the ground.

"Look what you've done to me!" Her robe was torn and red scratches ruined her arms. The tree had won after all.

Midian took her by the arm and pulled her away. "Never, never spy on Yahweh's Temple. You must never go near it."

"The entire city looks up at it every day! Why should I not, Midian? Does not my father worship Yahweh?"

"Is your mother not Athaliah? She forbids you to worship his God." Midian frowned then and stopped her in the path, looking around once more to be sure they were alone. He released her arm.

"Jehoshebeth, will you oppose your marriage to Ahab's noble?"

She nodded and tried to keep her eyes on his face. Something unspoken passed between them.

"There are secrets trapped within those palace walls, names that have not been spoken in years. If you refuse your mother, everything will change. The dead will find their voices, and she will become a woman you don't know. You will be in danger."

She took a step back.

"Promise me you'll always trust me."

Her heart beat faster and she was embarrassed.

"I promise," she replied.

"Give me then this one night to seal the good thing between us, so no matter what lies are told, we will know the other is true."

When she nodded, he reached down, taking her hand in his, and moved through the trees to find the path back down. They walked, her mind searching for little things to talk about, but she was dumbfounded by the combined wonder of this first freedom and his attention.

He followed the winding turns as they moved past the palace, past the citadel, into the heart of the city. Numerous buildings huddled in groups all looked the same to her, but Midian picked his way through them until he came to one wedged between a dying oak tree and the city wall. Together they stood before a weathered wooden door. It did not look to be faring any better than the tree. Midian knocked and a woman answered, staring at them with a harsh frown. He bowed, calling her by name, and her frown turned to a grin. She opened the door wide to him.

They passed through, and Jehoshebeth saw they had entered a secret market. It was the market for the Hebrews, Midian said, the ones who did not worship the idols Athaliah pushed upon the people. The finest fruits of the land were brought here, sheltered from those who hated the God who provided it. Everyone was careful not to draw the attention of the world outside as they entered, but in here, they let their carefully hemmed words unravel and spoke freely of Yahweh. Jehoshebeth listened with fascination; how could one god rule two worlds: heaven and earth, body and spirit? He sent death and blessed life, closed wombs and delighted in children? It made no sense. The many gods of her mother each had but one purpose and each would hear but one prayer. This God of the Hebrews was vast and unpredictable; if He would not show His face, how could a worshiper know Him?

Jehoshebeth studied His faithful followers, considered each deep line of their faces and their worn robes. She gasped when she saw a child, its jaw slack, spit running down its chin, resting in a wide basket lined with blankets. His mother stroked his head as she waited on a customer. None such as this would have been allowed in her mother's palace. Jehoshebeth tried to harden her heart, but she could not. Sorrow flared into anger. What kind of God would do nothing about this child?

She saw the people laughing and embracing and stopping with grins to wipe the dirty cheeks of children. Women carried jars on their heads as they moved between stalls, and they looked beautiful to her, though their hair was uncombed and they had no oil on their faces. She watched a mother lead her young daughter around the tables, showing her to the women and boasting about her charms. Jehoshebeth felt she shouldn't watch more and turned away. She did not like seeing the children unafraid to grasp their mothers' hands or beg to be picked up, or the mothers who stopped to listen to their children and offer a tender word. These were people at peace with their God and each other. Jehoshebeth felt her childhood coming undone, like a tightly bound scroll breaking its cords and unfurling.

Midian held her hand again then, turning her away from the women. With no language between them save for the roughened palms of his hands warming her own, he led her deeper in to the hidden vendors who supplied what the palace would never buy: the rarest apples fed with water brought from Mount Carmel, smug and gold; raisins soaked in wine, their slippery skins beckoning like a whispered secret; warm cakes from a wheat ground for hours into a fine white powder.

She blushed when he took a raisin soaked in wine and placed it in her mouth. His eyes never left her face as he watched her tasting wine made away from the shadows of the palace.

The juice stained her lips, and she drew them in to taste it. He raised an eyebrow slightly and smiled. He pulled her to himself and tasted her lips. She had never kissed a man before. His lips were salty, a hint of the wine-soaked raisins lingering. His hands steadied her when she leaned against him, unable to taste love and stand.

When she opened her eyes, an old woman was staring at her and began to rise from her bench. Midian saw it too and shoved Jehoshebeth, hard, pushing her through the vendors until they reached the door and were permitted exit. He would not tell her what had caused his fear despite her urging on their return to the palace. From the distance they could see the torches still burning high and hear the singers and musicians. It was still early in the evening, and the merchant Philosar would be looking for her.

"Let us not return until the feast is over. Show me something else in my city. Show me the Temple," she said.

"No."

"You could die for kissing me, for taking me through the streets like a commoner. One more offense will mean nothing," she argued.

"You do not know what you ask," he said.

"And you do not know what you refuse!" she snapped. "I want to hear their prayers, to see how they approach this God."

Midian sighed. "All right. One look, then you return to the palace and keep this secret between us."

Jehoshebeth nodded and took his hand. He led her between clusters of mud buildings, up dirt streets made smooth by many feet, following a winding path that led them around the palace. She saw the Temple rising above them on a narrow one-way street, but he moved her to another path.

"This is where the priests live," he whispered. "A staircase spirals up from the complex. It affords the best view of the Temple."

He led her into a dark hall lined by the priests' private quarters. Jehoshebeth pressed into him and felt safe. She felt her anger departing, felt it lift slowly and with reluctance, like a fat carrion bird abandoning its food. She breathed the damp air. They climbed the staircase undetected and opened a door that led to the roof of the chambers. The roof itself looked to be made of a straw-and-mud plaster, but it held firm under her feet everywhere she tested it. Here she could see the City of David and beyond. The sun was stealing away like the good servant it was, slipping quietly into the horizon. Its last red rays made the white stones of the city glow and the Temple's gold dome burn. Finally, she could see what had been hidden from her for so long.

"Such beauty," she sighed. She had so rarely been allowed beyond the palace grounds.

In the center courtyard of the Temple, she could see great bulls of bronze bearing a giant basin of water on their backs. The priests had to carefully climb narrow stairs to the stone altar, where blood pooled and a nearby spring continually washed it away. Beyond this courtyard was the Temple itself, standing behind two great pillars each cast from a single piece of bronze, etched along the sides and opening toward the heavens at the peaks.

It was magnificent, more beautiful than the palace. The gods her mother worshiped were serviced more humbly, on stone altars beneath trees, or in shrines tucked into a corner of the home. They were not so grand.

She leaned against Midian and he put his arms around her, kissing her hair as they watched the priests in the courtyard begin circling a younger member.

The priests encompassed a single man, who kneeled in submission. They sang, their voices deep like the waters of the first ocean, the hiding place of the unsearchable things. Another ring of men surrounded the first, musicians with instruments of many kinds. These were played as the priests waved their arms toward the sky, circling the man, their steps counted and moving in a pattern rather than a straight path.

Praise the LORD.
Praise God in his sanctuary;
Praise him in his mighty heavens.
Praise him for his acts of power;
Praise him for his surpassing greatness.
Let everything that has breath praise the LORD.
Praise the LORD.

"What are they doing to him?" Jehoshebeth asked.

Midian watched but did not answer.

"What is it, Midian?" Jehoshebeth asked again, but her attention moved to a man who approached the group from the steps of the Temple. The man wore long, washed linen robes with a sash of bright blue at his waist and a gold vest with stones set in the breastplate. Each stone was several inches across and a different color. He moved with dignity through the priests until he reached the kneeling man, who rose to face him. Together they walked toward the basin of water carried by the twelve bronze bulls.

The man who had kneeled removed his plain robe and stood nearly bare before the other.

Jehoshebeth's gaze went to the blood-stained altar, still burning with the last sacrifice of flesh, then back to the man. She gripped the arm of Midian and closed her eyes.

"Oh, no. Forgive me for not speaking sooner," he said, laughing. "Have no fear. The man robed in ornaments and gold is the high priest; he is about to welcome the other into the company of the priests."

"What then?" she asked.

"Nothing to fear, Jehoshebeth. The younger man will go in peace and live and serve in the Temple like all the others. The man's name is Jehoiada; many in the village have talked of this day. His father is the high priest now, the one who is ordaining him. Jehoiada will become the high priest one day himself."

Jehoiada bowed his head, and the high priest dipped his hands in water, pouring it over Jehoiada's head until the ground became a spreading shadow beneath him. Jehoiada, washed now, stood with his arms out. Jehoshebeth stopped breathing and heard the pounding of her pulse in her ears. Jehoiada had the appearance of a man formed in the midnight fires of the ironsmiths, his body too forcefully made to attend to the delicate matters of a God. His muscles were stretched tightly across his tall, full frame, and his long brown hair drew her eyes from his square jaw to his broad shoulders.

Jehoshebeth wondered why this man looked as if he could wage war when his destiny was only prayer and offerings. How inconstant this God of the Hebrews seemed. Her mind returned to the broken child in the market. Why did these people pray to one God who seemed to have so many different answers?

Two other priests brought robes and dressed Jehoiada. He looked to the sky, his lips moving, but Jehoshebeth could catch no sound. She was transfixed.

Jehoiada turned his face as if to look at her full on. She shrank back into Midian's arms, knowing the priest had seen her. She knew he saw her, even at this distance, even across the roof's walls. She could see his gaze trained on her hiding place. She could not pull back, though she wanted to. She was held.

The men's low, deep chants swept over the new priest, praise and prayer rising and falling like a tide. The high priest embraced his son and placed his hand on Jehoiada's head to give a blessing. Jehoiada bent to receive the will of his father.

Midian's tug on her arm pulled her back. "We must go, and run, for the priests will soon be returning to their chambers. No one can know we were here."

They fled down the spiral staircase back to the courtyard and through the door into the dusk. Together they ran down the main path toward the palace. Jehoshebeth felt the tilted world beneath her, but Midian was with her, constant and stable.

"Enter through the main gate and go through the garden," he instructed, "and I will circle round and use the Horse Gate by the stables." Jehoshebeth nodded and he left her. She inhaled for strength, steadying her nerves, and walked toward her gate.

"Jehoshebeth." She turned. "A good thing has happened today, has it not? For a brief time, we were free together."

She could not find the words to answer. Midian ran toward his gate and vanished in the darkness.

CHAPTER THREE

ATHALIAH RAN her hand over the ivory box that once contained her mother's hair combs. She had left the feast early, relieved at last of the burden of Jehoshebeth. It was too delicious a moment to share with the others who could never understand. She replayed Jehoshebeth's pained expression when the deal was struck, and Athaliah felt satisfaction to wound her daughter at last. She was only doing what a good mother would do by arranging a marriage; how could anyone fault her? Jehoshebeth's pain was sweeter than the wine they drank, and Athaliah's mouth watered to taste it again in her mind.

Her servants dressed her for bed and left. She was alone now as she studied the old treasure. Ivory was interspersed with black onyx stones, and the pattern held her eye as her hand ran back and forth across the cover. It is the wine, she told herself, it is the wine that summons these memories. She could hear her mother's voice from the place in her mind that held these terrors captive.

And the goddess, great in the palace, fair of face,
Crowned with glorious feathered plumes, mistress of pleasure,
May she live forever and always.
In her name we sacrifice this child.

A shudder shook Athaliah and her chin pressed into her chest. Memories came fast. Jezebel stood before her, eyes unblinking like a snake's. She was stroking Athaliah's hair as the servants prepared the girl's bedchamber. The sun outside dipped into the Great Sea.

"Shall I tell you of the great queen of Egypt, my darling? Shh, now, yes, let me tell the tale, daughter."

Athaliah tried to squirm away, but Jezebel seized her arms.

"Once a great queen ruled the world," Jezebel said. "She was beautiful, a rare gift from the gods to the mud people who baked their bricks and ground their wheat and lived without meaning or purpose. Like us, she had a long, graceful neck, with elegant black arches over her eyes and lips stained the color of a red sky before a storm. Yet no one knew the tribe she came from, if she was born royal or common, but she held the throne as no other woman had ever done. She would not sit at the feet of a man, nor give her body to the crown with nothing but mewing children as her reward. She reigned as a goddess and changed the course of the world. She was the first true queen, one who ruled and damned and broke and built. Nefertiti saw the future, and the future came to her as a woman."

Athaliah willed her mind to escape, down the dark hallways to another part of the palace where the servants cared for other children, where women did not bear such burdens, but Jezebel pinched her to keep her present.

"Do not wander, my child. I will finish our tale."

Jezebel held Athaliah by the arm. "In her land she was troubled by the priests of another religion. Their time was gone, but they would not concede, would not bow to the goddess in their midst. She offered them life, peace between gods at war, but Athaliah, what do you think they did?"

The girl made no response.

"They came at night and killed her. Afraid of this strange power a woman could wield in the courts, they slit open her veins and fed her to the beasts of the river. Yes, men try to master us by blood, but who knows a life of blood like a woman?" Jezebel's voice grew higher and sharper.

"Her tomb had stood prepared, ready for years to receive her. She would become more powerful in death, surrounded by the magic buried with her, amulets and offerings to the underworld. King Osiris, the king of the underworld, would meet her, and she knew her beauty would not fail her even in death. But this they denied her, feeding her to the animals in bits. She never arrived in the underworld, her spirit lost forever among the bulrushes of the Nile.

"Even now she is not fully dead, though she will never live again. She will never know the reward of her labors or see the punishment of her foes. Nefertiti speaks to me in my dreams and shows me that much work is ahead, dark days as we, too, face the stubborn priests of another religion who will not give sway. But we will listen to the voice of our dead sister, and she warns us to not repeat her mistake."

Athaliah tried to remain very still and wait for the end of the story. Jezebel turned her gently to face her mother. "Tonight, my child, I must know what is in your heart and if you have the will to do what Nefertiti could not. I must know if you have the will to conquer and destroy the world of men. For I would rather you die by my hand here tonight than by the hands of a man later."

Jezebel took an oil lamp from her table and held it under her daughter's face. Athaliah began to tremble, her eyes darting from the flame to her mother's eyes.

"And so I must ask you, my child, will you be queen?" Jezebel said.

Athaliah gasped, a small, quick breath.

Jezebel screamed. "Will you be queen?" The flame singed the delicate hairs around Athaliah's eyebrow. Athaliah whimpered and could not find her voice. She squirmed harder in her mother's grip, but Jezebel held her so tightly she felt her arm snap.

"*Will you be queen?*"

"Yes, Mother!" Athaliah screamed back, weeping. Jezebel threw the lamp onto the floor and seized the girl by the shoulders, her words coming in a rush.

"When I die you must do two things. Kill all who opposed me in life that they may never find me in the underworld, and promise me I will be buried immediately and only in the tomb I have prepared. I will be reborn as the red dragon men will fear even when the earth melts away. But the beautiful one who rules the dark place of cinders and lightning tells me I must destroy those priests who offend him. I swear to you, the days ahead will be filled with the blood of the prophets who call curses upon me."

The walls seemed to fall away, as if only Athaliah and Jezebel stood together in a land of dark ash and soot. Her mother's words came from a great distance, and the biting darkness grew heavier and thicker, choking Athaliah until she fainted into the flames at her mother's feet.

A voice outside her chamber door brought her mind back

to the present. Athaliah looked down and realized she had knocked over a lamp from its stand on her table, and the thick green oil had been dripping down her robes, searing her skin where the material parted to reveal her thigh. She wiped the oil off her leg and dabbed her brow with her other hand. She would never rule as her mother did, and she was grateful the other memories had not surfaced, the memories of children dying, the sounds of mothers choking on their grief.

She stood, careful to put the weight on her feet slowly, rolling each foot from heel to toe silently as she crept to her door. Solomon's palace was made from cedar and oak, with limestone supports. Each piece was smoothed and polished on all six sides like her gems, and Athaliah knew every joint in the floor that would betray her if she stepped on it. She was the only wife to have a chamber so near Jehoram. The other wives were housed with the royal children a floor beneath them. But Athaliah was not like the other wives, and after a servant died while serving her on the floor below, no one had opposed her move to the chamber next to Jehoram's.

Athaliah pressed her ear to the heavy door, crouching lions carved into both sides. She pressed her ear to the gap where the aged bronze hinges had begun to separate slightly from the wood. Athaliah knew the voice, and cursed.

It was Jehoshebeth.

"I DESIRE an audience."

She knocked on the door again, glancing aside at Athaliah's door. The lifeless lions frozen there forever stared back, their claws sprung and seeking flesh.

The guard posted outside her father's door stood aside and let her knock without interference. They no longer protested her visits to her father's private chambers. Jehoshebeth paid them for their cooperation, remembering them when she stole cakes from the kitchen at night or found a stash of beer that other guards had secured elsewhere in the palace. The rivalry between the men who guarded the royals and the men who guarded the palace grounds was a rich source of amusement for her, and she never minded stacking the odds in her men's favor.

The heavy door opened into a dark room.

"Why do you seek me?"

Jehoshebeth's eyes focused on a bed in the center of the room. She could barely see his form lying upon it, a beautifully carved frame of oak inlaid with ivory panels. It caught the weak bit of light entering behind her from an oil lamp recessed into the wall. Little else in the room indicated his rank: a simple toilet, made from a plank with a hole in the center, which emptied into a cesspool beneath the palace, a table with an oil lamp, unlit, and a scroll, probably a history of the kings. He had once read this to her at night, and together they had dreamed of what his story would be, what brave deeds would be recorded of his name in the annals of the kings of Judah. But it had all changed, though they never spoke of why. She had begun to dream of other tales also: of love, not wars, and of things that could not be.

But someone must have insinuated these dreams to Athaliah, because Jehoshebeth remembered the night her mother's grip became fierce, cutting into the flesh of her arm as she removed Jehoshebeth from his room. Unnamed bitter thoughts began floating between her and Athaliah, unnamed truths that made her feel shamed, and now these mysteries infected her father as well. She had bathed with vigor the first morning she became aware of their presence but had not felt clean since. Some love or trust had been lost between her and both parents. If only she could understand more of her mother's troubles, of what she had done to disappoint Athaliah, maybe the stain could be cleansed.

But there was no hope, she feared, to restore the breach with her father. The distance between them swelled like a gentle river turned to ice, cracking the soft earth of its banks. Jehoshebeth wished for nothing more than to return to the spring morning they had once known.

Jehoram sat up.

"Why are you not in bed? Where have you been?"

Jehoshebeth held up her hands. She could say nothing without revealing the truth. Midian would surely die before breakfast.

"Please, hear me," she said. "I needed time to summon my courage, to tell you that I do not wish this match."

He sighed. "I do not wish it either. But I need an ally in the north. And if not an ally, a spy."

"I do not understand, Father."

Jehoram motioned her to come near. Jehoshebeth moved closer.

"Athaliah made the match, but it is I who sends you north. This is the decision I have reached here in the darkness."

Jehoram lowered his voice and Jehoshebeth leaned closer in still.

"You can be the wedge I must drive between Jezebel and Athaliah. For Jezebel rules her husband and counsels Athaliah in mastering me. She would make me half a king, serving the kingdom and fighting my queen. I must find a way to break their alliance before it breaks us."

"There is nothing I could do," Jehoshebeth said. "I would be the wife of a merchant, nothing more. It is not a wise match, for your purposes or mine."

"You are so young." He sighed again. "You think this old man in the darkness cannot see. I look at you, with your bright eyes, and know how little is made plain to you."

A noise in the passageway made them both freeze. Jehoshebeth held her breath until her ribs burned, exhaling silently, watching her father's face. He looked to the doorway behind her, but his expression did not change. His shoulders began to relax and he spoke once more, but in a whisper only she could hear.

"Do you not wonder what could make Athaliah happy? She must long to be free of her mother. How many nights have I woken her from screaming, wiped her brow that ran hot with sweat, and heard her hoarse cries of terror as the shadows faded from her mind? She might break alliances if we expose Jezebel here in Judah."

Jehoshebeth crept closer. It was hard to hear his whispers, and he was spilling the secret she sought.

"Jezebel rules by blood. She demands the children of the poor, the nameless women who work without wages and must learn how to survive each day. From all corners of the city she calls them, and from every valley in her kingdom. The forgotten children born to such unlucky women, they are placed in a basket in the temple of Asherah, the great mother. Her fire never dies, and one by one the children are fed to the flames. In this way, Jezebel says her power is complete. It is said that on dark nights a greenish glow surrounds her, like a serpent of air coiling about her face. That is why her streets are always quiet, and the poor no longer fight her, for they are slaves of fear. They are broken and will never rise up, never, until one woman has the strength to hold onto her children, to refuse Jezebel at last. If Jezebel's reign is diminished, her hold on Athaliah will lessen as well. I would have a wife, not just a queen."

Jehoshebeth frowned, thinking on the words.

"Perhaps Jezebel's adversary has not yet been born," Jehoram said. "But you, you are a special child. I have known that from your birth."

"But I cannot marry Philosar."

"If you do not obey me, you will die."

Jehoshebeth's mouth dropped open. "You have never threatened me."

"It is not a threat, my daughter. It is a fact. You and Athaliah will unite in this decision or you will rise against each other. There is no other way among women."

Jehoshebeth put her face in her hands and tried to think of a reasonable excuse to resist. It felt wrong, this going away suddenly. Her father had omitted some important details, but she did not know what.

Jehoram laid back and turned away. "This is the difference between girls and women. Girls believe their love for a man is real; women see that it doesn't matter. When Philosar has finished his business here, you will return to Israel with him."

CHAPTER FOUR

A FULL MONTH passed, marking the time of the Feast of Trumpets, a day for the people of Yahweh to gather and prepare for the Day of Atonement. With Jehoshaphat's blessing, Midian returned to his home for his mother and father and brought them to Jerusalem for the feast.

Philosar was still in Judah, and Jehoshebeth stayed in her room, taking her meals there and praying for a wind of change. Her room was more ornate than her half sisters'. She had a bed with animal-skin blankets and woven throws, a table and chair to make herself comfortable as her maids applied her cosmetics, a toilet made of stone, and a basket filled with jewelry to choose from. The only thing denied her was an altar of her own to worship the goddesses she cared for. Her father had refused this, though he allowed her to give sacrifices at her mother's altar in Athaliah's bedroom. But she could not go and pray there now and wondered if any of those gods would still care for her or act to save her from Philosar.

Philosar passed his time growing richer and met with

many nobles from the kingdom and Jehoram's advisers. When Ramoth-Gilead was secure, it would be a strategic post for the trade route. Philosar had much to say about trade. He was a man of gold, Jehoshebeth muttered to her maids, a man as unyielding as his coins.

Twice Philosar had sent her gifts and tried to woo her from her chambers. She let her maids open the carved ivory boxes and admire the necklaces of strung rubies and anklets of little gold bells that would make a beckoning noise as she walked. The maids found them enchanting; she did not. She returned the jewelry to him without comment, and she did not leave the room. She dreaded each sunset, for it brought her closer to the day when he would demand entry, and what excuse could she give then?

She had sent a servant to fetch raisin cakes from the kitchen and instructed another to place these at the altar of Asherah, which stood in the garden of the palace courtyard, a simple stone altar beneath an oak tree. She must beseech everything and every god that might grant her prayer.

Jehoshebeth grieved Midian's absence. She had grown to love his shadow outside her chamber, grown to love falling asleep to the sound of his voice singing a psalm of their people. But he would return by dawn. Nothing had changed while he was gone, Jehoshebeth realized, except that now she was a prisoner in her room. It would be impossible to get away and be alone with Midian.

No words had been spoken openly between them since the day they spied on the Temple. Still, the night before he left, as she brushed her long rich hair, she heard Midian whisper softly, "Do not be afraid. I will return for you."

Jehoshebeth stopped the brush and felt his words wrapping around her. Her heart felt light as she drew them near her, hugging herself and nodding at the scenes that played out before her in her mind.

But he was gone now, and his absence made it hard to sleep. Twice during the night she bolted upright, fearing she had heard the footsteps of Athaliah's guards approaching to steal her away. The wing of the royal children was quiet, only the sounds of murmured dreams reaching her on occasion, or a few of the younger ones getting up to use the stone seats that let into the cesspools running beneath the palace. She smiled when she heard her youngest half brother. She could tell it was him when he said a harsh word, probably after stubbing his toe on the stone. It was a nightly habit for him.

It's a wonder he still has all his toes, she thought as she sighed. She would remind him again in the morning to stop drinking his juice before the sun set.

Silence returned, and she followed the shadows in her room as the moon moved across the sky, wondering about the man Jehoiada, about the sacrifices offered at the Temple. A vow made there before God could not be broken, she had heard the servants whisper. The women said it was a place of deep magic, where miracles of healing and unexplained blessing took place, where an unseen God heard every prayer.

The moon was still in rule, but she could dress and slip away before the day took its charge back. If she ran, perhaps no one would know she had been gone.

JEHOSHEBETH RAN up the narrow street toward the Temple, her legs burning from the climb as she approached the courtyard gate. A few women milled about, women whose veiled faces made Jehoshebeth uneasy. Men were there too, counting coins as they struck their deals with the women. There was a sorcerer on the street leading to the Temple. Her mother loved these people especially and encouraged their presence in the city. Worshippers convicted of their sin at the Temple often sought easier answers later, answers that gave them permission to enjoy their sin, not destroy it. These worshippers paid well, and some of this money flowed down to the palace later. Athaliah did not mind the distress of her people when it sparkled as a ruby on her finger.

Jehoshebeth would take no chances. Her business was grave and needed the full attention of this God. She would find a priest, perhaps even the high priest she had seen, and make her request known. She was glad she had worn a fat, weighted necklace. Perhaps requests were granted more quickly with gold.

Jehoiada was near the gate, talking with elders from the village, laughing good-naturedly as a wrinkled old man lost the end of a joke and gestured weakly. Jehoiada spotted her but gave no notice to his companions that anything was amiss. He waved his friends off and turned to walk alongside her.

"You approach to make an offering," he said quietly.

"Yes," she replied, looking straight ahead, willing herself to look certain of her business here and not so much like a frightened runaway.

"Are you not a royal? No one else wears a robe such as yours."

Jehoshebeth stopped a moment, startled by his steady tone. She looked down at her robe. She had never thought the gold threads woven into her sash were unusual. She felt foolish that she could not see what marked her so plainly to him. She was grateful her shawl was draped around her shoulders so he would not see her necklace too.

"I am Jehoshebeth, daughter of King Jehoram," Jehoshebeth said.

"He does not know you are here," Jehoiada observed.

"That is not my greatest sin against him," she replied. "As his daughter I must obey him. But I will not. My mother has made a strange, untimely match. My father insists I keep it to serve him. But it is wrong; I know it. Neither will hear me in this, and so I call on one higher to resolve the dispute. I hear your God has magic and listens to all who call on Him."

Jehoiada frowned. "You do not know what you ask," he said, "or the God you seek this answer from. But if you are willing to resist Athaliah in this small matter, then perhaps God is inviting you to a greater battle. Stay here and watch from the courtyard with your shawl covering your face." He motioned her to the place where women had gathered.

Seeing men leaving the Temple gates and coming toward them, he placed his hand on the small of her back. Through her garments she could feel him, as if they were alone in this moment. She did not like the way his touch seared through all the trappings of her life: her robes, her jewels, all that seemed to give her importance.

"Place an offering into the pot and watch from the outer court. I will offer a lamb on your behalf." He pushed her gently in the direction of the court and went through the gate toward the altar.

She held her shawl by her chin, up and over her hair. Few women were veiled, as it was not the custom of the people here, but some foreigners wore theirs, so she did not look out of place. Jehoshebeth, falling in with a group of sisters, moved easily through the people until she reached the offering place, the large pot with a narrow neck and wide base. Discreetly she removed her necklace made from strung gold coins and ivory, and placed it within. The necklace slid into the chamber, and she could hear the coins, one by one, slinking into the darkness and falling upon the coins left by others. She saw a few other women drop in their treasures while the men moved to an inner wall to purchase animals.

Jehoiada himself moved to the center of the main court, along with the other men who had come to present sacrifices. The priest on duty met him and took a lamb from Jehoiada, who looked at Jehoshebeth as he laid his hands on the lamb, repeating the priest's prayer of consecration:

See, O Most High
And may your peace rest on us.

In a slow, gentle motion, the priest brought the knife across the neck of the lamb. Blood fell onto the dusty earth until the lamb closed its eyes and sank, the priest catching it in his arms and laying it across the altar. He touched its young muzzle once, sighing, before the flames rose up and swallowed their prey. The priest walked down the steps of the altar and laid a hand on Jehoiada's bowed body.

It was finished. Jehoshebeth fled from the sight of the lamb and the flames, from the blood spilled for her.

She ran until her legs tired, down the path that ran wide around the palace, turning to run near the open market below. Away from the sight of the sacrifice, she tried to make a prayer to this God who seemed so alive. It was hard to find words; she knew only psalms the servants had sung, and each servant worshiped a different god. In her mother's house, many gods were perched in bedroom shrines, offerings of grain and perfume burning at their feet night and day, yet none ever moved except by man's hand. Here was a God unseen who seemed to move of His own will, watching her sacrifice at the Temple and then finding her here. She felt Him near and thought again of the blood offered in her name.

In the first morning light, she saw that there were no more shadows; night had passed. But she felt different now; she wondered if darkness would ever return. Perhaps this light would warm her forever. She threw off her shawl and drank in the fresh scents of dawn, the wind blowing freely, tumbling between the vendors just setting up their stalls for the day, careening down the warming stones. A bird followed it as if giving chase, and she laughed. To taste peace made her glad to be free of the weight of gold across her neck. How was it possible that she had asked for freedom and instead been lavished with this? She would have to tell her mother she had been wrong, so wrong, about this God.

She saw an old woman then, her quiet, steady eyes watching Jehoshebeth. It was the same old woman who had spotted her in the market with Midian. Her peace turned to unease under the gaze of this woman who watched her but none else. Jehoshebeth took a step back and started to run. Her servants would be looking for her soon, wondering who would dare confess to Athaliah she was missing. She knew their fear would buy her more time, but not enough. A group of women entered the market then, and she tried to get past them as they carried baskets of wares and squirming children, laughing loudly and planning their day. Jehoshebeth elbowed her way through them. The old staring woman stood in front of her now.

"I know you," the old woman said, raising a withered finger and shaking it.

Jehoshebeth put her finger to her mouth. "Shh! Come!" She led the woman by the arm to the edge of the market row.

"You are Miraiah's child," the woman said. Jehoshebeth started to laugh.

"No, Mother, you are wrong. Your eyesight must be poor indeed. I am not the daughter of Miraiah. I have never even heard the name."

"You are the daughter of Miraiah!" the woman snapped. "I am no fool!"

Jehoshebeth leaned in to whisper in her ear.

"I am the daughter of a foreign woman. There is no Miraiah."

The old woman took Jehoshebeth's face in her hands, jerking it too close to her own. Jehoshebeth could smell the woman's breakfast on her breath: dried fish.

"There is no Miraiah, this is true. Athaliah killed her and raised you as her own. Some say there is a prophecy over you, and one day Athaliah will find her reason to kill you too."

Jehoshebeth pulled her face out of the woman's grasp.

"Search your heart," the woman challenged, "and you will know it's true."

"No, no, you are wrong," Jehoshebeth stammered, then turned to run. The woman caught her by the arm, her grasp strong, and with her other hand she ripped her own necklace off and pressed it into Jehoshebeth's other hand.

"What is it?"

"It is your mother's necklace, given to her by your father Jehoram, when he first spied her in this very market, selling pomegranates. He was riding with his men out to a hunt. He gave her this, this necklace that bears the seal of the house of David, the house he would one day rule. He swore to return and claim them both. He did, and she was with child by the time the rains came that season. You are that child."

"That can't be true. My father has many wives; my mother has brought harm to none. And why would she kill this one if she was but a merchant?"

"Your true mother was a powerful woman. She prayed in earnest and God blessed her in all she did. She spoke loudly against the diviners who worked in the markets, against the strange gods Athaliah spilled among the people. They were natural enemies, like an eagle and a crow."

"It is a nursemaid's tale," Jehoshebeth said, shaking her off.

"Not a nursemaid's. A grandmother's." A tear came down the woman's cheek as she reached out to touch Jehoshebeth's face.

Jehoshebeth broke from her and ran.

The morning was late when the servants found Jehoshebeth sitting in the palace gardens, staring at the Asherah altar. The birds had eaten her raisin cakes. Rolling their eyes at this troublesome dreamer, but relieved, the servants called her to forget her unhappiness over her betrothal and come bathe at once, for a messenger from the battle had arrived.

ATHALIAH WAS seated in her chamber. A servant entered, bowing and wishing her blessings in the name of the goddess Asherah.

"A messenger from the battle at Ramoth-Gilead," he said, bowing again.

"Send him in and set a lamp upon the table for more light," Athaliah replied.

The servant returned with an oil lamp and bowed before

making his final exit. The messenger entered next, his clothes dirtied from hard and relentless riding across the countryside.

He took a deep breath. "I do not bring you good news. Will you spare my life? For I have ridden hard with no sleep to bring you this word. May you not falter in your attempt to make your husband, Jehoram, secure. May he reign forever as our king."

Athaliah covered her mouth with her hands clasped together and then reached for him. "I will grant you your life in exchange for this message, my friend and faithful servant. No more blood will be spilled in the name of man's war," she said loudly. The servants in the hall heard. "Shut the door behind you, so we may by modesty protect this secret and your valor," she said.

"Blessed be Athaliah for your mercy. Forgive me for this news: Your father, Ahab, is dead. Your mother, Jezebel, is in deep mourning and your brother ascends the throne under her good care."

Athaliah sat back in her chair, gripping the arms tightly to brace herself. Her brother would feel the weight of his crown but not its full power. It was Jezebel who would keep that, for sons could be swayed more easily than husbands. She was an ally who could not be trusted.

"Our own King Jehoshaphat survives," the man said, "but a prophet of God in the north speaks dark prophecies for the house of Jezebel."

"My mother knows this man," Athaliah nodded. "She will destroy him before he troubles us."

The messenger continued. "Jehoshaphat returns in a day, perhaps two if he has many wounded. Miss not my meaning. Your mother sends word: She has done all she can for the aging king, and she entrusts him to your care now. She says to think on how close you are to the crown."

Athaliah rose and kissed the messenger. "I thank you for

your service in this." He looked away when tears sprang to her eyes. He bowed quickly and exited. Jagur was upon him at once, running a thick blade through the messenger's back, keeping a hand over his mouth.

She walked to her window and stared at the harsh sun piercing the garden below. The evergreens appeared to wilt and brown; unrest disturbed even the soil around the palace.

A knock caught her attention. Philosar approached.

"Yes?" Athaliah groaned.

"My business here draws to an end. I must soon leave, but this girl will not have me. I cannot even call her out from her chambers, and I have already paid for her."

"If she is to be your bride, then learn to master her!"

Philosar's face flamed red, and he exited as Jagur smirked.

JEHOSHEBETH DID not want to hear a report from battle. Whether her grandfather reclaimed a trade route was a petty concern now. She went instead to her bed. Midian had returned and tried to catch her eye as she went past.

She did not look at him, uncertain she had the will to ask the question, but he caught her hand lightly.

"What troubles you?" he asked.

She paused, glancing to make sure none else was near. Reaching deep into her robe, she produced the necklace from the old woman and showed it to him, shadowing it from unseen eyes in the folds of fabric.

He frowned and closed his hand over hers, sealing up the necklace as he pushed her hand back into her robe.

"Put that away. What have you done?"

She saw in his face the answer to her unspoken query.

"You knew," she spat.

She entered her chamber and slammed the door. She refused entrance to all, even her servants. Night fell, but she did not undress, she did not sleep. She curled herself up in the bed, feeling a hollow break open in her spirit, like the trunk of a tree that had rotted and failed the child who placed her weight on a limb. She had been betrayed. Every foundation was suspect, every friend a liar. She tried to think of what she must do, but anger clotted her mind and tears nettled her cheeks, leaving them raw and cold.

The next morning she was startled by a noise. She could hear sounds of women assembling in the palace courtyard, heavy sounds, voices with no laughter.

Jehoshebeth summoned her maid. "What goes on?" she asked.

The maid hesitated before saying, "Queen Anna died last night in her sleep. The women go to bury her."

"Why was I not summoned?" Jehoshebeth asked, her voice too sharp. The girl shrank back.

"Athaliah wishes you to prepare for Jehoshaphat's return. Then you must be ready to journey north."

Jehoshebeth's eyes burned, clenching shut before more tears could spill over. She went to the window, needing the relief of a breeze. She saw clouds coming, carrying thunder, and wondered if Anna would be buried before the storm was unleashed.

ATHALIAH ENTERED her daughter's chamber without knocking and saw her at the window. The mourners' song could still be heard, though it was fading. Athaliah motioned for the maid to leave. Athaliah waited there, at the door, until Jehoshebeth sighed and turned away.

Athaliah saw her jump, saw the expression that swept over her face. But Athaliah was so close to getting rid of Jehoshebeth, it was better to ignore this.

"My father, Ahab, was killed in the battle. Jehoshaphat returns now." She spoke to Jehoshebeth without emotion.

"I am so sorry you have to face his death. Losing a parent must pain you."

"It is how kingdoms are built."

"The deaths are no easier to bear."

Athaliah turned to leave.

"You are forbidden to leave this room unless Philosar escorts you. You will receive him, entertain him at dinner, and go to Israel when he is ready. I will not see you again."

"I want to see my father then."

"But you already did. He approved the marriage."

"And this is how it ends? I slink away with an old merchant I despise, never to return to my home? Why have you done this? You cast me out with no explanation, no warning!" Jehoshebeth heard her voice climbing higher until she was screeching.

Athaliah laughed.

"Clearly you don't know what a desirable ending for you that is."

CHAPTER FIVE

WITHIN THE week, black banners hung low over the palace walls and King Jehoshaphat returned. He turned to one of his men and asked the meaning.

"Why does she grieve this way? It is Israel that has lost her king, not Judah. My son's wife must remember her place." Jehoshaphat was tired from the battle, tired from these confrontations the house of Ahab brought upon itself, even in death. He felt weary all over again thinking of Ahab's daughter sleeping in his palace, nipping at him like a pup who wants to lead the hunt, not content to live fed by another.

TRUMPETS HERALDED the approach of the king. Athaliah and Jehoram stood in the courtyard of the palace to receive him. Jehoram studied the men gathered with them.

"Where is Ethan?" he asked. "Why has he been absent so often from me?"

Athaliah shrugged. "Perhaps he realized the pointlessness of his counsel. I have not seen him for weeks."

JEHOSHAPHAT WATCHED Athaliah smile as he dismounted and was greeted by all. Jehoram kissed his father's furrowed brow and Athaliah kissed his hand, clutching it to her face.

"Welcome, Father, welcome. Peace on your name," they repeated, murmuring it over and over.

"Athaliah, I am sorry your father has lost his life in this vain pursuit of a city," King Jehoshaphat said. "There is much to tell you, Jehoram, of this war. It was not a war between mortals, between men who want roads and cities, but a war against the unseen. Jezebel's name is repeated by the spirits, and it is they who led us into this battle. There never was a city to be conquered."

Athaliah held her forced smile on him but he returned it with a cool glance. He was still looking at her when he spoke to his son.

"Jehoram, remove these banners at once," Jehoshaphat said. "Ahab's name was held above our heads while he was alive; I will not have it done again in his death. We are free of him, and we will now cut cleanly through whatever ties we have made." He continued to stare at Athaliah, who shifted her weight and then bowed her head. He wondered why she smiled, that hidden half smile he had seen too many times since she arrived.

"King Jehoshaphat," she said, "I came here to your palace as a lonely girl and was welcomed by the queen with such generosity and kindness that I loved her as my own mother. It is I who asked these banners to be laid out, yes, but not for Ahab. Forgive me for wounding you, but I must tell you, Queen Anna has died in your absence, her heart broken that you would leave her in her final days for another battle when your kingdom is already so full."

Jehoshaphat felt the blood drain from his face. He turned his eyes to the upper walls and windows of the palace, searching, then back to Jehoram, who nodded with heavy tears rolling free.

"She is gone," he said to his father.

Athaliah took Jehoshaphat's hand and pressed it to her cheek, falling to one knee before him. "I know I am a disappointment to you in many ways; I have none of her goodness or devotion. But I pledge to comfort you in her absence."

King Jehoshaphat remained standing, and a soft rain began to fall. He was unmoved for a long time, his entourage growing wetter and colder, until at last one soul moved forward and carried the fallen king to his chambers.

"KING JEHOSHAPHAT does not leave his bed," Jagur said. "We can do nothing."

"Jagur, if you cannot see the moon rising, do not ask me to point out the stars," Athaliah snapped at him. Her eyes were swollen and red this morning but she had lined them carefully anyway, and in the same way commanded her servants to paint the eyes of her Asherah idol. Her goddesses were often painted to make them seem nearer and alive. Alike now, the women surveyed the men with glittering eyes.

Athaliah reached out and wiped a trace of lip paint from his neck. She herself had not worn lip paint for several days. It was as she suspected last night. Men were redundant in one thing:

Some gave pleasure before betraying her, some only troubled her thoughts, but every man stole her sleep.

Jagur glared at her guards lest they relish the moment. "A true Phoenician charts a course and keeps it."

She slapped Jagur with full force. Blood shot from his nose.

"Do not speak to me again as if I were a mere woman. What I am, you have not yet seen."

She took a step away and looked at the men surrounding her.

"I have charted a course and I will keep it. The king will be dealt with, but not by me. I do not crave the light of men's affections to do my work."

Jagur tried to stop the blood with the hem of his woven belt and made his exit without further conversation.

Athaliah adjusted her necklace, a fat emerald slipping down because of its great weight. It had never sparkled so on Anna's wrinkled neck.

A WEEK LATER Athaliah summoned the wives to meet in private, her guards not present. She presented each of them with gifts and had her own servants attend to their feet and hair, spoiling them with luxuries they had not had for months. She gave them jewelry from the craftsmen in Phoenicia, pins for their hair and rings for their fingers. Baskets of choice fruits were passed around, and the women drank from goblets of pure gold with inset rubies along the rim of each cup.

"Forgive me, my sisters," Athaliah said. "When Queen Anna died and I realized I would soon have her crown, I only then realized what great distance I had let grow between us all. I was wrong to be indifferent to you. I believed you resented me because of my position and the assumption ruined my intentions. Please forgive me, as this is your custom as worshipers of Yahweh, because today I will pay back what I have stolen. Yes, I have fulfilled your own law of old, because I have repaid my debt to you plus some."

No one responded. The lesser wives studied their rings and goblets, and each watched the other to know what to say to the new queen.

"Please, can anyone find it in her heart to love me?" Athaliah asked again. When no one moved, she turned her face away and wiped at her eyes. "Is my sin so great," she pleaded, "that you would set aside the laws of Moses and harbor this enmity between us?"

A younger wife stood and kissed her hand. Athaliah embraced her gratefully, squeezing the young woman's shoulders and kissing her repeatedly on the cheek until both giggled. "What is your name?" she asked.

"Alma," the girl said.

"The first to offer such love will be the first to share in my goodwill," Athaliah proclaimed, motioning for a servant to step forward. The servant clothed the wife in a cloak of finest weave, with emeralds and sapphires trimming the neck, held in place with heavy ropes of gold. The women gasped and the young wife looked pleased to have gambled and won. The other wives kissed Athaliah's hand and were adorned with rich robes, and servants brought trays with more elaborate treasures, oils and perfumes exclusive to Athaliah until then. The women, feeling Athaliah's generous charity now, rubbed their dry and neglected hands and arms and legs with the aromatic creams and tried the perfumes, holding their necks out to each other for smell, and laughing. The mortar of darkness holding the palace stones together was now entirely changed; the women could feel it. This was a rich repentance.

"Let this be a new day between us, sisters. Open your hearts to me and let me tell you how we must care for good King Jehoshaphat," Athaliah began. "He has yet to stir from his chambers, the loss of his queen is so great a blow to him. I have not yet earned his pleasure at seeing me, I know, but I have seen how his face lights up when your children are present. They are the true treasures of your kingdom, wouldn't you agree?"

The women softened again, pleasure rippling through the room to have their children commended by the one who would soon have the throne.

"Now, I confess my intention in bringing you here today is not as it would seem. I asked forgiveness, but I would ask one thing more. Let us dispense with royal tradition, which separates wisdom from youth. Let us be rid of the servants who tend to him so often. Let us surround him with his children. He will recover his spirits, seeing his beloved queen's face echoed so sweetly. What I cannot do to mend his heart, they will."

The plan seemed right to the women, and it was arranged that the children would begin serving the old king his meals and keeping him company in his chambers. Only one daughter was forbidden entry to the king, but she was soon to be out of the palace, and no one objected to her omission. A reluctant, spoiled bride might lower the price of their own daughters.

Everything unfolded just as she said, an easy remedy that blessed them all. Jehoshaphat's grandchildren read to him and spread the blanket over his feet when it shifted and patted his hand if he cried in his sleep. He seemed to be revived, nourished in the presence of his dear grandchildren. His more frequent laughter attested to the possibility that he could yet live with the brokenness of his heart. The women loudly blessed Athaliah for this gentle move, her insight and humble admissions, and felt credited through their own children for this miraculous turn.

PRINCE AHAZIAH wiped the brow of his grandfather, King Jehoshaphat, with a rag steeped in juniper juice, hoping the scent would revive him for an after-dinner game of pegs on the board. He was young and thought old age was a strange and foreign thing that happened in a time before he was born and would never reach him. He pitied the aged king.

The sun had been setting earlier every day and winter was approaching, with its endless rain and clouds. Sometimes, if Ahaziah was lucky enough to escape the palace on a jaunt with the hunting men, he could move into the clouds on top of a distant mountain and, on the rarest days, feel snow landing softly. Hot breath from the horses would melt the snowflakes falling near them, and Ahaziah would laugh to see a horse try to shake off an irritating wet flake that landed inside a nose or eye. Together, the men would hunt and turn back down the mountain only after building a fire near a cave and telling stories to one another.

Ahaziah knew their stories well by now. There was David, the king whose passion both pleased God and disrupted his favor; Noah, the patriarch who had built a boat to save the animals and watched humanity drown; and Enoch, the man who never knew death but was spirited away like the smoke from the campfire, rising and disappearing into the heavens. The world was mystery and adventure, and one day he would lead the charge into this unknown future as the king of Judah. His father, Jehoram, was soon on the throne himself, and Ahaziah would be one step closer to the pleasures of reign. It thrilled him, the thought of the world unbridled and at his feet. Those dreamy adventures of winter were the best kind.

And yet the matter of an heir was already a reality. His mother pressed him to prepare for his reign by presenting her with an heir before he took the throne. She had summoned two wives from Phoenicia, but they were cold women and had produced no children as yet. He had not the heart to try again with another, though Athaliah promised to find women more to his liking. He wondered how any man wished to be alone with a woman and her many complaints. He consoled himself with the thought that wives were meant to please the man, and yet he suspected a better man would be more pleasing and suffer less complaining.

The present king stirred, bringing Ahaziah back to attention. A servant entered with a bowl of soup and bit of roasted lamb, carved for presentation but appreciated by no one; it would have to be minced before the toothless man could eat. Long ago, the king had complained of a toothache and the healers tried to cure him of what they said was surely a worm infestation eating at his gums. In the course of their cure, the king lost the essential teeth. He could smile at the plate set before him but not quite devour it. Ahaziah wondered again at the humilities of age, this upbraiding from life, blows against the pride of youth. Life was a patient, pleasant mistress, but she would slap all who endured her.

King Jehoshaphat sat up, rubbing the spittle from his open mouth with his bedsleeve. He was pleased to see Ahaziah.

"Was I dreaming, Ahaziah, or were you?" the king asked with a smile.

Ahaziah swung his feet off the bed and fetched the plate for his grandfather. "We both dreamed, my king, only I trust your dream was the richer for your years," Ahaziah replied.

"Good answer, my boy." The king laughed. "Your words are well selected and will serve you well as a king . . . or with your women." The king winked at him.

"What use are words with women?" Ahaziah asked as he parsed the meat again and again. "Mother is trying to marry me off again. Tell me your secrets, Grandfather, tell me your clever words: Is that what won the heart of Queen Anna?"

King Jehoshaphat looked away, seeing something in the distance of his mind. "No, my son," the king replied, "no, some women are not won by words, but by something they see in you, some reflection of God that you spend the whole of your life trying not to tarnish. It is a burden to be loved by such a woman, I tell you, but it is the only way to truly live."

"It must be easier to serve one God than many," Ahaziah mused. "You can know Him better. I grow tired of Mother explaining all her gods. I can never remember who rules what, and then I send prayers for rain to the god of cows, and prayers for my women to the god of thunder."

The king patted his hand. "She speaks of many gods but knows none."

Ahaziah handed the plate to the king. Though he loved adventure, he hated the politics of the crown and would not choose sides. He did not like this war of worship he had witnessed all his years; he preferred to jump nimbly out of any god's way and let all people go as they please. It bothered him that worship was made so personal, as if one man's choice was an insult to all others.

"Ah, yes," the king said, smelling the aroma of the lamb and the wine flavored with small shavings of cinnamon. "A perfect meal for a day such as this, to warm my body."

Ahaziah found his courage as he watched the king's shaking hands fight to hold the fork steady.

"My king, remember my youth and do not fault me for how I speak."

Jehoshaphat raised an eyebrow and gestured at him with his shaking fork to continue.

"My sister Jehoshebeth. Athaliah has arranged her marriage to the merchant Philosar."

"I had heard of this."

"My king, Jehoshebeth cannot bear it. She loves Judah, and though she will never wear the crown, she still wishes to serve this great nation. To send her away with Philosar would do nothing for Judah and would only crush her spirit. Can't you buy her back and send him away quietly? Athaliah would never know. She would think he found her displeasing, and another match could not be made so easily with a princess who had found disfavor."

The king considered this as he chewed.

"Take whatever money you need from my treasury and secure her release. I will provide for her all of her days, though her mother would cast her out." He set down his fork and placed a quavering hand over Ahaziah's. "Do not think Athaliah will merely be disappointed. If her intentions were other than marriage for her daughter, Jehoshebeth will be in greater danger for refusing the match."

Then the king called the guard from his post outside the bedroom door.

"Can you bring to me the high priest?" King Jehoshaphat asked.

"Yes, my king," the guard said, bowing low before departing.

"I have lain in my bed grieving the end of my life, but there is much work to be done yet," the king said to Ahaziah. "I have gone to God in my dreams. I know now where it was lost and believe there may yet be time to sweep the grass and disrupt the serpent's nest."

He stopped and looked at Ahaziah a moment. "You know that I love you, do you not?" he asked his grandson. "An old man asks such questions plainly where a younger man would assume he knows the answers plainly enough."

Ahaziah nodded. "I have always known that you favor me, even though I have not earned it."

"Good," said Jehoshaphat. "Leave me now, and I will go to work."

CHAPTER SIX

JEHOSHEBETH SLIPPED from her chamber down the hallway toward the back stairs, the stairs that would lead her to the stable and to her favorite of the horses, a huge, perfect black horse with love for no one but her. She had been allowed to ride him once and the event had gone without incident, but the stallion often threw inattentive riders and was fond of biting the stable boys. Not long ago she had fed him nightly, stealing from the kitchen treats and promising always to return with more. Too many nights had passed since her last visit.

She went barefoot through the limestone halls and down the smooth cedar steps. At night the palace had a warm scent, and the dense wood concealed her movements. The guards posted at the wing where the royal children slept had long ago gone blind to the nighttime exploits of Jehoshebeth and Ahaziah. When the guards were blind and mute, they received spoils from the kitchen at the end of the siblings' adventure.

Jehoshebeth entered the stable complex and let her eyes adjust to the light. Here the royal horses were bred and kept.

Other stables farther back in the complex held the more exotic captives: the lynxes, ostriches, peacocks, and once, in the time of Solomon, great apes. Years ago, by the light of a low lamp after all others had gone to bed, a nursemaid told Ahaziah and Jehoshebeth of these creatures:

"The ships docked in a great storm, and the men carried loot off the ship that no eyes here had ever seen. Spices, jewels, and gifts from the lands far beyond Egypt. There were beasts, some dead, having not survived the journey, but others still living, some so strange they made the villagers shriek and the children bury their faces in their mothers' robes. But then came creatures unlike anything a man had ever seen. They were called apes and were as big as the biggest man among us, covered in black hair, with large black eyes that pierced the very soul, and monstrous teeth as thick as walnut shells. Yet these creatures seemed so like us, it was as if we forgot for a moment who was the beast. And when these great apes were led forth, a silence fell over the village, for no one had ever imagined such a creature. The chief from each town was assembled in front to witness the gifts from a new world. One brave man approached the first ape led out and demanded to know his name.

"'What land did you rule over before you were captured?' the chief demanded, perhaps too loudly, because he was sorely afraid.

"The ape roared and struck the man with his hand, and all the chiefs scattered and ran in fright. The ship's men laughed so hard that they could not unload the rest of the cargo for a long stretch of time. They took to drink, still laughing, and the children of the village ran in and out of the ships for days, exploring, stealing, and playing. They found many more treasures, forgotten by the men or too small to be noticed, and they carried them into the village."

Jehoshebeth and Ahaziah sat up, their eyes wide in disbelief.

"The keepers said they felt a great peace as they tended the creatures, but the apes bore a heavy creeping sorrow from the land beyond Egypt, and they died of broken hearts."

"Why?" Ahaziah asked, defending himself from Jehoshebeth as she tried to poke him in the ribs.

"No one knows. Perhaps they died of sadness, being so far from home. Perhaps the savagery of men pushed them to their graves. But they were marvelous creatures. Some say when the moon is full you can still hear them stomping round the stables, their deep growls sending brave children running for the safety of their beds."

The nursemaid yanked the blanket over the squealing children.

Jehoshebeth sighed at the memory. Her nursemaid had not lived long after that night, and the midnight stories and shared secrets ended. Ahaziah had been moved at once to another room, and she began to understand the difference between an heir to the throne and a daughter.

But on these midnight journeys, as she slipped along the dirt floor littered with straw, she relived her wide-eyed childhood again. Tonight, no one stirred. The stablemen were above her in the loft, snoring. She wished Ahaziah had joined her. She could not send word to him to meet her, and she could not leave her room. She wished for nothing more than a moment with him, a moment to feel safe again, to believe her world could be mended. But it was only a wish, not a prayer. She felt sure prayers were heard because they were given with offerings. There was no god who heard wishes.

She crept along until she was in front of her favorite stable, then took a deep breath and carefully lifted the wooden bar. She eased back the door, trying to hold it steady along its track, and slipped inside.

Philosar sat on a wooden chair, cleaning his nails.

"You thought you were so clever, keeping yourself from me by hiding in your room. But do you know what's better than being clever?"

She shook her head, her hand still in her pocket to retrieve the fruit for the horse. He was not in the stable.

"Being clever and rich," Philosar answered. "I bought the information I needed that gave me access to you at last. What do you think I should do now? You have humiliated me, distracted me from important business, and driven the costs of the arrangement above that which was acceptable to pay."

Jehoshebeth opened her mouth to speak, but he shook his finger at her.

"Say nothing. I meant only to engage your mind, not your mouth." He rose from his chair and walked to her. She backed up until her body was pressed against the stable wall. He reeked of garlic.

He grabbed her hair, inspecting it and glaring until he dropped it and stepped back to look at her more completely. When his judgment was made, he moved closer again. She tried to hold her breath so his stench wouldn't infect her.

"I leave tomorrow," he said. "You will prepare to leave for Israel by packing one trunk. No more than that, so the animals will be good for selling when we arrive. Think wisely what you would have."

He placed his hands on her shoulders and brought his sweating face closer to hers, looking at her mouth.

"I will be repaid."

She screamed and tried to pull herself out of his grasp, but he was too strong. He used one leg to sweep her feet out from under her, forcing her to the ground. She punched but he caught her hands and pinned them above her head, his mouth reaching down for his first kiss.

He opened his mouth wide, and she jerked her face away. He landed with a dull sigh on top of her and did not move. She wrestled him off, but he did not resist, and when she stood she saw a blade run through his back.

Ahaziah stepped out from the shadows.

"Sorry I was late."

He held her and she cried, trying not to look at Philosar lying dead. She couldn't stop herself from stealing another look. She heard the heavy sound of gold as Ahaziah nervously shook a bag of coins while looking at the dead merchant.

"What do we do?" she asked.

"We're royals, right?"

She nodded.

"We bribe."

THE HIGH Priest was to serve God and the people that day and could not be easily summoned away, even by the king. He would send his son Jehoiada in his place.

Jehoiada came the following morning just after the first sacrifice. He could still smell the smoke from the Temple fires as he approached the palace. His clothes, his hair, his skin all smelled of the Temple incense and flames. To him, it was the smell of eternity. One day a year, God drew near and occupied the innermost room of the Temple, and on those days the smell was entirely different. The air hung heavily with the smell of air after a storm, crisp and fresh, the smell of dew just touched by the sun. God smelled to him like both a winter's night and a summer's morning.

And yet, God drawing so near made no lasting change in the people who watched Him from a distance. They tired of a god who did not change, though the needs and seasons of their own lives changed so rapidly. Jehoiada had no patience for them, the lost who pretended they didn't hear the call home.

Before the day had begun, many faithful lined up with their rams and doves and lambs to make good on their debt to God. One man, Balak, appeared in this same line every month, always with the same offering and always with the same story. He bemoaned to Jehoiada in shame as he passed him at the gates. "For the forgiveness of my lust, of taking my wife's maidservant against her will," he said, his eyes poor and downcast, voice strained at the pity of his sin.

Today when Jehoiada saw him, his anger burned. Balak drew close, offering the lamb, soft and warm, to Jehoiada. Jehoiada stared at him. Balak could only nod that yes, the sin was the same again. Jehoiada smiled with tender compassion, then struck him with full force so that Balak fell down. Everyone in line gasped.

"That is for the woman," Jehoiada whispered to the man, offering his hand to help him stand.

Balak lost his pallor of remorse and his eyes blazed. He got back on his feet without assistance and was forming a choice word when Jehoiada struck him again, sending him back to the ground. Blood ran from the split lip as Balak stared in wonder at this priest standing over him.

"And that was for the lamb," Jehoiada said, passing the small creature off to another priest, who carried it toward the altar. Jehoiada reached again to help Balak, who was too stunned to refuse the offer. Jehoiada smiled at everyone in line; they shrank back a bit with their offerings.

"Go in peace, my friend, and sin no more," Jehoiada said loudly to the bleeding man, who stumbled off muttering in shame.

"You are to revere the blood shed on your behalf, not trade upon it," Jehoiada told the crowd, who agreed very quickly. A few looked at the bleeding man walking away, then down at their own sacrifices, as if wondering if it would be best to leave too.

NOW JEHOIADA was called to the palace. It felt good to brace his muscles along the descending path. He watched with satisfaction as the animals scurried away from him. At the Temple he was surrounded daily by weakness, the weakness of men in resisting what was wrong, the weakness of bodies ravaged by disease, the weakness of men afraid to approach an unseen God. Jehoiada laid himself down daily for these people, but his great strength served only to carry them partially across the divide, edging toward God, never meeting Him fully. The gap was always too great for a man to bridge, even a man such as himself.

In his darkest moments, Jehoiada saw that it was all futile, the river of blood that never made anything white, the washing of hands that would turn, clean, to sin again. God's shadow stretched over a world of people doomed, and Jehoiada saw no way out. Every good experience, every taste and sound and texture, beckoned and baited man to know the divine, and every breath condemned that same man to sin and die apart.

A mute servant with dark circles under his eyes received Jehoiada at the gates and escorted him duly through the halls. The priest wondered what had happened within these cedar walls saturated with the odor of fear. Other palaces had been built with rosewater and herbs mixed into the mortar so that there was always a hint of something good. Here there was something else behind the pleasant cedar, something ill at ease and struggling for breath.

He was led directly to the king's chambers and announced. He entered to find King Jehoshaphat sitting upright in bed, alone. The old man did not look well. Jehoiada greeted him in the name of the Lord, and the king replied in kind.

Jehoiada walked to the bed and laid his hands on the king's head, giving a blessing of peace and life over the wilted hair and folded skin. He sat then and awaited the king's command.

King Jehoshaphat reached for Jehoiada's hand, which he held tightly until neither could tell their lifepulse apart, until the warmth from Jehoiada's hand had warmed the king. The king summoned a breath and began.

"It was a small thing that grew and took shape," he began, tears forming in his eyes. Jehoiada gripped the king's fingers more tightly and with his free hand, took a firm hold of the king's shoulder.

"God still considers you a friend," Jehoiada said, comforting the king.

"No," the king said. "It is not for me I weep, nor for myself that I repent. I would will myself to be cursed if I could bear the punishment to save the people. No, I have seen the angry, hungry end of life, the kingdom sliding away toward its open mouth, a pit of graves where dead women rise up with sharpened teeth to torment the living and gnaw away at the tenuous peace established in the land. And it is I who taught the people the laws of God, it was I who welcomed it," Jehoshaphat cried out.

"There is nothing you can do, good king," Jehoiada said. "It is time to pray and enter His rest."

Jehoshaphat brushed the words away as if they hung in the air before his wizened face. "It takes more strength to do nothing in the face of evil. That is one sin I will not take to my grave. I once loved my life so much that I thought I could tolerate a little wrongdoing for the sake of my children's contentment. I thought turning my back would give us all peace. Now I see that in so doing I abandoned them all."

Jehoiada considered this, shaking his head. He finally said, "I know of nothing you must do, for God has given me no visions or dreams."

The king nodded and relaxed against his pillows. Jehoiada released him and sat back as well, sighing. The king motioned for a cup of water, and Jehoiada helped him sip from it, a steady stream spilling from his mouth onto his bedclothes.

"There is something restless and dead here, and one girl has drawn its eye. It is this girl I can save, though not my kingdom."

Jehoiada motioned for the king to continue.

"When the time comes, you must take her from this palace, to the Temple. She will be your wife, and your mantle will protect her," the king said.

Jehoiada saw the purple veins that knotted and coursed across the king's arms and hands. Jehoshaphat had been a powerful man whose commands once rocked the kingdom to its core. But Jehoiada shook his head.

"You will do it," the king said, raising himself up with fire in his voice.

"The king does not command priests."

"You will do this."

"I will consider your words, my king, but I answer only to God," Jehoiada said.

"I'll see Him soon enough." The king laughed weakly and settled himself back in his bed. "I'll explain the whole thing."

Jehoiada stood and bowed.

"Jehoiada."

"Yes?"

"No man gives a daughter without a dowry. What should I send with her?"

Jehoiada shook his head and held up his hands. "I can accept nothing, because I have not consented."

The king settled into the blankets and closed his eyes, a smile on his lips. Jehoiada, confused, opened his mouth to speak again. Old Jehoshaphat opened one eye, still smiling.

"How you sound like a maiden and not a man! But I will send a dowry with her, the finest gift that will serve you both well."

Jehoiada left, his words boiling up until they spilled out. The servants watched him as he left, muttering a thousand stern oaths.

CHAPTER SEVEN

ATHALIAH WATCHED from an upper window as Jehoiada moved through the courtyard and out the gate, then up the steep path that would take him back to that holy place. She knew a priest from the Temple had been called to the king's chambers but could find no one to report their conversation. It was Jehoshaphat who had allowed her marriage to his son, but on her first night in the palace, he looked at her as if he knew what was in her heart. He had clenched his jaw as he reached out to welcome her, and from that night on they had battled to position their gods more advantageously.

A movement of guards down the hallway caught her eye, and she saw Jehoram.

"Jehoram, my love!" she cried out and approached the men. The guards stopped, and she went to Jehoram, bowing low. His eyes were spoiled with dark, heavy circles. His robes hung loosely from withering muscles.

Athaliah touched his face gently.

"Is my husband not sleeping well?"

"No, Athaliah, my dreams disturb me." He sighed, removing her hand. "It is something more than grief for my mother."

Athaliah looked at him with compassion and gave an order to the servants posted in the hall.

"Jehoram bids me sleep in his chambers from now on," she said, "for only I know how to sing over him in sleep so that he does not wake."

"Sleep is not the repose I most need, Athaliah." He moved as if he would walk away.

Athaliah blocked him, her mouth open. "Where are your other wives, Jehoram?"

He scowled in confusion. "I do not know. Why?"

"I know," she said bitterly. "They robe themselves with garments to seduce the men brought back from the war. They perfume themselves with scents the soldiers brought from the land of Ahab. They season themselves with delicacies you are never meant to taste."

Jehoram grabbed her arms, jerking her close, studying her face in anger.

She kissed him full on the lips, pressing her body into him and taking hold of his face.

"Wake up, my lord, for the red dawn is upon you," she whispered, each hot word brushing his cheek before leaving it cold. "They are aiming for you, even your brothers, can you not see it?"

Athaliah let him loose and warned him before she fled to her chamber. "Be ready."

JEHOSHEBETH STILL did not emerge from her chamber. Athaliah could afford patience now, though, and marked with satisfaction Philosar's bags loaded into a caravan below. Her servants told her he had been especially pleased with his last deal here, telling everyone he had found a way to master her at last. He would be leaving at any hour now, and the girl's name would be erased from everyone's lips.

JEHORAM SOUGHT out his father. King Jehoshaphat looked pained to see him.

"My son," the king said.

"Is there news for me, Father?" Jehoram begged. "There are whispers and shadows everywhere in this palace, and I am startled by strange murmuring. Tell me what you know."

Jehoshaphat shook his head. He had grown considerably paler since Jehoram had seen him last.

"I do not know what you see," the king said. "I see goodness surrounding you, light if you would have it, but there is darkness too, a darkness that demands your life. There may still be a way," he said, his voice trailing off as if he would sleep.

Jehoram sprang to his side. "There may still be a way for what?"

The king was weaker now, as if something heavy settled over his chest. He looked at his son through lenses of thickly salted tears. He tried to blink, to see again, but the clearer vision was leaving him. He pressed his hands against his chest to force air in, but none came easily.

Jehoram held the old man's head in his hands as if that would help the words escape the labored breaths. The guards posted at the entrance of the room exchanged glances as the children entered, one carrying a bowl of mushy figs stewed in honey for the king.

"He is near death," the smallest girl cried, pushing Jehoram out of the way, for she was too young to understand the politics of crowns and lineage. She began to cry and laid her head over his chest, but the king did not move. She pulled his limp arm around her, and Jehoram saw that the softness of a child would be Jehoshaphat's last touch of earth. In this way his father left him, taking comfort in another, and Jehoram wept.

He wept until his body fought against him for air and he attended to the necessary ragged breaths. He saw the figs, spilled across the floor, the silver bowl dented. He began picking up the figs, and they slipped between his fingers so that he had to scoop them, dripping, into the bowl. He felt grief coming back up through his throat, and he gagged, holding his hands over his mouth. He smelled them and then smelled again, his blood growing cold. More than honey spiced these figs. The child was sitting on the bed, stroking the old man's hair as she cried quietly. Jehoram knew the girl must be his, although from which wife he couldn't remember, and he watched the tiny hands that had unwittingly poisoned her hero even as she sang to him.

His children had done this. He would be blamed. His unseen enemies were drawing the noose closer and tighter, and he could not get free. He wanted escape more than life.

Jehoram stumbled from the dead king's chamber, not looking at the guards. His own guards escorted him to his rooms, where Athaliah waited with blankets soaked in rosewater and crocus buds before they were set out to dry. Perfume dripped from the torches all around the room, and this plus the smoke from the fat that cracked in the fire seemed to him to be a smothering blanket, pressing the shadows in, shielding his chattering, freezing spirit from the light. His father was dead, but Jehoram was never more a child. He needed someone to help him now and tell him what to do.

ATHALIAH RECEIVED him with a fragrant bed and spiced breath. His wine was cool and he tasted none of the powder she had mixed, powder that bought her magic more time. Philosar's caravan stood in the palace courtyard, the same place it had been that morning. Athaliah sent Jagur below to learn what he could of the delay. The cedar walls groaned in the coolness of the night, and the darkness swallowed Jehoram in sinister sleep.

MIDIAN KNOCKED on the door, begging for an audience, but he could not get Jehoshebeth's maids to speak to him. He could think of nothing to say or do, and the silence of the palace on this night unnerved him. He prayed, propped up against Jehoshebeth's door, slipping in and out of dreams, asking God to make a way for them, that Jehoshebeth would be free of the strange suitor Philosar, that she would be delivered from a life neither would choose.

Athaliah had already sent her good-bye to her daughter in the form of a small figure of Asherah and incense to burn for prayers. These were already loaded into Philosar's bags. She had chosen to remain in her chambers and see her daughter no more, though Jagur entered and left several times. Midian saw that on this night only the guards moved through the halls, and for the first time in his service here, he felt alone.

ATHALIAH ROSE in the darkness and swept back the curtains from the chamber. Jagur met her there. He shook his head so she would understand there was no news. He offered the vial she requested, then disappeared again into the shadows.

She crept silently, her small feet easy across the stone floor, and drew Jehoram's sword from its sheath. She used it to prick her finger and watched as the bubble of blood rose at her sharp bidding, then she smeared it across the blade. The vial had a stench unlike anything she had smelled, but her priest Mattan told her that evil spirits have such a smell as this, the odor of hopelessness mingling with the sourness of grief. She wrinkled her nose as she poured out the libation and lifted the blade high above her head in the moonlight. A cloud passed over the moon and she closed her eyes. Somewhere in the hills beyond the palace a wolf bayed, heralding a living thing now scented and tracked, its prey doomed to die by morning.

Jehoram stirred in his sleep and Athaliah returned to him, ministering to this man before his first day as the new king, willing him to taste malice and crave blood. The dawn rose and Athaliah knew the wolf was running, his prey stirring and yet unaware. "Wake up, my love," she sang to Jehoram. "Stir yourself and remember. You are the king."

He blinked heavily, his strange sleep having stolen more strength than it gave. But he had escaped his dreams, even if for a night. He saw his sword unsheathed, a glint of blood on it. He had never seen blood on his sword before, and the sight moved in him something terrible, a rotted seed that split open and sent a creeping thing toward the surface of his soul.

"Do it," she said as she stroked his hair. "You know it must be done. They have betrayed us all."

He got up from their bed and walked to the sword, studying it in the new light.

"They may even now be in their beds, dreaming of your blood across their own swords. They killed Jehoshaphat, you know that. Kill today and live in peace at last." Athaliah stroked his back, moving her head side to side like a serpent finding a willing ear on each side to test.

"Go now, before the mighty sun rises and sees you weak," she hissed.

Jehoram put on his cloak, though his fingers fumbled the cloth and he could not hold his vision steady. Not sheathing his sword, he walked from the room, his guards already prompted and ready, waiting for him to emerge and begin his reign.

ATHALIAH WAITED for Jehoram to leave, then called Jagur.

"The palace is almost ours. Only the problem of Jehoshebeth remains. Is Philosar gone with her yet?" she asked.

"He is nowhere to be found. Jehoshebeth is still in her chamber."

Athaliah cursed under her breath and drew her lips in, rubbing them together slowly back and forth.

"Draw your sword and follow me," she commanded.

Jehoshebeth would still be sleeping. The work would be fast.

JEHOSHEBETH WOKE as if something had tugged at her bedsleeve, but all was still in the room. She could hear the steady breathing of her servants sleeping in the far corner, glad to return to their mistress' service, and could detect the rustling of a guard standing post outside her doorway. All seemed well. The air this morning was especially cold and bracing, like the first bite of a tart apple, and she pulled the bedclothes closer around.

Suddenly something else made her sit upright against her wishes in the cold air. Something stirred in the palace, something new and unwelcome; she could feel it.

Wrapping a heavy lion-skin blanket around her, she got out of bed, moving to a wall that was connected to many others. She pressed her ear to it and detected nothing amiss, the strongest noises only the usual ones. Her servants stirred in the corner, seeing her behavior, and asked her what she was doing. Jehoshebeth motioned for them to be quiet as she pressed her ear to the wall again.

As she strained for a hint of what had disturbed her, a scream tore through the air and sent her flailing backward in shock. "Murder!" was the word Jehoshebeth understood plainly from the sharp screams that rose up, one after the other, like spirits from the cedar walls and stone floor, each moan shifting shape and tenor. She began to shake as the screams of agony poured through her chambers from every direction. Her maids rushed about, trying to dress Jehoshebeth as fast as they dressed themselves, sputtering prayers to every god they could remember.

The women screamed as a guard burst through the chamber door, his sword drawn. Jehoshebeth was the first to know him.

"Midian!" she cried, "What is happening?" Midian ran to her window and looked out. He took a rope from over his shoulder and tied a knot in the end, then grabbed the princess and shoved her roughly to the window.

"What is it, Midian? What is happening?"

He wrapped the rope once around her waist, tightly, securing it with another knot, and lifted her to the window's edge. "King Jehoshaphat is dead and your father Jehoram is killing his brothers. He will be the only son left to rule."

Jehoshebeth slapped at Midian and struggled to get down. "This is untrue!"

He slapped her back, and she was stunned into quiet. "Quiet yourself and listen if you want to live! What I tell you is true: the king is dead, and your father is slaughtering his brothers. Now flee, for no one knows what set his sword off and where it will swing next."

"My father would never harm me!" Jehoshebeth said. "Why are you saying these things?"

Midian stroked his hand along her face and kissed her, their tears and breath touching, leaving their faces cold in the morning air. He had looked upon her in all her ages, from child to woman. Jehoshebeth felt him so close and saw all the nights he had greeted her in her ornaments and robes and all the mornings he had seen her disheveled and sleepy.

"Even now, do you not understand?" he asked. "You know that Athaliah is not your mother, but now let me say the worst: She has no love for you. You were born of her enemy, and she has waited many long years to see you dead. It is she who is at work."

Jehoshebeth shook her head. "She was a good mother to me. She wishes me gone, but not dead."

"She kept you close to know what was in your heart toward her. She decided you were too weak and stupid to ever rise against her, and so she slowly forgot that you had ever troubled her. But you changed, Jehoshebeth. You grew up. The prophecy that you would become her undoing gathered length of bone and strength as you did. Athaliah will remedy her mistake today. You will leave with Philosar or she will see you dead. It is not as I would wish, but it is the only way."

"Philosar is dead."

Midian exhaled. She watched his eyes darting side to side as he recounted something in his mind. Then he whistled, soft.

"Your grandfather outsmarted us all. Before his death last night, the old king gave orders in secret that the black one be saddled and ready for you. See, the one they call Gabriel awaits."

Jehoshebeth looked down and saw her black horse waiting.

Midian shook his head. "I thought it was a wedding gift, meant for you to take to Israel. I wondered why he did not command the donkeys be readied for you. They're better for a long journey." He shook his head. "He knew you would have to run."

"Where will I go?"

"I don't know, but I see now there must be a plan in place. You must ride away from here and trust your grandfather's hand in this."

"But what of you, Midian?"

"I will find you."

Midian shoved her through the window and lowered her in jagged bumps until she was close enough to jump. She swung herself onto Gabriel and he burst for the open gate.

THE DOOR to her chamber swung open. Midian dropped the rope and turned to face Athaliah's closest servant. Jagur used his sword to push back the linens on the bed. Seeing it empty, he drove his sword through the bed, cursing.

Athaliah saw the maids cowering in the corner and Midian at the window.

"Who is responsible for this?" she growled.

Midian bowed. "Jehoshaphat. He arranged it last night. The servants who attend him were drunk after his death and told me everything when they returned to their chambers this morning. I ran here to stop her, but I was too late."

Midian bowed before he drew his dagger, pointing it at his neck, and took a breath.

Jagur sneered as he watched. Athaliah stopped Midian.

"The servants tell you things?"

Midian nodded.

"Put your knife away. You may serve us well yet."

Midian exhaled and lowered his dagger. Jagur shook his head.

"I can always kill him later, Jagur," Athaliah said. She looked at Midian.

"Find out where she went. Find who has given her shelter and report back to me."

CHAPTER EIGHT

THE LYRES played a slow, sad song, like the cry of the last bird before nightfall. Athaliah watched as the dancers moved, their scarves trailing in the air among the mourners who must be paid later in the afternoon.

The women stood in groups behind the procession, keening loudly, chanting:

> *Death has stolen once more*
> *That which we held dearest*
> *Rescue us, O Lord, and*
> *Receive our beloved.*

The chanting made it easier to walk along the dusty, rocky path, as everyone's feet seemed to move as one, their pulse and breath matching the chants.

Jehoram and his son Prince Ahaziah together held up the dead king's head, and two advisers took up the other end of the woven mat. Jehoshaphat was draped in royal purple robes, his sword in his frozen hands, his shield across the body. Athaliah and her maids carried all he would need for burial: spices and nard to burn at the tomb, his royal seal on a pillow.

The tomb of the kings was deep inside the earth, a sandy womb for the dead who would never be reborn. Athaliah despised this place, these burials that marked the end of life, that gave the body over for the earth to devour. She herself would never be buried this way; she would go with her jewelry, her face painted, with clay goddesses and gifts for those who had all power to deny her admission to the underworld.

A wide, deep stairway led the way into the tomb. Water flowed along either side and collected at the bottom of the stairs in the ritual baths for the mourners. The procession began the long descent. Athaliah cursed the stonemasons who had cut so many steps into this place; she counted to a hundred and had begun again when the men carrying Jehoshaphat stopped. They rested the body on a stone slab and purified themselves by washing their hands and faces, their tears mixing with the water.

Before them, the stone had already been rolled away. Inside the deep chamber, a new place had been dug out from the wall to lay the body. Jehoram washed first and, with the help of Ahaziah, eased the dead king off the mat and carried him to his final resting place. All behind them stood silent and watched. Jehoshaphat slid easily into the cut rock. Jehoram pressed his fists to his eyes and sank to his knees. The mourners resumed their songs and chants, watching as Jehoram shook with sobs. He was unable to find his feet again. Athaliah pushed her way through the advisers, who stood stupidly and watched, and past Ahaziah, who shrugged when his mother approached. Placing her hands on Jehoram's shoulders briefly, she then moved to the dead king. She pressed her face against his and kissed him on the cheek so all could see. Letting her robe fall to cloak her next act, she slid a stone into his stiff hand.

"Sink and never rise," she murmured, her face turned away so that no one could see her lips. "May your God die with you."

She turned then to Jehoram, whispering in his ear too, lifting him to his feet. She dabbed her cheeks for the benefit of the gathered witnesses. Jehoram, clutching her as if he had no strength apart from hers, let her lead him to face the king one last time. He bowed low and kissed his father. He touched the sword across the king's chest, then turned to walk out of the tomb.

He stopped and looked at Athaliah.

"What of my brothers?" he asked, his voice high and frightened.

She shook her head. "We do not bury traitors with kings."

Athaliah nodded to the attendants of the burial site, and they loosed the boards that braced the stone at the opening. The heavy rock rolled into place, the final moon to set on King Jehoshaphat's days. Jehoram cried aloud and clung to Athaliah again as she helped him along the steep path back toward the palace. The musicians and mourners circled and waited for Athaliah's cue. She smiled on them and they began to mourn once more.

"Strength now, my darling," Athaliah urged Jehoram. "You have buried your father and destroyed his enemies. See that it is good to be king."

JEHOSHEBETH RODE, and Gabriel followed the narrow winding path she had once traversed with Midian, a shrill whistle sounding once, leading him in the direction he traveled. She felt like a child's toy being pushed along by a strong wind.

She kept looking through the trees, expecting someone to step out, to take the reins, to motion her to come near. The heat of the day was nearer now and she saw a wolf trotting back to its cave, a broken, dead thing in its mouth.

The horse took her below to the edge of the city. She held Gabriel's reins tightly and looked for somewhere to pull him off the path. She could not ride into the city and be seen. If her grandfather's plan had failed, if no one found her and gave her shelter, then she would keep herself hidden until Midian could get to her. There was no other sound, not another whistle or call.

Gabriel wouldn't leave the path. She pulled at him, harder, and still he picked his way along, his head low, moving toward the open city road. As they rounded a broad, sprawling tree that hid the view beyond, she saw him. Abel, the man who fed Gabriel every morning and never complained about midnight visitors who spoiled his appetite, sat on a broken tree stump, his hands folded in his lap. Abel looked up, then stood and whistled once more for Gabriel, who walked to him.

Abel put a finger to his lips, smiling, and gently took the reins. Gabriel followed him. Jehoshebeth tried to hold herself up by pressing her hands against Gabriel's thick, warm neck. But even her arms were too weak and she leaned down, resting herself against him, willing her racing heart to match his slow, bumping stride.

She watched the ground change from rocky path to even street marked with footprints in many directions. It was quiet, and she summoned the strength to lift herself and see.

There were square mud-brick houses, clusters of them in all directions. Some of the bigger clusters had courtyards surrounded by low walls, where chickens and goats bickered and laughing children scattered food for them both.

Abel led Gabriel past these houses to what looked like the tiniest dwelling in the tiniest square of them all. Bits of straw poked out from the mud walls, and jagged slits formed its only windows. He motioned for her to get down, and she obeyed. She walked to the door, a rough wooden door on rotting hinges. She turned back and saw him leading Gabriel away. He motioned for her to go in. Jehoshebeth felt she was in a dream. But if she was in a dream, it was her grandfather's, and she trusted him that it would end well.

She held her breath and pushed against the door. It slipped on its hinges as it swung open, scraping the earth. She cringed and pushed it harder. There was no sound inside of voices or protests. She peered in and then entered. She had never felt a dirt floor under her feet, and she moved a toe along the swirling dust. Her maids had dressed her so quickly that none had thought of shoes. Most of the royal children went barefoot in the palace unless called to the court. Seeing the condition of the home, she wished she had sandals now.

Three long, narrow chambers faced her. The main room was in the middle. It was clear of all furnishings. Stone walls stood on either side of it, coming up to the height of her chest, with cedar beams extending from there to support the cedar beams of the roof. The floor of each room that flanked the main one was lined with straw, looking like the stables she had at home. At the back of the room on the left she saw a wooden staircase leading up to a small loft, where a straw mat and a table were perched. She wondered who lived here and if they were happy. It was odd to her that the home, with its dirt floors and straw bed, seemed fresh and peaceful. She looked around and realized this home had no shrine to the gods her mother worshiped.

The mourners' cries reached her door, calling their praises

for Jehoshaphat, and the hairs on her arm stood. She knew her mother and father were near. Why would Athaliah wish her dead? And the mourners — the mourners did not cry for the dead brothers. Had she dreamed that? Her gentle father could not have been persuaded to kill them. She wrapped her arms around herself and wept, stifling her moans. She felt she was falling, the faces of the dead sweeping past her, their eyes telling her what she would not hear. She held herself tightly, settling to the floor and rocking herself. She wondered how she came to be in this poor house. It was wrong. It was corrupted and wrong, like a broken bone set by a fool.

She wondered if Midian knew where she was, and if he, too, would be forced to flee the palace. She tried to imagine him coming to her here and rescuing her, but her mind had been stretched too far in one day. She sat in the dirt and could see only that. She sat, staring, and barely noticed the light in the room, her only companion, move from one side to the other. But soon it failed her too and began to fade.

She realized she was hungry, but there was no one she could call. There was an oil lamp near the mat in the loft, but she did not know how she would light it. The darkness grew heavier and darker. She felt something move near her foot and cried out, trying to jerk herself up and get away from whatever could stir on that floor. It was too dark in here, she told herself. She couldn't breathe. She had to get out. She eased to the door and looked outside.

A fog had settled heavily onto the streets like a drunkard unwilling to move, unaware of where he fell. Looking up, Jehoshebeth saw the moon's glow as it rose. She heard from a great distance the sounds of the Temple, the melody of psalms, and the crack of wood being cut for the fire. She pulled her robe tightly around her shivering body. She would go there, where she wouldn't be alone.

A hand caught her arm, pushing her back inside. Fear clutched her stomach before she could scream. In the moonlight she saw Midian.

"This is not a proper time for the princess to travel alone," he said.

She gasped and threw herself into his arms, burying her face in his neck, weeping.

"Where were you going?" he asked.

"To the Temple. I was afraid."

"You did not trust me? I said I would come for you."

"What is happening, Midian?" She felt as if she were losing her mind. Everyone she thought she knew had been unmasked; what had she failed to see? What else had they hidden for so long?

"How much have you known? And when?" he asked.

"Known of what?" Jehoshebeth took his hand. She tried to press it to her face, but he pulled it away.

"I will escort you." He grabbed her arm like a guard would instead of a lover, her flesh aching under his grip. Neither spoke. Jehoshebeth did not know if he led her to her death or her grandfather's intended salvation. They seemed the same to her now.

They came to a different home, larger and well-built. It marked the intersection of two paths. He stopped and forced her to look at him and she saw tears on his cheeks.

"Did you think my world began and ended outside your door?" he asked. "That for years I lived only within the three cubits I was assigned to guard? Why did you not tell me? My post was to protect you, not love you. I failed at both."

A noise from a darkened home nearby startled them both

and he shoved her roughly again, moving her down the path. She had no time to respond.

"Run until you see the tree split by lightning," he said, "then look for the women to meet you. They are waiting." Midian turned his face away so she would not see it.

"Midian," she said. "Where am I going?"

"To your marriage. Now run!" he snapped, sending up a clamor from sleeping mothers now disturbed, rising to curse him.

The sound frightened her and she ran, running until she saw the split tree and the women Midian spoke of. They moved toward her slowly, draped in dark garments, like the ravens who did not take flight when approached. She saw they had been waiting and knew her from a distance. As they rose, she saw the old woman from the market, the one who had first claimed her, and the woman nodded at her with an uneven smile. Jehoshebeth saw she leaned heavily upon a cane now, and one side of her face hung limp. A younger woman wiped her mouth and felt her brow for fever.

She spun around but Midian was gone, not even an echo of him left behind. She was alone in darkness with these strangers. She fell to her knees, raising her hands to beg this God to stop His work, but she knew no prayers. She only cried out, and the women smiled as they took hold of her wrists, raising her and encircling her so that she could see nothing but where her foot should go next. As they walked, few spoke, and her mind made no thoughts. She had seen captives brought from war into the king's Hall of Justice and they behaved as she did now, stumbling and dumb. She had made fun of them, she remembered, thinking they were poor creatures, blessed to lose a freedom they were not strong enough to have held onto.

Silently they held her hands, giving her a bit more room to walk, because she faltered often. They were moving along the outside streets of the city, closer to the double wall that guarded it. They worked their way up, swinging far past the palace and ascending to the Temple. She tried to remember if she had ever passed this way with her father by chariot, before Athaliah had forbidden her such outings. She could smell fires burning down as dawn approached. A few older men had already risen and sat outside the courtyards, watching her with mild interest. A baby's hungry cry seeped through the fog.

A priest's song, low and deep, came to her.

Be gracious to me, O God, be gracious to me,
For my soul takes refuge in you;
And in the shadow of Your wings I will take refuge
Awake, my glory!
I will awaken the dawn.

A priest exited the outer courtyard now, his bronze incense bowl swinging in front of him from a heavy chain, pitching a thick yellow smoke against the sluggish fog. She did not recognize him, but he was older than the other priests she saw going out from the Temple. His eyes were pale with disease and age, and his face was lined with heavy folds like the tapestries she had seen bunched together at the market. He nodded to her with an easy, gentle smile and waited for the women to follow him. His voice rumbled ahead. She saw the early vendors moving to set up their booths in the common market. The women scuttling about smiled at her. As she went by, they nudged one another.

A few of the weakest and oldest, sleeping in the spots where they would surely beg later in the day, held out their hands to her, crying, "Pray for me, sister! Pray for me!"

Jehoshebeth turned to question a woman who walked alongside her, a woman of many years but still lovely, her face smooth and at peace. "Why do they cry this way to me?" Jehoshebeth asked.

The woman kept her eyes on the path. "A prayer said in ecstasy is the first heard by God," she replied.

It made no sense to Jehoshebeth. She walked on with the women, led by the priest.

The priest led them to a small house, far from the Temple and the quarters of the priests, lit with oil lamps and waiting. Whispers and giggles escaped from the windows, and Jehoshebeth stepped inside, followed by the women who had guided her. The priest remained outside, still singing to the morning. Greetings were exchanged with kisses by all, and words passed so quickly between them that Jehoshebeth was not sure what was said. She stood and waited, no longer a royal who knew how to command.

The women sang of a beloved bride as they ran their fingers along her face and shoulders, examining her the way a cook might examine his spread. One woman swept the floor and sang a hymn inviting God nearer, to witness and bless the marriage bed. Another woman began massaging her stomach and inspecting her gums, consulting with the others on whether Jehoshebeth would conceive right away and what foods she must eat. They argued among themselves how to dress her hair, which flowers should scent her tresses and body, and how to stain her lips and eyes.

Jehoshebeth knew nothing to say, and tears ran down her cheeks. Her mind was torn in so many directions that it could no longer attend to any one thing, and she was left without the will to run or beg for answers. She closed her mouth and eyes, trying to feel her heart. It was there, somewhere beneath the ruins of the deaths and betrayals, but there was no time to drag the heavy fallen stones away. And so she stood, the final betrayal being her own, and let the women do as they wished.

They bathed her in the middle of the room with water heated over a fire just beyond the house. If it felt odd, being undressed in front of these new women, when attendants had seen to these chores for years, she did not know. She was sure she could not feel her skin or move herself freely any longer. This was their work, and she would submit. They wove flowers into her hair and scented her breath with lemons and softened her skin with ground almonds, the white milk from the meat seeping into her flesh. Whole beads of lavender blossoms were scrubbed on her body, leaving their sharp, smoky-sweet scent. A bit of nard between her breasts and on her neck was their crowning touch, the women giggling to themselves about the pungent, fetching aroma. They dressed her in a clean white linen undergarment, followed by a tunic of light blue with sashes of darker blue wrapped tightly around her waist.

The youngest woman now bent and retrieved a pot of color for lips and made a motion to open it when the matriarch, who had sat in the corner drinking a hot brew of cinnamon and lemon, spoke.

"No," the old woman said. "It is enough." The young wife frowned and closed up the color.

Rising from her perch, the elder clapped her hands, and the women quickly gathered at the door. The old woman walked to Jehoshebeth and approved of her appearance. She held out a large white veil and draped it over Jehoshebeth's head. It covered her shoulders and tinkled with tiny bells sewn along all four edges. This last step taken, the woman grasped Jehoshebeth's hands and led her from the home. The other women gathered around the pair, and together they moved through the city, following the priest who had waited outside the home while they worked. He led them through narrow dusty streets while the women sang under their breath, careful to call no more attention to the group.

The old woman still held Jehoshebeth firmly, leading her along by linking arms.

"My name is Sebia," she said quietly.

Jehoshebeth nodded. Her legs felt weak and her stomach was tying itself into a tight little knot with every step. She looked to the sky but could see nothing beyond the square mud-brick homes clustered along the path like gossiping servants. Trees blocked her view; she could not see the palace and tried to remember it. This was a world removed from all she had known, and she questioned what she knew to be true.

She questioned everything she remembered, as if that life had been a dream. They moved up and up, circling west until the priest stopped in front of a complex of homes joined together, rising up around a spiral staircase. She knew this place from that dream-life she once had. She heard the voices of men singing to God and knew if she climbed the stairs and looked to the other side, just beyond this courtyard, she would see the Temple.

The priest's incense bowl swung for a moment as a morning breeze blew past, and she saw Jehoiada emerging from the darkness. The fog swirled around his feet as if it would hold him back, the earth-mother goddess claiming him for her own, but he kicked it carelessly away with each step, having no eyes but for her. All sound was muted in the fog and Jehoshebeth could hear her heart pounding again in her ears. She imagined she could hear his breath as he came near, breath like a lion panting, like the lions her father had brought back from the hunt and kept chained for sport. The dark, wet earth was beneath, the awakening sky above, the sun now beginning to plead its cause. This dream did not end and took its steady, strong steps straight for her.

He wore a white tunic, no color in his robes at all save for the gold clasps on his shoulders pinning the robe into place. A shorter white robe encircled his waist, woven with threads of gold that looked like small chains. He stopped outside the door and kissed the elderly priest on his cheek. The priest began walking away. The women gathered around Jehoshebeth, kissing her hands and blessing her. Sebia, too, blessed her, and the women departed as a group, casting glances back over their shoulders and letting little laughs escape as they walked.

He stood before her, and she did not have the nerve to watch his expression when he spoke.

"This is as your grandfather requested."

Jehoshebeth tried to form an answer, but she had none. She looked at the entrance into the priest's quarters and felt her body beginning to shake once more. Somehow, the thought of marrying a man such as Philosar had seemed so laughable, so far from her heart, that she had never troubled herself with imagining his touch on her bare skin, alone in a bedchamber. And the thought of Midian — it was not a thought at all, just a hunger that remained, as if she had been pushed away from the fullness of a first love too soon. But here was a man so unlike them both that she found it hard to think of either. His hard edges and muscles were so different from her own frame that she felt a desire to know him stir within her, a new appetite that cared nothing for what had passed. It infuriated her. She felt angry that she could feel desire, angry that she would be pulled into this marriage by a dark current that had dragged her past two others. She shook her head and backed away as he lifted his hands toward God and prayed:

Our times are not our own; we are in Your hand.
Look with favor on this union,
and grant us safe passage through the days ahead.
May You love us, may we keep faith,
until we rest with our fathers in the bosom of God.

With a short step toward her, he took her hand and led her into the quarters. He led her through the courtyard, to the right, and down a hallway. He paused and looked down at her before he pushed open the simple wooden door set into the limestone.

"This is my home. When you enter it, you will become my wife."

Jehoshebeth nodded and tried to swallow. Her mouth was dry and she could feel the edges of her lips cracking as she tried to open her mouth for a deeper breath. He entered and turned, holding out his hand to her. She looked at his palm, held out as if to receive an offering from her. She looked at him and felt herself beginning to faint. Everything began to go black, with the light becoming smaller and smaller, until it was just a pinpoint in the center of her vision. Her legs gave out and she fell, but he caught her and she clung to him as the room spun and she tried to open her eyes.

When she could stand, she saw they were in the doorway, but she had not yet entered his home. She closed her eyes again, this time to summon the strength to run, and saw everything then in a tangled flash: her grandfather raising his arms to worship the God she had been forbidden to seek, a God who had shadowed her with a strange kindness since that day in the market. She saw too her father reaching to embrace Athaliah as he was drawn into darkness and drowned. Could it be that her fathers had all grasped for the things that had blessed or destroyed them? Was it all so simple, that someone could choose a love and command fate? But she felt her father's weakness now; suddenly it was as familiar to her as the sound of her own breath. It would be so easy to run. Athaliah could surely be persuaded to love her once more, and Jehoshebeth could live again with the certain ease of a royal. She didn't have to suffer. She might even find a way to marry Midian if she was clever enough.

Jehoshebeth looked again at the man standing before her and thought of the invisible God he served. Her grandfather had said this God was a God of justice who had compassion for all living things, a God of mercy and life. It was this God who had swept close to her in the market after she had witnessed the sacrifice made on her behalf. He had poured peace out in exchange for blood; sacrifice was His only answer to the pleas she could not voice.

She took Jehoiada's hand and stepped inside.

CHAPTER NINE

JEHORAM SAT in the Throne Hall, staring ahead at an empty court. Beyond him was the Hall of Justice, which led to his throne, but it was empty too. Only his guards were near. Jehoram studied the cedar supports of the roof, the rubbed wood planks of the floor. It was odd, he thought, that such wood was used for his throne hall. Wood severed from the life of the tree must burn or rot, but it will never feel spring again.

He sat, his sword having opened wide a dark door, sending a draft roaming through the rooms of the palace. The stones here waged their own battle. Twice as tall as many men, they groaned as the outside winds struck them. The weight of the Hall of Justice seemed too great for them now.

From a distance, Jehoram heard the sound of footsteps. An adviser, one from the lesser courts of the people, sought an audience. The guards held their swords at attention.

Jehoram gave no indication whether the man met favor or disdain.

The man kneeled before the throne, his face turned aside

in respect. Turning it only so that his voice would be heard, he entreated the king as he kept his head low.

"Jehoram, son of righteous Jehoshaphat and heir of David, long may God bless you and the rule of your house. I speak on behalf of the people, your people and kinsmen who love you and seek your honorable face." He waited.

Jehoram replied without lifting his gaze from the paintings on the far wall of the room, paintings of seas that once parted and a pillar of fire that led frightened sojourners. Jehoram wondered how these images that brought him so much comfort as a boy troubled him so greatly as a king.

"You may speak," Jehoram murmured.

"The people, my king," the man began, looking on the king now, "the people are greatly alarmed by the sudden rush of events. They mourn for Jehoshaphat, as you do, and fear that his sons met an unlawful end, though not by your hand, of course. The people are frightened. Will you speak to them, to us? Will you assure us of the throne's love for all things righteous and the continued reign of peace in the kingdom of Judah?"

"Are you a prophet of Yahweh?" the king asked. Fear hemmed in his full voice as if he saw danger from a distance.

"No, I am a magistrate and adviser," the man replied. "I do not speak for myself or my interests. I speak only for the people."

Jehoram squinted at him. "Not a prophet of Yahweh," he said. "Speaking for the people but not for God."

WHEN JEHORAM summoned her, Athaliah was in attendance in the queen's court, which had joined his at her suggestion. She walked from her throne to join him. He whispered in her ear.

"This man speaks for the people, my king," she said. "They want a sign of what your reign will be, that is all. It is a small matter, not to trouble my lord. Shall I instruct him for you in the reply?"

Jehoram's gaze returned to the paintings. "Yes, Athaliah, give them a sign of my reign, for I am lost to dreaming for the moment."

She turned to a guard.

"Cut him to shreds and throw the corpse from the south wall," she commanded. "Let him fall like ashes on the city beneath us."

The man screamed as the guard's sword flashed and sprayed the golden mosaic at the foot of the throne with blood.

"Not here, you idiot," Athaliah snapped, "or his screams will ruin the peace of the morning." She turned to glare at the rest of the guards. "Where is Jagur?" They glanced between themselves and then one by one shook their heads at her, shrugging. The bleeding man moaned, and Athaliah whirled back around.

"Take him to the outer hallway to finish your work," she commanded. She grunted in disgust as two guards moved forward to help carry the bloody man out, his eyes wide with terror and accusation.

Jagur entered as the man was dragged away. He noted the blood on the floor, its salted smell still in the air. Athaliah walked toward him, her robes swaying behind her, catching the stray drops of blood, leaving a red wake behind her. Jagur stood still and she moved around him in a circle, looking at his body. She came round to face him and reached for his face. Jehoram still studied the scene painted on the far wall.

Jagur did not move. He crossed his arms and stared down at her. He reeked of another woman. Athaliah clenched her jaw and wished to strike him, but the fool would think it jealousy. He did not understand their situation.

Turning, Athaliah raised her arms in an embrace as she approached Jehoram again.

"My king and husband, how regal you are on your throne! It is well you have called for me today. We do indeed need to instruct the people as to our reign. Let us send that man back out to begin the speech, although he does go in little stutters and not as a whole." She laughed. "We will make our plans while the people collect him."

"This seems well to you?" Jehoram asked as unsteadily as a child taking new steps.

Athaliah sighed, turning so she could catch the eye of Jagur as she bowed before Jehoram and took his hand to her mouth for a kiss.

"Oh, yes, my lord," she said. "Tomorrow we will adjourn to your gardens, where we will seek the will of the one who will guide us as we set our nation on the edge of glory. My mother intends we should join her; I intend we shall surpass her."

He nodded and stood, holding his arm out for her to join him and to lead.

"Where is my daughter, Jehoshebeth? She was not among the mourners, was she? I would have her join us, for I long for her smile."

Athaliah stroked his arm. "She took your offer of marriage to Philosar and has left by now. She would have said good-bye to you, do you not remember?"

Jehoram sagged under her touch and began shuffling toward the door.

She let him move a few paces without her, turning to whisper to Jagur. "It is not over. Philosar was a weak little fool who could not master his woman, and it vexes me that he left her for us to deal with. But Jehoshebeth will not live long enough to enjoy her freedom."

AT MIDNIGHT Jagur was standing by the fire burning in the kitchen courtyard of the palace. The fires burned throughout the night: fires in the courtyard of the kitchen, fires outside the royal bedchambers to keep insects away, fires at the palace gates so that all who approached would be seen clearly.

Midian watched him. Jagur did not move, even when the flames blew too close to his thick legs. It was not a good night to approach him, but it had to be done. Midian tried to ignore the guilt crushing his chest and constricting his throat. He was betraying her, but only in small measure, so that she might live a little longer.

Jagur turned with a smile to face him, although no noise had given Midian away.

"News?"

"From the stables. The black horse they call Gabriel went missing the night Jehoshebeth fled. He has not returned since. Abel says he had orders from Jehoshaphat to saddle Gabriel during the night but he was not told who would take him, or where. It is clear the old king found shelter for Jehoshebeth in a faraway land. Tell your queen to search for her no more."

MATTAN MET them the next morning in the garden before a low table spread with a purple cloth, a flask of wine, and a bowl for crushing herbs. He was the high priest of Baal and Asherah, and Athaliah had furnished a temple for him with much gold from her husband's wealth. It was Mattan who found the best healers and diviners to serve her. Though she found him distasteful, a man whose lazy eyes took in all women but seemed to enjoy none, she had also found him to be an excellent judge of the divine. They never spoke of the earliest days, the days when he had, at Jezebel's request, ushered her into the darkness.

Mattan saw her smile and returned it, offering up his hands in a prayer before sprinkling them with water. Athaliah and Jehoram sat on their folded legs before the table.

He crushed the herbs with mortar and pestle, then poured olive oil in the bowl as well. Mixing carefully, he applied the mixture to their hands, then wiped them clean. He clasped their hands together and poured the wine over them, letting it fall to the ground, which swallowed the red stain. A tiny river of wine caught Athaliah's eye as it escaped between a row of roses, running to tell her dark secret to the listening winds.

Wiping their hands clean again with a towel, Mattan now produced an ink and a needle from his robes. Carefully, he pierced their skin in frantic little stabs, holding their hands near his face as he worked. Athaliah felt his stale breath. From time to time Mattan would look up from his work and smile, keeping a firm hold on the flesh. Jehoram sat silently as Mattan worked on his, and Athaliah felt her husband's skin growing cold as the needle punctured his flesh and the chilled breath entered with the ink.

Soon it was finished, and Jehoram pulled back his hand to see what was done.

A cobra coiled around an ankh, both now a part of him.

Athaliah smiled. "The symbol of unity." She raised her own hand to admire it more closely. She kissed Mattan on the cheek and was pleased to notice him flinch when she darted so close to him.

"Beautifully done, my old friend," she proclaimed, taking hold of Jehoram's hand, holding it out for a brighter inspection.

"I will be a king who unites?" Jehoram asked, looking from between his hand to his queen. "How can I unite if I have broken with the laws of Yahweh?"

She willed his very last memory, the old blood that once ran freely, to surface now so that she could surprise it like a hunter coming upon his sleeping prey.

She took hold of his shoulders. "I have seen the wisdom of unity born of the freedom, of allowing all things in all forms. Such openness brings us a peace that Yahweh holds beyond our reach."

Jehoram rubbed his temples and groaned. Athaliah lowered her voice.

"You did well to rid yourself of your brothers. But we have been betrayed by a new rival."

Jehoram raised his eyebrows with some effort. She felt his weakness like a bruise that burst easily beneath her grip. She drove her edge into it, pleased that he did not need details. Athaliah could still dispose of Jehoshebeth quickly, quietly if Jehoram knew nothing. But the priests of the Temple would suffer. Jagur had told her everything.

"The priests of Yahweh. They gather strength and will resist you. They invoke the name of their God to curtail your power. Do not let it be so. Do not let them go unchallenged. This is a land of very old gods; yet they cling to one and deny all else. They breed discontent, and a wise king would sever himself from them at once."

Her words found their way to Jehoram more easily today.

He stopped rubbing his temples and listened, his eyes following her mouth as she spoke.

"Your priests say we must deny ourselves in this life to be blessed by Yahweh, but who among us has ever returned from the dead to say what is true? We have only the word of priests who want our money today and promise better things tomorrow. I would rather live and love now and be lost later than deny myself everything and be no nearer the bloom of the rose as I return to dust. I have seen the graves of the great men of God, and their bones rot as well as the next man's."

"And yet I know this Yahweh exists," Jehoram said.

Her eyes narrowed, but she leaned in close, as if for a kiss.

"I will not argue that with you. Who am I to doubt what you feel? But if you choose the path of one God, one way, you will travel alone and the nation will perish. Jehoram, you have loved me with all that you are. And this is all that I am: the spirits of Baal and Asherah. They have consumed me. And you have known me fully and thought me rich. Do not lie to the nation about that."

Mattan spoke, handing two bowls to the couple. "I offer two bowls, peace and war," he said. "Choose then a faith, and you will choose the destiny."

"It is the sin of men that makes wars," Jehoram said weakly, fading.

"Not of men, but of the jealous God who denies all else and then commands you to deny yourself. That is the cause of war." Athaliah spit the words out. "I will drink peace to the kingdom and bear the sign of unity."

A sound descended from the sky: thunder made from hooves and heaving short breaths, of wings that beat the clouds back. Birds screamed and dived low to the ground. The trees were bent back by something unseen, their uppermost boughs snapping and breaking clean as the wild wind roared. Moist fruits, the last of the harvest, fell. Scavenging, detestable creatures eyed them from their holes, a certain meal.

Jehoram cried out, his hands stretched out toward the heavens, and he fell at Athaliah's feet in a faint. Mattan fell over his table, protecting his ministrations and magic. The blast swept past them and was gone.

None spoke for a moment. The only movement was from Athaliah's thin robe, her heart pounding and shaking her chest. Jehoram began to weep, his face in the dirt. Athaliah looked at the sky and felt Someone near. She remembered the Presence from a birthing room long ago. The hair rose along her arms and she felt the dark rage climbing in her chest, ready to spring out and meet Him. But she swallowed it, looking at the two pitiful excuses of mankind on the ground. She helped Jehoram to his feet, her jaw set.

"You fell faint, love, from the heat and burden of such a day. That is all," she whispered. "Let us go to our chamber. You need rest."

"Did you hear it?" His wide eyes took in the sight of her heart pulsing rapidly against her thin flesh, her veins in her trembling hands standing out as blood was forced through like the floodwaters of the Nile.

Athaliah hardened her expression as she caught Mattan's eye. "I heard nothing," she replied. "A wind swept the trees, a sudden and soon winter gale, that is all. It took us by surprise. It is my fault for allowing you to push yourself this way, to take so much ground so quickly as king."

She laughed, stroking him as he walked. "Never has a king turned his house right side out so quickly. In a matter of hours you have righted the wrongs of many generations! Blame my pride and fear of you that I did not speak up and bid you think more carefully of your health. You rule as a god, my lord, but I must remember you are mortal."

Jehoram held her hands tightly, wrapping her more closely to him, and stumbled toward his chamber, stealing furtive glances at the sky.

When he was in bed and sleeping at last, a thick brew of heavy beer from the kitchens speeding the work of dreams, Athaliah crept from the chamber and called for Mattan. He had not returned to his temple of Baal, but was still in the garden, staring sullenly at the dead plants.

Athaliah slapped him, hard.

"What is this magic visited upon us?" she demanded.

Mattan shrank away. "I do not know, my queen," he said.

"A weak and foolish priest is what my mother has saddled me with!" She cursed him, pacing.

"Our baru has fled," he pleaded. "No one knows where he is, but there is a girl. The spirits of many gods speak to her."

"Something stirs that is not of men. Find out what it is."

CHAPTER TEN

THE GIRL'S eyes rolled back and she jerked against the chain that had chafed her neck into a raw red sore. She fought it, screaming and pulling with both hands until she fell limp on the floor before Athaliah.

"What now?" Athaliah asked.

Her keeper held up his hand for silence.

The girl sat up, opening her eyes and staring at Athaliah. Athaliah met her gaze without flinching.

"What do you see, my sister?" she asked.

"The prophet Elijah in the north was taken by God and wind. He will not return," she said. "It is this thing you heard in the garden."

"Elijah is gone! It is good news then!"

"No, an evil omen. For before he left, his disciple asked for twice a portion of his spirit. Another prophet comes."

Athaliah frowned and rubbed her arms, which seemed to belong to someone else's body. The nerves along her arms throbbed as if remembering what it was to be bitterly cold.

Yet she felt nothing.

"Say nothing to Jehoram," she instructed.

The girl jabbed her finger at Athaliah.

"Your mother is killing the prophets of Yahweh. Why do you not make war on Him as well? Already His priest has stolen your daughter; the kingdom is not far behind." She scowled at Athaliah and spit out a taunt: "Will you be queen? Will you be queen?"

Athaliah jumped up to grab her, and the girl shrieked and launched herself to meet the queen. Her handler jerked the chain at once, yanking the girl backward to the floor. She watched Athaliah's fists curl and uncurl, and she began laughing, her mouth open, many different sounds of scoffing pouring out. Athaliah was grateful when she closed it at last, and the keeper dragged her away.

JEHORAM SANK low in the blankets. He had not slept soundly for weeks nor received anyone from court. He turned in his bed, over and over, finding no comfort. When he was awake he imagined he could hear the sounds of the spirits who attended Athaliah, the sounds of gaping mouths inhaling in long drafts, of serpents whose scales rasped together as the coils constricted, the hollow sound of bones snapped clean. It was the sound of the dead. It was this, this silence that was not quiet, that stirred terror and drained his life when he most needed strength to run. Instead he turned his back to the sound and tried to sleep, in vain. Night brought him dreams that were worse than his days; every morning he weakened, and the battle seemed too great.

Though he knew righteousness called out to him, the

gulf between them was made deeper with every hour, until he began to hate it. He pressed his hands to his ears and cried out for relief. Finally, after an unbroken row of night-filled days and horror-filled nights, he lowered his hands and discovered an unexpected stillness in his room. He was alone, with Athaliah at the window. Nothing wrestled in his spirit; nothing moved at all. He stood and joined her, looking out at the world.

Beyond them, a great hawk circled and they were both drawn to such force and beauty met in one creature. He circled in silence, not even causing the wind to whisper as he swept it away in great rushes beneath him. He dived then, his fury centered on the starving, thin mouse below that had stupidly crawled out for a grape rolled loose from the kitchen. The hawk dug its talons into the soft meat and screamed as it lifted its writhing prey high into the air, giving it a vision of a new world, before it was devoured and the dream snatched away.

Jehoram breathed deeply. Strength came to his limbs and he looked at Athaliah.

"It is time," he said.

Athaliah wiped the bead of sweat threatening to topple off her brow and lifted her face to his lips. Her mouth was wet, and warmth returned to her flesh as if she had been in a very cold place.

"Did you hear the little one scream?" he asked, a smile on his lips.

She smiled too, tasting him gently and pressing closer. The strange new power worked its way through the last of him and he found a new life wholly entered him now, the hissing breath of a liar in an orchard, bidding him to taste after her, to know what she had partaken of, to see that it was good.

"I heard the scream," she said as he forced his mouth to hers.

THE PEOPLE assembled near the palace to hear King Jehoram's first public address. A month had passed while he was nurtured by Athaliah in secret, like a splendid spider growing fat, hidden in her silken shadow. Today he would reveal himself to the people. Jehoram knew some, those faithful to Yahweh, came only to silently accuse. Others came in hopes of gold coins thrown for favor. But all would listen.

King Jehoram came to the center of the waiting crowd, announced by the royal trumpets. Hired girls laid palm branches across his path. Athaliah did not stay behind in the palace, as was the custom of Queen Anna, nor did she walk behind him. She stood proudly at his side, staring down anyone who looked twice. The guards with their swords and double-edged axes made sure every glance was respectful and brief. Jagur was behind her in the procession.

A child from the crowd ran forward carrying a blossom and laid it at Athaliah's feet. She bent to kiss him on the head. Whispering to a guard, she produced a coin and pressed it into the boy's palm. His mother blessed Athaliah loudly.

King Jehoram motioned for silence and attention, receiving both right away as only a new king can. The people were most attentive at the beginning and end of each reign, but wished largely to be undisturbed in between. But this king, with his strange Phoenician bride, would hold their attention considerably longer.

"Good people, my brothers and sisters of Judah, the house

of David rests secure on the throne," he said.

The people responded, "Long may a light from the house of David shine before the Lord!"

"The world is shifting, is it not?" Jehoram asked. "What enemy has not grown in power? What fortress has not been threatened? What vassal state has not rebelled? Even little Libnah has taken a nibble at us!"

The people booed and hissed. Little insurrections were a petty complaint, but in the absence of real war, they needled at the complacency of the people and harassed the mothers, who were loathe to send their boys to die in a minor valley.

"We have grown up together, you and I. We were children together, we were raised on the milk of the prophets and the judges, the laws of Yahweh stitched neatly into our hems. I was raised at the knee of the great King Jehoshaphat, who ruled as one under the authority of God. But I have seen a wrong turn taken. I have seen arrogance bubbling up from our once pure springs. I have grown into a man and from my new stature, I can see the way of our fathers is killing us."

The people looked at each other.

Jehoram continued. "The Temple tells us there is one God, one law, one truth. Why must this be? The Temple condemns anyone who will not recognize its law, and it breeds discontent as it promises peace."

A few in the crowd began to whistle in agreement.

"That great thorn of the north, Elijah, who spent his days pitting king against God, is gone forever. We have a moment's peace, but can we stretch it now to an hour, or to a lifetime?"

Only a few in the crowd were not cheering. Jehoram turned to them.

"I bless Yahweh. I praise Him. His name will always be

honored in my courts! But He is one God among many. I will recognize all men and all ways, but let us share the rich blessings of earth now rather than dream of them later!"

"Loose yourselves, then," Athaliah called to the crowd. "Be loosed, and go to the Temple of Jerusalem, the Temple of your fathers, the Temple that houses the gold, the silver, the turquoise that once lay across your mother's gentle neck! This God has stored up your wealth — today, go and receive it! Proclaim that a king reigns in Judah, and that all are bound by his law now and none else!"

She flung her arms high, yelling, the people feeling her stormy voice surge through them, their legs compelled to move. One man ran for the Temple, calling out the name of the high priest. If he was going to warn him, or rob him, no one ever knew, for his sudden movement ignited the whole crowd, and he was trampled before he could raise his voice again.

The storage places of grain and wine were broken open first, hungry families diving in for their share alongside the wealthy and the gluttons. They stole the priests' goblets and the money given for sacrifices. All were broken, chipped away clean, and carried off, save for the mightiest pieces. The guards took those, striking any priest who stood between the things of God and the men of swords. The priests were running, trying to stop the thieves, begging the people to let the sacred things be. The guards killed only a few of them. Most of the priests were simply restrained and tossed outside the Temple gates. They were too old to fight well.

JEHOIADA HAD been preparing his father, the high priest, for the Day of Atonement. In the inner court, near the giant bronze bath, his robes were laid out with the breastplate of twelve stones. As the high priest approached the inner sanctum, into the very presence of God, he might be killed if he had not completed the ritual cleansing perfectly. The priests were careful, but God was unrelenting, and some had died.

After the preparation for the next day was complete, father and son mounted the steps into the massive Temple. The two had just finished the ascent and stepped inside when they heard the crowd tearing through the Temple gates. Jehoiada made as if to see what was happening, but his father held him back.

"We will guard the Holy of Holies," he said. He began to recite a prayer, his eyes closing in supplication.

"Father!" Jehoiada protested. The sound of the priests outside the gates, some dying, stung his ears.

His father turned to him and kissed him once on the cheek.

"You have always been a good son, more than I had a right to ask for. I hope I have served well as your father. Now, let us each go to his destiny."

The massive doors swung open and the guards from the palace, pushed from behind by the people, stormed the Temple. They began hacking and destroying, stealing and running. Jehoiada recognized Athaliah's personal guard, who was a head taller than any of the others. The kohl-eyed man approached Jehoiada and his father as they stood in front of the entrance to the Ark. The beast grinned, revealing brown decay where each tooth met the next. Then he drew his sword.

"Betraying the queen costs many lives," he grinned. "Which of you should die first? Give me the one who married Jehoshebeth."

Jehoiada's father stepped between them and raised his hands to reason, or pray, but at his movement the guard lunged and slashed his stomach open. The high priest fell as he died, the whites of his eyes reflecting gold as they closed. Jehoiada tried to catch him, but the guard drew his sword back for a new strike.

Jehoiada screamed and charged, knocking the man off balance, both of them falling backward. The crowd pressed in from all sides now, and nothing was spared from their greed. The noise, the precious treasures being slammed together and tossed into robes turned satchels, the laughter and calls from unattended children, all rose above them, echoing off the gold walls in a fearsome cacophony.

Jehoiada held Athaliah's guard by the neck, one hand pinning the sword to the ground. Another guard rushed to the man's aid, climbing on top of Jehoiada and ripping his head back by the hair as he tried to free his friend. Jehoiada's enemy was losing air, but not his strength. He struggled and slipped free of Jehoiada's grip. He saw a priest standing guard over a gold lampstand and turned to kill him, leaving the other guard to kill Jehoiada.

Jehoiada wrestled the guard off his back, his veins near bursting as he forced the guard's head against the stone floor, pinning him as he had the first. The guard tried to claw with his free hand, but Jehoiada slammed his forehead down into the man's nose, causing a thick popping noise before the blood began to spill. The guard blinked, trying to focus on Jehoiada, who caught a glimpse of himself in the gold paneling and froze.

Just then, the table of shewbread crashed to the ground behind him. He looked at the man beneath him, whose blood was running down his face, perilously close to spilling on the floor. With a yell, Jehoiada let go of the sword and dragged the guard with one hand by the tunic. He dragged him out of the Temple, down the steps, through the courtyards, only stopping outside the gate.

"I will not desecrate the Temple with your death," Jehoiada said.

"That is good," the man said weakly, the beating having nearly killed him already.

"We are not in the Temple now," Jehoiada replied, cradling the man's head. The snap of his neck rang clear and true through the crowd that stopped to watch the priest kill one of Athaliah's men.

The crowd's courage died with the guard. Their faces fell when Jehoiada saw them carrying the stolen pieces.

And so it was that within an hour, the Temple was swept clean, its high priest murdered, and the wave of people at last receded. The priests, now released, cried out, rending their robes and falling over the altar's steps. The people scurried back to their homes to inspect their prizes in secret, a hushed guilt draining their anticipation. Jehoiada saw in each eye that met his a question, a loss as to how they had broken with the way of their fathers so readily, how long that dark thing had lain in their hearts unannounced. But it was done now, and they might as well toast the grain and use the goblets.

JEHOSHEBETH WAS in her bedroom when the surge of people overwhelmed the Temple. Long accustomed to hearing voices through thick walls, she knew at once it was a savage crowd and rushed for the roof. She watched the Temple being ransacked and abandoned. If this was only Athaliah's spite for her, she could hope it would be short-lived. Instead, she felt the dead, stiff-boned grasp of this woman's evil ways curling around the Temple. Kings and men of God had always shared power in

Judah. It was to be no more.

She wept and looked for her father or Jehoiada among the people but did not see them. She closed her eyes and felt her father's absence. He was somewhere in the crowd below; she recognized the royal guards at once, but she could feel him no more in her spirit and knew he was lost to Yahweh completely. She wrapped her arms around her waist and, in a vain attempt to escape her grief, set her mind on the tiny, bare room downstairs that was now her home.

CHAPTER ELEVEN

A FEAST WAS declared, and the priests of Baal and Asherah, including Mattan, were seated at the queen's table and served with the utensils from the Temple. Jerusalem was the heart of both kingdoms, Judah and Israel, and there was no other Temple like the one she had raided. Athaliah relished knowing her gold now outshone her mother's. Why shouldn't she one day rule Israel too?

And so the palace was opened to the people, who came in great numbers.

"There are great pleasures at hand tonight, my friends!" she cried out, and tables were filled, bowls rimmed and spilling with good wine. "Take what is before you and drink from the vine while it blossoms!"

Rugs embroidered with purple and scarlet and gold threads were arranged around the tables, which stood a modest height from the floor. Everyone sat on the rugs, surrounded by pillows, and laughed as they made room for more.

Jehoram sat on a large gold couch, with Athaliah on her

throne at the edge of this couch. Servants gathered around
the king to feed him as he sat. They offered food and wine to
Athaliah, who waved them off. She watched the crowd and
wondered who would be easiest to pull into her service when
the time came. She had learned long ago that leaders and gossip-
ers made the best allies.

Jagur stood on Athaliah's right. He wore a new chain of gold
around his neck, thickly braided cobras, each biting the tail of
the one before it, emeralds inset for eyes. His eyes did not stay
long on any one maid, and he attended her carefully. She smiled,
her first full smile of the night. All the royals sat on carpets
behind Athaliah and Jehoram: the lesser wives and the children
of these women who had so recently served the dying king.
All were quiet and pale with fear but were present at Jehoram's
command. The crown of the king sat plainly on Jehoram's head
and Athaliah was at last the queen. Ahaziah was seated behind
them and did not meet the eyes of the other royals or look long
on the nobles gathered before his father.

The people drank deeply, refilled their bowls quickly,
carelessly, the droplets falling away to form a dark spreading
sea underneath them all, a sea of the blood of the earth with
the flesh of lambs and fattened calves roasted and fed to all.
Bellies filled as eyes lit, each surveying the better-looking guests
and trying to move closer to desire. Athaliah laughed under her
breath to see the young ones jostling their elders. The old laws
slipped away from the room like disgraced suitors. Everyone
felt their bands of servitude to these laws fall away, freeing the
pale flesh to a new world of taste and experience.

The red sea rose behind their eyes and their hands moved
about, grasping, first with caution, a hand carefully placed to
steady the spinning room; then with intention, to take what

their eye desired. Laughter from the ones too young to hold their drink came easily and feasting from the ones too old to be desired. Athaliah and Jehoram laughed, too, enjoying the sights of a people free at last, reveling in their appetites. An exquisite hunger seized them all, a craving that surged through their veins like fire through a field left dry too long.

The doors to the main hall swung open on swift, screaming hinges, and Athaliah felt her heart contract violently as all heads moved as one. The royal priests of the temple of Asherah and Baal, led by Mattan and in full dress, filed in, three columns wide by ten deep. They were men and women, priests and priestesses, dressed in gowns cut away to draw the eye, gold and jewels resting across their headdresses, hands weighted with sapphires and rubies. The people laughed, their hands clutched against their hearts, as they watched these marvelous creatures approach the royals.

A space was cleared in the middle of the hall, and the priests and priestesses gathered round in a circle. A minstrel called from a corner. He played a slow, throbbing song, and the servants of Baal and Asherah swayed. Across the hall, other musicians caught the tune and joined, building upon the steady rhythm. The temple priests and priestesses were dancing now, eyes closed in ecstasy as the music grew louder and faster, and the people clapped in encouragement, spellbound. One of the priests cut himself across his chest, smearing blood across his muscles. A priestess seized him, kissing him and letting the blood stain her gown, not acknowledging the catcalls of the men in the crowd. They danced, spinning in tighter circles, more cutting themselves, more tasting and spreading the blood, falling prostrate when they received a vision.

The priests and priestesses began moving through the

enraptured crowd, laying hands on them and prophesying. Full harvests, new children, love returned, these were the promises given to the people who opened their pockets and threw coins and praise into the temple servants' outstretched hands. Athaliah, seeing the gold given so freely, held Jehoram's hand and brought it to her lips. Loosed from their God, what wonders these people might do! How much more could the money buy when it did not have to go into the Temple's flames!

Only Athaliah noticed the servants' entrance open quietly. A man entered unannounced, and watched the people. Athaliah's body froze. She squeezed Jehoram's hand, but he did not react. She felt a great crushing weight on her chest, pushing all air away so that she could not inhale to scream a warning, and still she crushed Jehoram's hand in her own. He drank more wine, calling out to the priests for another prophecy.

The man hid his eyes, his head low as he approached the throne. Athaliah felt her legs twitching as if she should run, but she was pinned by her terror. She squeezed Jehoram until her rings cut into her skin, and only then did he turn to look at her. She could not meet his gaze and felt herself staring, mute, unable to breathe or close her mouth. He jumped up and shook her by her shoulders but she did not respond. He slapped her, breaking her gaze. She found her breath and screamed.

Everyone saw the man now, and the wild activity paused. He was dressed plainly but in the fashion of the prophets, an animal skin across his hips and a loose robe. It was a sparse covering, plainer in the light of all that sparkled here. He did not bow when he handed a letter to Jehoram.

The king faltered as he reached for it. The scroll shook, a scratching together of the dried leather being heard throughout the great hall. Athaliah felt corrupting fear enter behind the man and begin to move through the people. It slipped into their bowls, slid into the sinews of the meat, so that all became detestable at once. The people looked at what their own hands were holding and moaned, setting the accursed things far back on the tables.

Jehoram unrolled the scroll. No one moved. He read, his eyes moving across each line and growing wider with each return. The blood drained from his face. His mouth fell open and he stared at the man in skins. The torches grew brighter, their flames dancing higher for no clear reason. Athaliah snatched the scroll and read it, cursing and throwing it at the feet of the man.

The room grew fiercely cold with a chill that no winter here had ever brought, as the man recited the contents of the scroll from memory:

"This is what the Lord, the God of your father David, says to King Jehoram:

'You have not walked in the ways of your father Jehoshaphat or of Asa king of Judah. But you have walked in the ways of the kings of Israel in the north, and you have led Judah and the people of Jerusalem to prostitute themselves, just as the house of Ahab did. You have also murdered your own brothers, members of your father's house, men who were better than you. So now the Lord is about to strike your people, your sons, your wives, and everything that is yours, with a heavy blow. You yourself will be very ill with a lingering disease of the bowels, until the disease causes your bowels to fall out.'

"It is signed by Elijah."

"It is a lie!" Athaliah screamed. Jehoram sank into his couch.

"Elijah is dead! He has been dead a long while, and we approach peace at last!" Athaliah screamed again, tearing the air with her hands as if she could tear up the scroll from her perch.

The man made no reply.

"Elijah is dead," Jehoram said. The prophet made no reply.

"Kill him!" Athaliah screamed to the guards. The unnatural chill launched itself against their backs, forcing them to move, dividing the people from the guards. The man gave no voice to pain or fear as the guards sliced him into bits, finally carrying it all away in a borrowed robe, bundled and dripping.

Jehoram stood and stumbled, then wandered to his door toward his upper chamber, leaving Athaliah with the people and the priests of Asherah and Baal. She raised her hands over the crowd to announce their benediction. The people shifted against their wooden lounges, looking at the doors.

"Peace is ours, walk now in it," she proclaimed.

The people shot toward the open doors, crowding onto the rose-lined paths for home, garments tearing on thorns, skins pierced in the rush.

Inside the great hall, the sea of red had grown larger, the blood of the prophet mixed well into the wine of the feast, and all the stolen gold was dipped in red.

THE FIRES in the hillside burned low and were replenished with thick logs, the armed men not caring which trees came down for their comfort, for they intended not to pass this way again. The ancient trees, planted in the days of David, crashed with a groan and were fed upon by the axes of their enemies. No cooks or attendants accompanied this group of rogues. They had heard an old voice calling to them and followed it, knowing what was to be done, knowing the shepherd stepped away now from his flock. All these wolves moved closer until they were almost upon each other at the base of the mountain. They would set on the palace — tonight.

They painted their faces by the firelight as the moon rose to power above them. Their eyes became burning coals, embers alive at the center. Dark stripes moved down their cheeks, through hollowed-out places where fat would have been in prosperous times. Their swords had been sharpened until they brought blood from the driest of skin. A chill swept into the camp, and the last of the men was ready. Each knew the cold touch of the master, knew how he loved the warm blood of men.

Silently, they abandoned the fires, moving unseen toward the palace. The clouds parted as if the moon herself would whisper a warning to those who slept within her walls, but a thick and yellowed cloud swept over it, causing shadows to shift and restless servants in the palace to think of days past, or of their mothers, of whatever shreds of happiness they once had.

ATHALIAH PACED in her chamber as Jehoram stared out the window sullenly. With the end of his days announced, the unbearable pain approaching, he found no strength to reach for what might save him. He felt he had awakened from a dream of torments, only to find he must live through worse. Over and over he formed the words he would say to the priest, the offerings he could make, until Athaliah seized his hands. She kissed them, but Jehoram knew he was condemned by this comfort.

He let Athaliah pace and plot. He saw the strange shadows in the garden, saw the creeping shapes along the far wall, but was silent. A dead prophet had decreed for him a bitter destruction. Jehoram could feel Sheol opening to receive him and was mute.

The screams below snagged him out of lost thoughts, and he cried out. Athaliah ran and barred the door. They could hear the hiss and explosions of swords meeting. They could hear the new swords of iron piercing their own guards' old armor, and the men's last desperate pleas to Baal, and sometimes Yahweh. Jehoram stared out the window again. He removed his crown and placed his face in his hands.

Athaliah pressed her ear to the inner wall and listened. She stumbled back and pulled Jehoram's sword from his side. He stared at her a moment before turning his gaze back to his palms.

"Do not resist," he said. "It is a judgment upon us all. We must receive the blows and pay for our sins."

"Have you lost your mind? Ahaziah is out there!" She shouted for a guard as she swung open her door. The guard shook his head in fear and made no move to help her. At any moment the horror would be up the stairs.

ATHALIAH RAN down the passageway, taking no time to kill the guard for his hesitation. That would be done later if the war raging below did not swallow her up. She ran down the hallways, uncertain at times of her steps and cursing herself that she had always walked behind the guards, never minding which passage they took. A few adjustments and she found her way back to the inner hall that led to the royal children. At the far end, a shadowed figure moved into a nursery and lifted a screaming woman onto his back, ordering a boy to march in front, prodded by a sharp sword that nicked his back and made him yelp. The intruder was leading them to the outer chamber when he saw Athaliah and stopped, grinning so that his white teeth took all the moonlight for themselves. She lost her breath. Athaliah had not felt this fear, this fear of mortal man, since she was a girl, and now she felt the rush of blood to her stomach and knees, felt the sword grow so much heavier now in her hands. She raised it, slowly, above her head and challenged him across the distance.

"Take whom you wish, but you will not have my son."

The man grinned wider.

"When I return I will take more than him," he yelled. He turned and rushed his captives down the stairs.

Athaliah popped open door after door searching for Ahaziah. She found him pressed into a corner. Grabbing him, she placed his hand on his dagger.

"Find your courage or I will kill you myself!"

"I saw them murdered," he moaned. "They dragged them from their beds while I watched." He pointed to the blood on the floor, and her eyes followed the trail to a pile of bodies behind the door, the bodies of his half sisters.

He looked at her and started to cry. "They didn't see me. I hid until they went to another room, and then I ran in. I tried to save them." He showed her his hands covered in blood.

She crept to the door and stole a glance out of the room. She could hear the raider taking the steps upward two at a time and she fled, pulling Ahaziah out of the room. A man jumped out from a passage at the far end, and Athaliah ran him through with her sword, not losing her stride.

A scream from below on the stairs stopped them, fear rooting mother and son to the floor. They heard a man cursing as he swung his sword, and it was met with a sharp reply of iron. The struggle lasted but a moment, and in the sudden silence Athaliah snapped to her senses, urging Ahaziah to run faster. But the man who had just fought and killed on the stairs was upon them now, running straight for them. Athaliah did not have time to raise her sword. Jagur did not slow his pace, but grabbed Athaliah's hand and kept running, dragging the pair behind him as he raced back to her chambers, where the guards paced like horses caught in a fire.

Jagur slowed down only then, and Athaliah motioned him aside.

Letting go of Ahaziah's hand, she lowered her sword and faced the guard who had made no attempt to help her. He made a motion to grab his weapon, but Athaliah struck him down with a violent thrust between his ribs and stomach. His torso leaned over at an angle and blood ran down his leg. The other guards took a step backward and let him fall as he might.

"Kill all who approach my chamber," Athaliah commanded Jagur. He stared at her, and her chin trembled but for a second. Jagur grabbed and kissed her and she pressed her body tightly against his. Ahaziah looked between them and reached for his mother's hand. Breaking away from Jagur, she swung open her door and shoved Ahaziah into her chamber. She looked back at Jagur and then followed, bolting the door behind her. Only then, inside her chamber with her son, did she sink to her knees, the adrenaline that had strengthened her now ebbing, leaving her trembling and afraid. She lifted her hands toward the ceiling, to cry out for relief from whatever was eating away at her house, but Yahweh's name was the only living name to penetrate her fear, and this name she would not say.

The screaming did not last much longer. Athaliah clung to Ahaziah without speaking, hearing the storm below recede and move away.

❄

JEHORAM, AT HIS window still, saw no more shadows. The clouds rolled back and the stars shone again. He saw a bird sitting on a dead branch near his window and looked away as it sang. He had lived through the first judgment. Hope stirred that he could survive the next.

"Is it raining?" Ahaziah asked.

Gentle waves moved through the walls, much like the sound of a rain after a storm had spent its fury. Jehoram looked at the boy, listening.

Jehoram shook his head. "You hear the sound of grief," he said.

Ahaziah strained to listen and rose to a near wall. He pressed his ear against the stone to hear weeping and moans from servants. Ahaziah withdrew and frowned.

Ahaziah watched his father, and with the back of his hands he rubbed at his eyes when they filled with tears. His lips parted in a sob he could not control. Athaliah slapped him with her full force.

"Do not waste your tears on those soon dead."

Ahaziah held his flaming cheek and looked at her. She stood and unbarred her door.

"Let us see what has been done and who is left alive," she said.

Jehoram stood to accompany them and cursed when he saw that he was sitting in a pool of his own blood. A bolt of pain hit. He grabbed his stomach, falling to his knees. He began to retch uncontrollably, holding his stomach and trying to reach his son with the other hand. Yellow bile spilled onto the floor as Athaliah pushed Ahaziah behind her, staring at her husband in horror.

"What is that smell? Have you been poisoned?" She covered

her mouth with her robe and glared at the yellow pool.

Ahaziah pushed Athaliah out of the way. Jehoram's eyes tried to flash something to him, perhaps a regret or a warning. Ahaziah reached for him.

"You cannot save him." Athaliah scowled.

Ahaziah looked away from his father.

Guards rushed in and tried to help Jehoram to his feet. When they realized he could not stand, they carried him to the bed.

"All below are dead," Jagur said, bowing to Athaliah.

"Then send for the healers to come to Jehoram. They will be glad for work," Athaliah commanded.

"Come, Ahaziah, let us survey what is left of our palace." She took his shaking hand.

CHAPTER TWELVE

ONLY A FEW people sat in the stands alongside the courtyards of the Temple, watching as Jehoiada was anointed high priest. The surviving priests had worked through the night to restore or repair what they could. Two more men had succumbed to shock and were in their bedchambers tended to by family. The priests who remained tried not to weep as they anointed Jehoiada.

"We have so little strength, my brothers," he said. "Save it for our work. Do not spend it in your grief for me and my father."

The men worked in silence then.

They watched as he walked toward the inner rooms of the Temple, averting their eyes from the stories that the walls told, the treasures missing. The table of shewbread had been uprighted and the loaves of offering were there, but a spirit of despair moved among the men.

Jehoiada walked, not looking to either side, and approached the Holy of Holies, the inner sanctum that would bring him into the Presence of the living God. Jehoiada turned, his eyes going in the direction of his home. He would labor alone before the Ark, then return to the priests for another week of service before coming back in. He prayed for Jehoshebeth before entering. Every day he offered sacrifices to God; he understood sacrifice as the only currency in the unseen world that ruled king and beggars alike. He had given his life to this woman to save her, not knowing the sacrifice would save him first. He had long been unmoved by the women of the city, wondering when one would finally stir in him the love he saw other men display toward their wives. It was Jehoshebeth who gave him the answer. His sacrifice for her split the stone of his heart, and now he knew what love was. He had saved her from the palace, and she had saved him from the half life that haunted him.

She was beautiful to him, more beautiful than the sum of her features or his first impression of her, because she was his own life poured out. He did not pray that she would be merely content with him. He prayed that her sacrifice would open her heart to him too, that she would know the power of his love and of life redeemed.

IN THE PALACE, the ashipu healer and asu herbalist attended to Jehoram. They had heard of a disease such as this, where the bowels died bit by bit, until at last they sagged and were passed out. The ashipu promised a cure and left to consult with Mattan, to arrange for sacrifices to Baal and Asherah and to create ointments from the offerings that might be of some use. The asu made no such claims but studied the king carefully, noting each symptom in detail before excusing himself to go and learn what had been written on the subject. The king lay in agony but commanded all to account for the losses and return to safeguarding the palace. He refused to send a war party out.

The asu was nearly to the door when the king spoke to him. "How long do I have?" Jehoram asked.

The herbalist shook his head. "I have heard of people living a full year after the disease makes itself known. Most, of course, last only a few weeks or perhaps months, if they have the strength."

Jehoram nodded and closed his eyes.

ATHALIAH RETURNED within a few hours to their chambers. Ahaziah had returned to his own room with extra guards posted for his reassurance. Athaliah was glad to be free of him for a moment. He had never seen children die. She had forgotten what work it was to comfort.

Jehoram's advisers were stationed outside the chamber, consulting among themselves on the state of the kingdom. If Jehoram died, Ahaziah would be next on the throne.

"We have not spent much time with the boy," the limp-haired Ornat said. "A regrettable oversight."

Another concurred. "We cannot know if he will be a hindrance to our plans," he said.

"I can vouch for the boy," Athaliah said. None had heard her coming behind them.

Ornat bowed. "Our concern today is only for the kingdom. We meant no disrespect."

Athaliah brushed past him.

"The kingdom is my concern, not yours. Do not take it upon yourselves to do my thinking," she said.

Inside Jehoram's chamber, she saw that he was weak, but

a brew had been sent from the asu's chamber servant. It was simple, a clear broth from meat, garlic, and leeks, mashed and boiled and then poured through a sieve. It seemed to have revived Jehoram enough that he could receive Athaliah. She entered and walked to the window, rubbing her head, rubbing her eyes with the backs of her hands.

"Athaliah?" Jehoram said. She did not reply or move.

No birds were visible near the palace. All of life had fled. Still, she heard the cry of one and strained to find it.

"You cannot bear to look on me?" he asked when she would not turn her face away from the window.

Athaliah laughed a short little laugh and shook her head. "Think on someone other than yourself," she said.

Jehoram laid there with no reply. Athaliah turned to face him.

"The prophet spoke the truth when he proclaimed the destruction of your house, for all the children of the lesser wives are dead. Many of the wives themselves are dead or carried away, with only the ones displeasing to the eye left alive and here. I felt sorry for you, thinking it was with these that you would rebuild the kingdom, but I see now you have not the strength even for that."

She slapped the window's edge and clenched her jaw as she exhaled.

She walked to the bed and peered down on him. Jehoram tried to pull a cover around him.

"Ahaziah will be our hope," she said. "He will marry again tonight and begin the work of rebuilding our house. I have sent my men for girls who will please him, and I will collect as many as needed until we replace the children of his brothers lost today."

Athaliah turned back to the window and watched as armed riders were dispatched with lengths of rope and swords to subdue anyone who resisted. A small white bird flew near her window, but she cursed it for disrupting her view.

AHAZIAH DID NOT stay in his chamber. Instead, he arranged his bed so that it seemed to hold him, sleeping, then he gave gold pieces to each of his guards. He ran to the stables. All the keepers were there, alive and unharmed. The raiding party had not even cared for the fine horses and animals kept here. There was a stable hand named Abel, older than the rest, who had never taken his bribes. Ahaziah sought him out, finding him resting on a high pile of straw, wheezing from the exertion of the morning feeding.

Ahaziah embraced him, and the old stable hand clapped him on the back with a weak laugh.

"There is someone to see you." He led Ahaziah to Gabriel's stable, which had remained empty since the night Jehoshaphat died.

Jehoshebeth was there. She stood when Ahaziah threw back the stable door. Both began to speak at once, until they waved each other to speak first.

"You, sister," Ahaziah insisted.

"What has happened?" Jehoshebeth asked.

"The raiders killed all the sons and took most of the women. It was a curse from Yahweh."

Jehoshebeth blew a long breath out.

"Where did you go?" Ahaziah asked. "Athaliah thinks you have run and will never return."

"Nothing is as it seems. I am not your true sister, Ahaziah."

"What? Don't be foolish."

She held his arms. "Athaliah is not my mother. It was all a lie. She wanted me gone as soon as I came of age. I have married the high priest of Yahweh's Temple. I will never return to our home here."

"You speak like an idiot!" He shook her off and would not listen to more.

"No! I see more than you do, for I am broken free of her spell. She is not as we think she is. She is the end of all that is good in Judah."

Ahaziah now gripped her by the arm. Her breath caught in her throat, both knowing his grip was too firm.

"You and I have always loved stories whispered in the dark, my sister. I grew out of them; I suppose you did not."

Jehoshebeth removed his hand, not taking her eyes away from his.

"She has turned her plan over and over in her mind since the day she was brought here. Our father's slaughter of his brothers was only the beginning."

"What? You cannot call it slaughter! It was a righteous act!" He stopped himself and rubbed his forehead. "You did not risk being seen back at the palace for a fight with me, did you?"

She gave him a half smile. "I do not know what she will whisper about me to our father. Tell him I am alive and happy and that Jehoshaphat arranged my marriage to the high priest. I will be safe there. Tell him I know the truth now and am at peace. Tell him he, too, can find peace before he dies."

Jehoshebeth started to say something, then stopped. Ahaziah motioned for her to speak.

"Does he ask about me?" she asked.

Ahaziah's face fell. Jehoshebeth felt tears burning her eyes. She forced a smile, nodding. "Athaliah has worked her magic on him well."

"No," Ahaziah said. "I will agree that she is cunning, and she pushes me to act like a king when I would rather sleep and drink, but she is none of the things you have said. She is scorned for her worship and seeks only peace for all people. She has her eyes on no other reward than justice."

Jehoshebeth did not reply.

He groaned and punched the wooden wall. "How is this happening? We've never fought like this. Someone is turning you against us."

She stood and opened the stable door, looking behind her before she departed. "You will marry again tonight, for many girls are being taken from their homes and brought here in great haste. This, then, is the reason I have sought your face: These girls will not be safe, and neither will your children, Ahaziah. God be with the woman who gives you an heir. You are Athaliah's child, but the blood of David runs through your veins, as it will through his. Athaliah hates the power God holds over this palace, power that makes no room for her many gods, and His covenant with the men of David's line will not go unchallenged. Every time you make love to a wife, every time a belly swells and she is delighted by her good fortune, know that you have delivered a child into fear and shadows."

THAT NIGHT, riders could be heard driving their horses toward the open gates of the palace. Small girls, ages from thirteen to seventeen, clung to the riders, burying their faces in the backs of their captors to shield them from the wind that froze their tears against their cheeks.

Athaliah had all the torches lit and burning high for their arrival, though it was raining and a strong wind rose. The cook had worked with his servants to prepare a wedding banquet for the girls who would soon become wives, and the banquet hall was prepared to receive them.

Athaliah met the shivering brides there, striding up and down between their ranks, surveying them. Turning to a servant, she gave instructions and he dashed out, heading up a long limestone staircase visible from the room. He ran to the top, to the quarters of the previous wives and their children. All afternoon the servants had worked on sweeping the areas clean, gathering personal things and throwing anything worthless out into the back area of the palace where it would be burned later. The rooms were then tidied and fresh flowers set in each. The servants had walked for almost a quarter mile before finding any living flowers in bloom.

The clothes from the former wives were brought down. Athaliah chose a gown for each girl and tossed it to her. She chose their jewelry, ripping off cheap necklaces given to them by their mothers and setting upon them the stones of Judah. She smiled at her work, even as they cried.

"Call Ahaziah in," she commanded.

Ahaziah had turned nineteen that year. It was perhaps late to give him more brides, but she knew he enjoyed the women he bought in the city.

Ahaziah looked at the rows of girls, some quite beautiful. All were his.

"Bless you, Mother, for you have done exceedingly well!"

"Your patience with me is rewarded in full tonight," she

replied before she touched his cheek. "I am proud of you, my son. Proud to begin building a kingdom through you."

He nodded, not taking his eyes off the girls. One in the front caught his eye, with long black hair and eyes like wide dark stones. Athaliah saw the look from Ahaziah and traced it to the girl.

"What is your name?" Athaliah asked her.

"Zibia," the girl replied. Her accent was unfamiliar. Athaliah raised her eyebrows, expecting an explanation. The girl was quick to understand.

"I am from Beersheba. I was here visiting my father's family, for my mother has grown sick and my father is worn from caring for both her and me," she replied. The girl cast her eyes down.

Ahaziah moved to her side. "My father has taken ill too," he said. "I understand."

She did not look up until Athaliah spoke.

"Well chosen, my son," she said. "Zibia, you will become his first wife tonight. The rest of you will live in the wives' quarters and be called to my son as he pleases. Welcome now, and by my word, the word of Jehoram, you are all made wives and subjects to the crown."

The girls looked at each other, but none dared to speak. Athaliah commanded them to eat and set the guards to watch over them.

ZIBIA WAS led to a chamber freshly prepared for her and Ahaziah. She blushed when he began disrobing and pulled her own robe more tightly around her small frame.

"This is madness," she said.

"No," Ahaziah replied with a grin. "This is my birthright."

CHAPTER THIRTEEN

JEHOSHEBETH WAS freshly bathed with a flower tucked in her hair. A modest meal had been set out. She had asked for help from the other priests' wives in preparing it, but it was her own offering to him. Jehoiada sat at the small table in their small quarters, his eyes away from hers, and drank straight from the flask of wine, not bothering with a bowl.

Jehoshebeth rose and walked behind him. She had heard tales of priests who emerged from the Holy of Holies, their faces glowing, radiant from a surreal light that had penetrated them and lingered in the world of mortals. Jehoiada had none of that glow; he looked aged, flecks of new gray around his temples, lines etched over his forehead. His weary face moved her. He had been so patient with her, and she had not let him have her wholly. She had given him her kiss, and let him trace the curves of her body when he held her, but she pulled away when he desired more.

God had delivered her so perfectly, and she withheld all that was asked of her. Guilt set upon her and she lifted her eyes to ask forgiveness. If God granted it, she did not know, but she pushed back the heaviness in her heart and asked instead for courage.

Jehoshebeth removed his outer cloak and began to massage his unyielding shoulders with an oil of myrrh, his eyes becoming heavier, but resisting sleep. Her hands grew tired from trying to smooth the knots out of the muscles across his back. She dropped her hands in her lap and laid her head against his back.

He turned and held her until the afternoon passed. She started to speak now and again, but her mouth would only slightly open and then shut. He had taken a bride from the palace, and the palace had taken her bride price out of the Temple. That was how it seemed to her. She had no defense for the ransacking King Jehoram had allowed. Her father had brought this evil into their midst. The people's disdain for him would grow, she knew, even if their pockets were lined and their bellies full. The truth soured everything.

It would destroy her too. The people would always see her face, the likeness of Jehoram, and never her heart. She wondered how long Jehoiada could love the reflection of the one who destroyed what he had first loved, and loved most deeply.

Jehoiada moved closer, his muscles spreading over her like the wings of a great bird, sheltering her from the accusation and reproach.

"Shh," was all he said, although she had not spoken.

He kissed her gently, and she silently asked God for courage once more. Lifting her arms, she ran her hands over the length of his back, feeling the muscles and bones as if they held the secret to all her days to come. The sharp edges along his spine, the soft valleys between taut muscles, every place was her refuge. Her pulse quickened. Here was her life, and as she ran her hands down his back, here, she felt, was the length and meaning of her days. She wondered if it would have been this way with Midian and flinched. It was wrong to think of that time, before all had happened. She had been another girl then.

It took the only courage she had left, the bits she had borrowed from her husband, but she refused to turn her face again toward her dark questions. Instead, she lifted her face to Jehoiada and kissed him back, sheltering him now from his burdens, her hands along his back freeing him of the weight he had carried home. Their bodies and hearts were woven at last together in the quiet of their chamber, God loosed to do His unseen work between husband and wife.

A soft rain began to fall as they slept for hours, each of them waking in turns and watching the other. Jehoiada ran his fingers over her face and lifted her hair to smell it before he settled back on his pillow. Jehoshebeth woke once to find his hand still resting on her face. He had fallen asleep stroking her cheek. She bent to him and kissed him softly. His deep, low breaths did not break their cadence, and she rested her head and listened to the sound, the sound of her husband in her bed. She slept again, and when she woke, she felt his strong warm hand on her stomach and him leaning over her. She sat up slightly, trying to blink back the curtain of sleep that still hung around her.

"May God grant you a child, so that you will grieve no more," he said softly.

She placed her hand over his.

THE BARU who had once read livers and divined secrets for Athaliah was now a tired man made too old from his fear. He no longer could see the future and had closed his eyes forever to his past. He had fled Athaliah's chambers with his life and run to a settlement far in the north, where Athaliah had no spies and her mother knew nothing of his existence. He lived in a mud-brick home, kept a few goats on the lower floor, and grew vegetables behind the house. He had no friends, save for the girl who brought him eggs from her fowl. He had a fondness for the girl, who had a strange appearance, a malady he had heard of but never seen. Her forehead was high and round, and her eyes were shaped like almonds, the eyelids folding in around them at the corners. She was simple and asked no questions, but she smiled easily and he found his heart opening to her without effort. Her smile was the only pleasure he had, and being away from the shadow of the palace made it richer.

She would come today. He looked out and saw the sky darkening, a storm coming from the coast. It made him uneasy. He went inside and was preparing a little cake to serve her when he heard the thunder. The light began to fade, and he felt his legs growing weak. Unable to find a support, he collapsed with a cry.

WHEN THE girl found him, he was thrashing wildly, his head snapping in every direction. His eyes were closed. A hoarse cry parted his thin dry lips, and she saw blood filling his mouth. She sat, confused, and waited for him to wake from this dream.

"He is here!" he moaned. "It begins."

He drew a wet, rasping breath, and the thrashing stopped. He spat the blood from his mouth, gagging. She placed her small hand on his arm, and his breathing slowed.

"My friend," he gasped. He opened his eyes. Both had gone milk white. A quick movement beyond him caught her eye, and she saw a serpent disappearing into the darkness of the goat stalls. She started to cry and he groped blindly to find her, but she scooted away on the dirt floor.

"What is happening?" he screamed. "Why is it night?"

She stood and ran.

NEAR THE baru's home in the northern kingdom, the man was praying. He saw them again, his heart racing and sweat beading across his upper lip. He remembered falling on his knees onto the dirt road as they passed overhead. . . .

He thought he had died that day. He could not explain why he was still alive. For he had seen horses made of fire, their nostrils sending hot ash showering over him, and chariots of wind and flame. The creatures from the whirlwind made his stomach churn with fear. For a moment, the veil between the worlds had been lifted. The other world disliked the eyes of men. And yet, he had seen. His eyes had been opened and they burned. He had wept, muddying his face in the dirt until he was exhausted.

He remembered rising with much effort and seeing the cloak of his master left behind. His knees had gone weak when he considered his last words to the man. It was one thing to ask for mercy, another to ask for it fully understanding the fierce work of the God who delivered it.

"Give me a double portion of your spirit." That was what he had asked. Nothing seemed different at first. He inspected himself carefully, but he looked much the same. He picked up the cloak and walked to the river. No creatures were about and he saw no other men. He felt alone, the kind of loneliness brought by the deep winter rains, and the pain turned sullen and sad. His shoulders dropped when he thought of a lifetime ahead without the comfort of his friend.

"Where now is God, the God of my master Elijah?" he cried into the stillness. No reply came, and he watched the fast waters racing past him. The cloak slipped slightly from his hands, its hem touching the water. At once, the raging river split with a great scream. A path appeared between the halves, and a great wind slammed against Elisha. He fell forward, reaching his hands out to steady himself, and saw that he was braced against the wall of water. He cried out, righting himself and staring.

Trembling, he took a faltering step into the void. As he crossed between the walls of water, he was aware that he could feel the eyes of all living things in the river staring at him. All remained still, watching, as he crossed.

When he reached the other side, he could hear things — such things as no man had ever heard, except perhaps his master Elijah. Elisha gripped his ears, twisting his head round to see where the noise was coming from. He could hear it all — sounds of children sleeping in the afternoon heat, the maids laughing in the houses of the nobles, the sounds of food being chewed slowly and swallowed. Behind him, the river screamed closed again, and the living things fled to their caves and murky shallows.

He roused himself from remembering now and returned to his prayer. He stood and looked north toward Jezebel's palace.

She was laughing. He heard her first, then closed his eyes and saw her. She was holding a goblet sent from her daughter, a beautiful piece of exquisite workmanship from the Temple.

"It is a little golden herald." She laughed again.

Her male servant, brushing her hair, asked, "And what does it tell you, my queen?"

"That a new age has come to the land of Yahweh," she said.

"Indeed, it has," Elisha whispered across the distance of sand and stone.

Jezebel went white and threw the goblet away from her. She saw him and reached out her hands, shaking, to see if he was real, if the voice was from heaven or earth.

He opened his eyes now and began walking toward the palace. He threw his master's cloak around his shoulders and straightened his back.

"HOW IS my son?" Jehoram asked hoarsely from his bed. The asu stopped grinding an herb for a moment and thought about his reply.

"He is well, my good king," the asu said. "He has a favorite among the wives brought to him by Queen Athaliah, although he has not stopped himself from having a night with each of the girls in turn. Many of the women are already with child. I suspect he finds it well to be the prince right now."

Jehoram coughed out a little laugh. Seconds later, he doubled over and gripped his stomach. He bore down and his body released blood.

The asu took note of this.

Jehoram clenched his teeth and cursed. "The ashipu bring me sacrifices from Baal to eat at night, great chunks of vegetables and new grain, unroasted, with meat that they refuse to identify. Their cure is killing me, I swear," he moaned.

The asu nodded. "The ashipu make sacrifices every night for your health," he said. "But their remedies are meant to chase spirits away. I do not believe it is a spirit that haunts you."

Jehoram raised his eyebrows and laughed weakly. "No, it is a God."

The asu drew a chair near and listened. "I will do what I can, prepare my herbs and teas for you, but if there is something of the spirits to attend to, you must do it soon. There is not much time, King Jehoram."

Jehoram looked out the window.

"I used to play in the garden as a boy," he told the asu. "I loved every plant, every flower and the fruit that fell so willingly into my hands. The world was a song played for me, and I delighted in the thought of a God so near. And all I did was to love the woman my father sent me." Jehoram's face grew red and he frowned. "Why does God torment me for that? Was it not my father's fault?" he asked.

The asu shook his head, having no answer.

"She is what is wrong in the house of Judah, not I," Jehoram finished. "How odd that in her absence, as I draw nearer to death, my mind clears and I feel the strength of my heart returning."

The asu stood to leave. "I am not equipped to hear a king's confession, nor will I offer advice on love and the heart. That is why I have served in so many palaces and always left with money and my life." He bowed with a sad smile.

"Then bring her to me. There is something I must say," Jehoram commanded.

The asu looked at the doorway, considering the guards who were no doubt listening. He looked then at the king, who was losing blood at every hour with every meal. He decided to speak.

"King Jehoram, this is my last visit to you. Athaliah has commanded that no one enter or speak to you. You are meant to die here, alone."

Jehoram's mouth fell open. A shock of pain and another discharge of blood and tissue racked him. He laid in the waste, tears streaming down his face, his mouth moving in a voiceless prayer.

THE CLERIC finished the report to Athaliah and Ahaziah, who were seated together dining. "Most of the treasures that the people seized were returned to the Temple, with great remorse I might add," he said.

Athaliah sat her goblet down and wiped her mouth. Ahaziah reached to dip his bread in more honey and she slapped his hand away, moving the honey bowl.

"This does not surprise me," she said. "We were distracted by the prophet and we lost our place for a moment. Let nothing be said of the treasures. Perhaps their guilt may even be a useful thing in our hands."

The cleric agreed. "Even so, my good queen, we are enriched by your bold move and have created much discourse among the people about their God. This is marvelous work. It is so much easier to sway those who are not gripped firmly to some other thing." He patted his scroll against his chest as if to congratulate himself on the oration.

"Let the people who worship there be at peace, Mother," Ahaziah snapped. Both cleric and queen stared at him, their mouths open. Ahaziah cleared his throat. "I meant, we should attend to other matters."

Athaliah leaned closer.

"Why do you have an interest in the Temple?" she asked.

Ahaziah shifted in his seat. "You can run the kingdom well

enough on your own, Mother. Let me get back to my wives." She held his arm and stared at the cleric.

"The crown thanks you for this report," she said. "Give me a moment with my son, and then I must engage you for more information on the state of my holdings."

The cleric bowed and left.

"Have you made any progress in your task?" she asked Ahaziah. She leaned back against her cushion and finished her wine.

"I work at it every night, Mother."

"Don't be foolish. Have any of the girls shown signs of promise?" she asked.

"Yes, Mother, Zibia has not bled yet, and her servants tell me she sleeps often in the afternoon, complaining of weariness."

Athaliah ran her finger around her bowl of wine and pursed her lips, nodding. "This is good for you, as she is your favorite. But do not neglect the other wives until an heir is secured. In fact, do not neglect your other wives even then. We need many heirs to strengthen our cause."

Ahaziah agreed, wiping his mouth with his sleeve and standing.

"This I will do, Mother. May I ask a question of you now?" She raised her eyebrows to allow it.

"When can I see my father?" he asked. "I must talk with him."

Athaliah's face flinched and she covered it with her hand, waving him off for a moment as she was unable to speak.

"Ahaziah, you are a man now, are you not?" she asked.

Ahaziah nodded.

"Then I will tell you the truth, and you will need the strength of a man to bear it. Your father is very ill indeed, but with a most contagious disease. Every servant I have sent to him has died within hours, a horrible, bloody death. I will not even go into him myself, though I weep with grief when I must sleep alone. That your father has held onto life for this long shows promise. We must wait, my son, a little longer, and if he survives, we will all rejoice. Only do not go near him or his chambers, lest you die and leave us with no one to rule when he is gone."

He was silent. He searched her eyes and, seeing her heavy tears, bowed before her, then left.

She watched him go and reached for the honey bowl. Lifting the ivory spoon, she studied the thick gold syrup as it fell in a great pool onto her bread. The cleric returned and waited for her to run her finger through the mass and taste it before he spoke.

"My queen?"

She did not look up, but watched the reflection of the burning wick distorted by the glistening amber.

"What of the girl, Jehoshebeth? Did they kill her husband? I have heard a widow without a family does not live long in this land."

The cleric's mouth twitched. "Jagur killed the high priest."

Athaliah sighed, then slapped the table. "Yes, that is what Jagur said. But he described an old man who died, and the priest who visited Jehoshaphat was young. It must be this man she married."

"What would you command me to do?" he asked.

She lifted the spoon and let another mass cling and fall free.

"Nothing. She knows my intention plainly enough. She will think on it every day while they restore the Temple's losses and bury the dead. Fear will drive her back to what is dearest, and then we will act. With Jehoshebeth returned to the God who wants her, perhaps He will move on from this place at last."

WHEN ALL were in bed for the night, Ahaziah stole up the back staircase, careful to avoid the steps that creaked as the slate shifted under someone's weight. He had made it to the top of the chamber when a shadow from an oil lamp passed over the wall at the end of the hall. Ahaziah ducked into a room until he could see who it was and know when the person passed. He heard no further sound. He tentatively stuck his head into the passage.

Jagur was waiting.

"Good evening," he said.

Ahaziah shifted his weight from one foot to the other and cleared his throat. "I am going to see my father."

"No."

"You will not give orders to a future king."

He tried to shove Jagur aside. Jagur pinned the prince's arms until he flushed and winced, then escorted him back down the stairs.

"No."

ATHALIAH WATCHED from the shadows until her son was safely away. Then she entered Jehoram's chamber.

He was lying in his bed with soiled linens, empty wine-stained bowls thrown to the floor. She had to pick her way to his bedside. His eyes were not open and she studied his chest to see if he lived.

Something stirred him and he awoke.

His eyes followed hers, and he looked on his waste and on the broken and used bowls near the bed. His skin around his mouth was drawn tight, and he looked as if he had drunk nothing for days. The skin on his lips had begun to peel. Athaliah shook her head and spoke.

"What God would let someone die in his own filth?"

He watched her and licked his lips. She winced to see his swollen, blistered tongue.

"I wouldn't even let an animal die in such disgrace," she snapped. "I'd sever its head and free it."

He smiled through a grimace of pain from the cracks in his lips separating.

"I believe you would." He sighed.

His hand gestured weakly, barely rising above the bed. He motioned for her to come near. She took one step, one step only, kicking a bowl from her path.

"Tell me," he said.

She waited. He took another breath.

"Did I ever love you?" he asked.

Athaliah smiled.

"Let me think back to my first night here, so alone and frightened. My hands shook and I could not meet your eyes when we were alone in your chamber, but this you did not notice. You simply began with my breasts and continued until all was finished with your contented little snort a short time later."

He nodded. "Yes," he said. "I did love you that night, before you first spoke."

"Your love was brief indeed." She smirked. "And if I hadn't

conceived Ahaziah on that night, no doubt another woman would be your queen today."

"Ahaziah will rule now," Jehoram said. "Will he be a good king?"

"He will be what I make him."

She saw his chin quiver and his eyes blink, but he had no tears. He let his mouth fall open as he took shallow gasps.

Her heart softened as she watched him. She had never seen a man so humbled and it loosed a rare sympathy in her.

"There were moments," she said, "moments . . ." She leaned closer to him, near his face. "I felt I could . . ." He lifted his face slightly and she saw it in his eyes, a need for her, even now.

She inhaled a sharp odor and recoiled in disgust. "You stink."

She left his chambers.

CHAPTER FOURTEEN

SPRING AND summer passed away as unnoticed as a beggar dying at the city gates. Jehoshebeth heard them whispering as she went to market. She loved the women who had taught her to roast and use spices, to prepare the simple dishes that made her home such a pleasant refuge for tired souls. But their lessons were far shorter now: just little gestures toward the fresh herbs brought from the mountain or a quick nod of approval when she chose the cheese that had a mild flavor. She heard only bits of their conversations, but they pierced her heart nonetheless, little biting things that were so hard to remove, like splinters too small to see.

"King Jehoram was wrong to have married her. He disgraced his family, and us."

"King Jehoram is enlightened, but a coward. He has not the stomach for his work, so he hides behind Athaliah."

"Jehoram is cursed by God. That is all I need to know. I care not for him."

She heard all the worst, her ears searching out what she

shouldn't know and dutifully reporting it back to her heart. She often returned home in tears. On this afternoon, it was her weary body that caused her to cry. Jehoiada reached her at the door and eased her onto their bed, which was a few steps away.

"What is it, Jehoshebeth? What has happened today?"

She rubbed her swollen stomach and rested her head against his arm.

"I am so weary," she said, "and lonely. Forgive me, Jehoiada, for being inconstant, but sometimes I miss the palace. I miss servants who could bring me what I wanted, even before I thought to ask. I miss servants who would heat the water before I bathed or bring me blankets if I called out at night."

Jehoiada listened. "Are you unhappy with me?" he asked.

"No, no. But the love of a husband is not like the love of a father, and I miss him. I think of how Athaliah separated us as I grew. Now he is dying, and he seems a strange man that I have not been reconciled to." She sighed again. "I complain about the lesser things to save me from thinking on that."

Jehoiada stroked her hair and kissed her on the top of the head. "We must be patient and see what God is willing to do."

A knock at their entrance made them both start.

Jehoiada opened the door, and a young priest entered. "Peace be to you," he said to them.

"And to you," Jehoiada replied.

The priest looked between the pair and took a deep breath. He moved so that his back was to Jehoshebeth and lowered his voice.

Jehoiada took him into the courtyard.

OUTSIDE THE Door, the man spoke quickly.

"King Jehoram is dead. All was as the prophet said it would be. He had much strength and lasted longer than anyone could anticipate, but last night one of Athaliah's guards discovered the body of Philosar. He was little more than bones, dug up by animals and scattered along the outside wall of the palace, but his seal was still within his robes. Athaliah accused King Jehoram of betrayal, but when he heard of the discovery, they say he went crazy, calling out for Jehoshebeth. The guards posted outside his chamber said his screaming did not end but went on and on for hours. Athaliah withheld his remedies and would let none enter until he was dead. One guard fainted when he entered the chambers, there was so much blood. He said you could trace every bone in Jehoram's body and his eyes would not stay closed, even after a guard drew them closed."

Jehoiada looked back inside the room at Jehoshebeth, who was beginning to rise from the bed, trying to hear.

"The funeral is right now," the priest said. "They mean to bury him in disgrace — no fires, no incense, and not even in the royal tombs. This is a thing that has never been done!"

Jehoiada pushed him away.

"What is it, Jehoiada?" Jehoshebeth called. He took a deep breath and faced her.

When he had shut the door, he went to the bed and sat, shaking his head.

"For the first time in my life, I am afraid."

"Of what?" Jehoshebeth asked. She touched his face and he took her hand in his.

"That I cannot protect you from this, this news of your father," he said.

She groaned and moved away from him, shaking her head.

"No, no, this cannot be!" She began stumbling around the room, trying to collect her outer robe and sandals. "I must go to him."

Jehoiada took her gently by the arm but she struck him and tried to wrest herself away.

"I never said good-bye!" she cried. "They never let me say good-bye! I must see my father. I must tell him what is in my heart. They say if the body is still warm, the dead can hear your words."

Jehoiada held her, not letting her past him. She hit him, and hit him again, sobs choking her words as she fell against him.

He cradled her head against his neck. "He is gone."

Jehoshebeth sobbed, letting her weight rest against him. He kept an arm around her waist and held her gently as she cried.

"Jehoshebeth," he said, "there is one thing more I must tell you, though it grieves me to even say it. Your father is being dishonored in the city. They say he brought the curse of Yahweh upon them all. They will not light funeral fires for him, nor will they give him the burial of kings. He is being taken outside the city and will be laid in a commoner's grave. Ahaziah will be made king."

She sank completely into his grip, unable to bear both the weight of this death and the new life within her. He moved her to the bed, where he held her and brought her water to drink between sobs and cotton to wipe her nose and eyes.

At last, as the hours passed and she could breathe enough to find words, she was able to speak.

"There is a space in the heart of every girl that she shares only with her father. But this grief, it is a window to a room that is no longer there, and from now on, every time I go past it, I will look in and know that my father is with me no more."

ATHALIAH POUNDED on the door to Ahaziah's chambers. "It is time!" she shouted through the heavy cedar. When she received no response, she motioned for a guard to break it down. Before he could, the door swung open about a hand's breadth, and she frowned. Entering, she saw Ahaziah lying on his bed, empty flasks of wine scattered across the covering.

"What are you doing?" she hissed.

Ahaziah rolled his eyes away from the window to stare at his mother. "It is a heavy burden I am about to bear. My father has died and I must become king. I need my strength." He took another drink from his flask.

"What you need is a mighty slap, but I won't leave a mark before I present you to the people," she said. "Now get up and walk out of here like a king."

Ahaziah grimaced and threw his last flask down on the floor. The wine poured out and made a fast river toward Athaliah, who stepped back neatly without breaking her glare.

Ahaziah groaned and stretched. "I will go, Mother!" He stood then and fell, planting his knees and hands in the wine. He barked like a dog and then lapped up the wine, laughing and rolling his eyes at her. Athaliah cursed. Turning to a servant lingering outside Ahaziah's door, she commanded, "Get him bathed and dressed and meet me below." She could hear Ahaziah laughing as she moved back to her chambers, her guards marching in what little silence they could manage, their armor banging and creaking.

AHAZIAH FLINCHED at the sunlight that struck his eyes through the window as his servants finished dressing him.

The light was dimmer now as the earth prepared for sleep, but sundown was still an hour away. Already, people were gathered outside the palace. After the final belt was tied into place, Ahaziah managed to go downstairs, supported by two servants. The procession began quietly, the people staring rather than cheering. Ahaziah continued to stumble until Athaliah ordered him put on a horse and led to the Temple.

"Lash him down to it if you have to," she commanded.

As they approached the Temple, Jehoiada watched silently. The priests, ashen-faced, were gathered behind Jehoiada, holding their instruments to play the traditional coronation music. Jehoiada held the anointing horn, a slender cup carved from ivory with bands of gold at its rim.

Ahaziah slid off his horse and was half carried to the Temple. Athaliah assumed a position behind him as he was led through the entrance.

A priest held his hands up as Athaliah approached.

"No one who is unclean may enter."

Athaliah would not look at him, keeping her head high as she stopped and chose to wait just outside the entrance. The priests began playing a tune with harps as they sang:

God is our fortress from everlasting to everlasting
God, look with favor on Your people.
May God grant the king long life!

ELISHA APPROACHED the palace of Jezebel. The wind carried him, pushing at his back, making each step light and swift. He did not know how long he walked or how many voices he heard.

The prayers and petitions of the people alighted unseen, even as the birds followed him and sang. He stopped, his eyes growing wide, for now he heard in their songs the words of the prophets and saints, the glorious hope of another King still to come.

Elisha raised his arms in the air, spinning around and around, the sounds hitting his ears now indescribable.

"I have lived my life here but I have never heard!" He laughed. "The earth is alive with Your song!"

A company of prophets approached from the east and found Elisha there, laughing as he lay on the ground, exhausted from his journey.

WHEN THEY had built a fire and roasted their dinner, the prophets passed around flasks of wine. It was not strong but refreshed each of them from their day of walking. They began to tell lighthearted stories, although a few kept an eye on Elisha. He did not eat or drink with them, though he listened to their stories with interest. One by one, they began turning in, each man finding a smooth spot in the dirt and picking away troublesome stones before he laid down. The stars overhead were crisp and bright, and the men watched for shooting stars as they fell asleep.

Elisha was alone by the fire now, watching the embers burn low. The pops and sparks sounded off only when he stirred the edges of the wood. Another prophet, the youngest of them all, Jonah, came and sat by him. Elisha welcomed the boy.

"Did you hear me calling you?" Elisha asked.

The boy frowned. "No, sir, I heard nothing. I came to sit with you because you looked lonely."

Elisha shrugged and stirred the fire again, then rose and fetched a last piece of wood to lay across it. He sat down again next to Jonah and smiled. "Much has changed for me since my master, Elijah, went away. But I see that the gifts he left are mine alone," he said. Jonah nodded as if unsure what he was agreeing with.

"You sit with me to keep me company," Elisha said. "That is kind."

The boy edged a bit closer. "Sir, it is not that I am a noble youth, although I esteem you much. Truthfully, I was hoping to hear stories of Elijah, of the wonders he performed, of the great battle with Jezebel that he waged."

Elisha looked at the boy. The boy blushed and faced the fire. "I did not mean to overstep my bounds," he said quietly.

Elisha patted him on the back. "You have a taste for adventure, do you?" he asked. The boy nodded shyly.

"Well, you shall have an adventure then, one that will be talked about for generations to come," Elisha promised.

Jonah looked at Elisha. "I carry sacks for the prophets as we travel. What kind of adventure did you have in mind? I'll have to be back before we set out again."

Elisha laughed at the joke and produced a flask of oil from his robes. He handed it to the boy. No one was stirring now in their camp, and the fire was the only witness as Elisha gripped the boy's hands, Jonah's eyes growing wide.

"You must tuck your robe into your belt so that you will run swiftly," Elisha said. "Take this flask of oil to Ramoth-Gilead. Follow the trail of stars over that mountain and be careful to make no noise. When you find the city, you must find Jehu, the son of the warrior and captain of the armies. King Ahab chose Jehu to lead the armies in his name while he was alive. Find Jehu, but do not speak to him until you have him alone in an inner room with no witnesses. Then pour this oil over his head and tell him, 'This is the word of the Lord: You are now the King of Israel. For God has declared an end to the days of the house of Ahab, and all who once loved him will die by your hand, Jehu.'"

The boy stood still for a long moment, then asked, "What do I do then?"

"Run for your life." Elisha cackled so loud he disturbed the sleeping men, who groaned and rolled over.

The boy looked at Elisha and then at the flask. Elisha pointed to the moon's position in the sky, indicating that time was already moving against them. The boy followed his gaze, understanding. Then he ran.

AHAZIAH APPROACHED Jehoiada in the center of the Temple courtyard. Ahaziah was steadier on his feet than he had been moments before, and his eyes searched the crowds gathered in the surrounding courtyards. The people were still silent and staring. He saw his mother surrounded by her maids, her guards being cut off from her, waiting outside the Temple gates.

"She looks so small from here," Ahaziah said.

"She is of no consequence," Jehoiada replied. "There is another who loves you. If you look again, you might catch a glimpse of her too."

Ahaziah looked into the outer court, and his gaze was drawn to a woman he had overlooked at first. Her hair was swept clumsily back and she wore heavy, plain robes that only partially hid her swollen abdomen.

Tears filled Ahaziah's eyes. "I have never seen her without

her jewels," he murmured.

"She is well and she is blessed. She will give birth before another new moon begins."

Ahaziah nodded and kneeled to begin the ceremony. As Jehoiada approached, ready to raise his arms in prayer, Ahaziah grasped one. "Protect your child, Jehoiada, and if you find I serve God well, protect mine as well."

Jehoiada poured the anointing oil over Ahaziah's head. "God be with you as you rule."

As Jehoiada rested the crown on his head, the people bent their heads in prayer.

"I am now made king over the southern kingdom of Judah by the hand of God," Ahaziah began.

ATHALIAH WAITED outside the Temple gates for Ahaziah to emerge as king. She saw the crowds from the city going in to see him receive the crown, and one woman, heavy with child, brushed past her. The hair rose along her arms. She lost the woman in the crowd as a dread stirred her stomach. Jehoshebeth was here; she could feel it. Athaliah had been so pleased to see so many people here to receive her son, but she cursed the same crowd now for sheltering her enemy. "Celebrate your brother coming to power," she heard herself murmur, "but it will be your last smile, or I am not the queen my mother raised."

"FASTER!" YELLED the men from inside the tent. "Faster!"

Jonah stood trembling outside until he caught a glimpse of

the moon racing, it seemed, above him. He took a deep breath and drew back the tent curtain. Inside, three men were guzzling wine in a contest. The smallest of the three seemed to be hollow as he emptied the giant flask of wine into his throat. Men stood around a table piled with coins, shouting as their favorite came closer to victory. The small man finished first, wiping his mouth with his cloak's hem and belching loudly. He made a start to collect the coins, but then the largest man sat his flask down and unsheathed his dagger, and all the men grew quiet. Little beads of sweat broke out on the small man's forehead.

The giant edged toward him, raising the dagger now until it was across his own throat, his thick vein straining against the blade. The men were still as they watched, no one among them visibly breathing. With a flick of the blade, he loosed a chain from around his neck and handed it to the small man, who staggered backward in relief. Shouts and laughter went up.

"Long live Jehu!" they cried.

Jehu bowed before his opponent. "Let no man say he lost more gold in this battle than did I." Turning back to the tables of food and wine, he caught sight of the young boy standing in their midst. Seeing Jehu's expression, everyone noticed the boy at once and quickly encircled him.

"It's a little late to be out of bed, don't you think?" Jehu needled. "Aren't your parents worried?" The men in the tent roared. The boy did not speak, but Jehu noticed his knees were trembling. Jehu took three steps forward until he was breathing down on the boy, who looked at him with surprising courage. Jehu reached out and the boy flinched but did not move. Jehu patted him down. "I feel no weapons," he announced. But reaching into the robes of the boy, he brought out a vial of oil and stepped back, wary.

"You are one of the prophets, are you not?" Jehu asked. The boy nodded.

"Why do you come to us?" Jehu demanded. The boy motioned quickly for Jehu to follow him out of the tent. Jehu did, and the men broke out chattering in speculation. The boy led Jehu to another tent, then into an inner room separated by veils hanging from the center beams.

"Kneel," the boy said meekly. Jehu frowned but knelt. The boy poured the oil on his head and cleared his throat.

"This is the word of the Lord," he said. "'You are now the King of Israel. For God has declared an end to the days of the house of Ahab, and all who once loved him will die by your hand, Jehu.'"

"You ask me to destroy the house of my master?" Jehu gasped, bolting up. But the veil was lapping at its cords, the boy already out of the chamber and running.

CHAPTER FIFTEEN

ATHALIAH PACED outside Ahaziah's council chamber. The advisers scurried in and back out, their faces cast to the ground.

"What is it?" she whispered to Ornat as he left.

He shook his head. "I cannot discuss the king's business with a woman, even his mother," he replied, not slowing down.

Athaliah pounded a fist against the wall. A spider slipped out from the mortar and raced down the limestone. Athaliah stared at the crack she had made and hit it again. Mortar and stone snowed down on her arm. Only the cedar beams held steady against her blows.

"Call my mother in," she heard Ahaziah command. Athaliah was escorted to him, sitting in a chair near the window. The remaining advisers rolled up their scrolls and departed.

"What has happened, my son?"

He stroked his chin and frowned, lost in thought.

"King Hazael of Aram has besieged Ramoth-Gilead. Your brother, King Joram of Israel, calls me north to fight with him,"

Ahaziah replied.

Athaliah sat. "You grandfather fought to secure that city for you," she said. "But he was a weak man, and now you must finish what he could not."

Ahaziah shook his head. "I feel unwell, somehow, as if a shadow has passed before my eyes and my vision has not cleared. I do not think it a good thing if I go."

Athaliah clapped her hands together. "Do not think that because you wear the crown you have grown into it yet. It weighs only a few shekels, and yet the burden is still too much for you, my dear. Take comfort in my counsel as always, and I will help you bear up."

"Mother?" Ahaziah asked. "Why is it so much harder to think clearly when you are near? While you were outside, I had so many questions, my will coursed through my veins. Yet near you now, alone, I feel your thoughts to be stronger than my own."

Athaliah rose and kissed him on the cheek. Her lips left a white mark as the blood beneath retreated under the weight of her touch.

"You are weary, my son. And perhaps more than a little afraid. You are a new king facing a very old battle. You must rest and trust that you will be ready for the moment. All you need is already inside your strong heart." She rested her hands on his shoulders and bent to whisper softly near his ear.

"You are sufficient, my son."

He reached up, laying one hand over hers. "I am sufficient," he repeated.

"Now rest, while I direct the letters to my brother. You will leave within the week and secure the claim on Ramoth-Gilead forever."

Ahaziah stood, and his servants prepared to escort him

back to his chambers. Athaliah watched him leave as a scribe entered the room, ducking his head as if the air were too thick for him. He edged closer to Athaliah and waited.

Athaliah instructed him to take a letter to Jezebel, Queen Mother of the North.

Greetings to you in the names of Baal and the Queen of Heaven, our goddess Asherah.

You know now that Jehoram is dead and my son Ahaziah is king of Judah. Our husbands ruled and died under the hand of this mysterious Yahweh, who allows no one to see His face. Yet our own power grows unchecked as we are dismissed as mere mothers, no longer queens. I am holding the southern kingdom tightly and have met no resistance.

Baal be with my brother, forged of the same iron of Ahab that I am, as he reigns in the North, with you giving him all good counsel. Pray to Baal and Asherah for my continued health and wisdom as I oversee the kingdom while my son reigns in the South. We will stay in the shadows, you and I, and do the deep work of a mother, promoting our sons in all they do, so that through them our names will be established. Through them a new kingdom, a new way, will emerge in this land: that every man may worship the god who calls his name first and loudest. Then wars will end and women rule.

Athaliah thought for a moment and addressed the scribe, who was writing feverishly, his quill smearing the kohl and fat across the dry leather.

"Send a letter as well to Joram, and send it by fast dispatch so that he will know to expect Ahaziah before the month's end. When you have finished the letters, bring them to me for my ring's seal and make sure a rider is carrying them north by tonight."

A servant knocked.

"Yes?" Athaliah snapped.

The servant entered and bowed. "Queen Zibia is having birth pains," she announced.

Athaliah frowned. "She is not due to give birth for another three weeks by my calendar. She should not labor early."

The servant looked uneasy. "I do not understand. Do you wish me to bid her stop?"

Athaliah groaned. "I only meant this is an inconvenience for Ahaziah and not well for the baby. Of course, some babies can be replaced."

The servant nodded.

"Very well," Athaliah said. "I will go to the chambers and be ready for the announcement. Tell the ashipu if the baby is a male, all other considerations, including Zibia, are unimportant."

The servant nodded and left. Athaliah left as well but not without hearing the scribe breathe a sigh of relief.

ZIBIA'S SCREAMS crashed against the stone walls. She begged for her mother, but the ashipu only yelled at her more loudly. "Bear down!" they screamed while she wailed and groaned. The door to her chamber would open, an ashipu would extend an arm, and a waiting servant would place fresh linens or a bowl of water into the hand. Ahaziah stood outside the door, a sick feeling in his stomach. He saw that his crown was of no importance in this struggle.

Zibia screamed for God to save her, to save her child, as the night air moved into the palace like a muzzle. After the moon established itself in the heavens, her screams turned to low moans, and the ashipu emerged, holding a child to present to Ahaziah. Athaliah rushed forward. The ashipu smiled, little flecks of blood on his face in the deep wrinkles around his eyes and mouth.

"A boy!" the ashipu said. "Ahaziah has an heir, and his throne is secure."

Athaliah turned to leave.

"How is Zibia?" Ahaziah asked.

The ashipu frowned and backed away, taking the baby toward the chamber again.

"It was a breech birth, very difficult for her. She called often for her mother, but we grew so tired of her screams we told her that her mother was dead. It seemed to work, for she gave us no more trouble then."

"Will she recover?" Ahaziah asked. The ashipu pursed his lips and shook his head, not giving a clear answer.

"She named the child Joash before she fell into unconsciousness."

"I must go to Ramoth-Gilead with King Joram," Ahaziah said, grabbing his arm. "Tell her I love her. Tell her to rest until I return."

The ashipu opened the door and stepped inside. Athaliah tugged Ahaziah away from the room. The ashipu stuck his face back out and found a servant walking down the hall.

"One of the attendants did not fare well during the birth. Would you send a servant for the body?"

"At once," the servant replied.

Ahaziah tried to look back, but Athaliah's grasp was too firm.

THE RIDERS at the Horse Gate were checking their horses and provisions. The fastest rider, a lightweight man whose every contour seemed to be a sharp bone, held the letters from Athaliah. He placed these in a leather satchel near the neck of his animal, who swung its head impatiently and snorted. The other rider, not much heavier himself, held other letters bearing the seal of the new king, Ahaziah, bound for nobles throughout the upper end of the kingdom. Another siege at Ramoth-Gilead would mean more expenses, but Ahaziah had reminded the men in his letters that the depth of their pockets would determine the height of their glory when Judah was at last victorious.

As the last of preparations were made, a kitchen maid ran out with two satchels of bread and two flasks for the journey. She bowed before the riders, telling them what other provisions she had laid inside. The riders mounted and as they turned for the gate, she caught the slower man by his leg. He bent low to hear her words.

"There is a letter in your satchel, between the bits of bread, that must go into the city, to the wife of the high priest. Her name is Jehoshebeth, and you will find her in the priest's living quarters just beyond the Temple. King Ahaziah gave it to me last night and asks you to deliver it in confidence."

He looked down at her.

"How is it you came to see the king last night?"

She would not answer but slapped the horse to make it run.

TWO WEEKS had passed since Jehoshebeth had received the letter from her brother. She kept it tucked into her robes and often reread it as she rested between chores. At first, she had read it over and over to Jehoiada as he washed her feet and rubbed them, the center of her discomfort, although every inch of her body was weary from carrying firewood in and food from the market. But Jehoiada had learned the letter well and moved on in his heart now to other considerations. So she was alone again with her brother's words, and she felt her childhood was folded up in her robes with the letter and the many hushed and secret words they had shared.

Jehoiada entered and found her on their bed.

"Resting?" he asked.

"I am sorry. I should be preparing the evening meal, I know."

Jehoiada sat next to her. "A blessing for us both that you rest," he said. She hit him on the arm and he laughed.

"The women in the village spoke to me today about the birth," she said. Jehoiada raised his eyebrows.

"Did you tell them to, Jehoiada? Today they drew near to me and told me what I must do to prepare," she said. "They say they will be waiting for a summons to come and help me deliver."

Jehoiada stroked her hair. "You are one of them, and it is only right that they care for you as your day approaches."

"I don't want them tending to me out of guilt," she replied.

"I will be preparing for my time of service in the Temple," he told her. "I must entrust you to their care. You cannot be angry with me if I have made sure they will look out for you."

"I have had my fill of women who tend to me out of duty," she said, rolling over, trying to find a comfortable position.

"When Ahaziah returns, do you think I will be allowed to see his son?" she asked. "I try to picture the baby in my mind, but I long to see him. Ahaziah says he looks like our father."

Jehoiada began rubbing her back and listened.

"I have had a dream of the baby," she said. Jehoiada stopped rubbing.

"It is a strange dream. I am deep in sleep, a black sleep with no color or noise, as if I were floating in a lost sea, until I hear a baby crying. I try to reach out to him, but the darkness is so heavy around me, I can't move. A wave lifts me up and I see that I am in a sea of children. The waves carry us apart, and I grope blindly in the wind and waves to grasp and pull him to me. And then I see that I do shelter a child in my arms, but when I wake, I do not know if I was dreaming of Ahaziah's child or my own. I feel afraid when I awake, Jehoiada, so very afraid. It is not a good omen."

Jehoiada turned her so she could see him. "I will not have you speak of omens and curses. It is not the way of our people to live in such fear of darkness! You are nervous before the birth; what woman is not? Do not breathe too much life into your fears or they will nibble at you for all of your days."

Jehoshebeth blinked back tears at his reproach. He kissed her cheek, his fingers gently brushing a loose lock of hair away.

"I can live with your cooking, but not your imagination."

"You've grown no smaller in stature since we married, I've noticed. How bad could it be?"

"KING JORAM has been injured, King Ahaziah," the messenger said. His horse, sweating and pawing the ground, nudged him, and the messenger pushed the animal away.

Ahaziah frowned but did not dismount.

"What now?" he asked his advisers. The men behind them, most on foot but some on donkeys, were anxious to complete the journey and see their king safely to Ramoth-Gilead.

Ornat looked at the messenger. "What else must we know?"

"The siege against Ramoth-Gilead goes on, but it is strange. King Hazael of the Arameans seeks to reclaim the city but only a little at a time. He wears us out, tests us, but does not overrun us. He is worse than a young child, teasing and biting, but without the strength to strike whole and completely. So Ramoth-Gilead stands. It is safe, and we continue to protect her against the daily attacks."

Ornat got down to study the messenger, who grew nervous to have him so close.

"And the king of Israel?" he asked.

The messenger blushed and bowed.

"The king of Israel is injured, but not mortally," the young man said. "He has retreated to his mother's palace in Jezreel, where he bids you join him."

"Very good," King Ahaziah replied. "Fall in with my men." He grabbed his reins.

"Oh, no, good king, I must return to Ramoth-Gilead, where my commander is waiting." The messenger raised his eyebrows as if it was a question.

King Ahaziah motioned for him to move aside. "I'll not keep a man from the front, then, my good fellow," he said. His entourage made ready to go to Jezreel and spurred their horses. They would cross the Jordan, turning west, and arrive in three days' time.

JEHOSHEBETH HELD her breath and then exhaled, hard, with a little grunt, wincing.

"I am so frightened, Jehoiada," she cried. He wiped her forehead and then kissed it.

"All will be well," he said. "The women will be here in but a moment."

Jehoshebeth stood and walked around the room, arching her back a little and taking another long, deep breath.

"Let us hope it is a short labor," she said.

The sound of women in the courtyard brought Jehoiada out. He returned in a moment and led Jehoshebeth by the hand. "The women are taking you to the birthing home of the midwives. It is not far. I will follow behind and will be just outside until my time of duty is called, although I will not be allowed to enter. Don't be afraid. All will be well," he said to her. "God holds us all in His hands."

She walked slowly outside and the women looked at her, each face as kind and pleasant as she had once remembered it. She questioned herself that she had ever thought their faces stern in the market.

"It is good of you to come, sisters," she said. The women held her hands and together they walked to the home.

AHAZIAH AND his men arrived in Jezreel at the winter palace of the king of Israel at dusk, when the palace was in shadows and the light was fleeing.

As they dismounted and walked through the courtyard gate, their horses shied away and refused to enter. The men shrugged and dropped their reins as servants ran out to draw the horses to the stables. The servants showed no signs that the horses were acting in a manner strange to them. Ahaziah led the men through the great gates, double-walled in the style of the Phoenicians. A Phoenician bride had once ordered this place built, and he wondered if she would be about.

A pack of dogs, their ribs and hip bones jutting out of their thin coats, rushed at them, their animal eyes wild with hunger and madness. Thick pus had crusted in the corner of each eye, and their tongues moved loosely about in their mouths, a yellow crust falling away from their bared teeth. Ahaziah yelled, startled, and fell back into his advisers. They pushed him ahead as he laughed under his breath.

A figure just above them looked down. She had long hair, let loose in the moonlight and blowing about her softly. Her thin arms and long fingers cast shadows on the ground and seemed to draw them near, scratching at them as they stared.

"Do not be afraid of the dogs," she said, her voice the rasp between a moan and a whisper. "They are chained to the palace wall."

Indeed, each dog stopped just short of the men. Ahaziah stared at the animals, then looked back at the woman above them, but she was gone.

A servant appeared at the door of the palace, his white hair falling about his shriveled shoulders, a man of so many years they wondered how he still served. He motioned them in.

"Enter, friends of the South, we have been expecting you."

The men entered, Ahaziah first, each man looking about him as the torchlight danced.

"You can feel the shadows here as they brush past you," one adviser whispered to Ahaziah.

The old man cackled. "It has been too long since we had visitors. You must forgive us if we seem eager to receive you," he said.

The adviser who had spoken jumped as a dark thing rushed past him, and Ahaziah laughed at him. "A shadow made from the torchlight in the night wind," he chastised. Then a cold thing touched him too.

"There is no night wind inside a palace," the adviser snapped.

The old man swung open heavy doors made of wood overlaid with ivory. The torchlight made the ivory seem to be molten and swirling, and Ahaziah traced the edge of the door with his fingers as he walked past it. A feast had been laid out, and King Joram was seated at the head of the table. His arm was in a makeshift sling. He smiled broadly to see the war party from the South joining him at last. More foot soldiers would be no more than a day's journey behind.

"Welcome, my brothers!" Joram said. "Welcome, but forgive me if I do not rise in your honor. I am recovering from a wound I received at the front."

"God's health to you," Ahaziah replied, and the men tipped their heads in respect.

Joram nodded to the servant, who walked back to shut the doors, holding his outstretched hands to hold something at bay until the doors could be secured.

Joram turned his attention back to Ahaziah's men.

"Let us eat, my friends, for you must surely be tired and in need of refreshment." He motioned the men to eat. Servants stepped forward to fill their bowls, their heads kept low so that their eyes would not meet any other. The men ate and drank with relish, but Ahaziah noted that each man kept his knife near, not setting it down between bites. They cast glances around the room, but it was hard to see beyond the table's lamps, so heavy was the darkness.

Joram seemed perfectly at ease, and this helped.

"I have never seen dogs chained to the palace wall," Ahaziah said. Joram grunted and chewed his meat, holding it with his one good hand, his teeth sawing at the bit that stubbornly clung to the bone.

"Yes, well, my mother loves dogs," Joram explained. "She thinks it good to leave them chained near her, for no one can climb to her chamber without meeting them first. It gives my mother such peace to enjoy her window and know she is kept safe by those stalwart creatures."

The men nodded and drank.

Ahaziah watched his men, then drew a breath and spoke. "We've had a long ride, brother," he said to Joram. Joram stopped chewing and looked around the table. His expression began to change and Ahaziah spoke quickly again.

"It is our honor to be called in service to the North, and I discipline my men to stay alert and ready for our enemy," Ahaziah said. He felt his men nudging each other under the table.

Joram considered this, then agreed. "Yes, you need sleep tonight. I will have you shown to your chambers, and tomorrow we will map out the strategy to finally be rid of Hazael."

Ahaziah stood, and his men bowed before Joram as the heavy ivory doors groaned open, shadows rushing in on them. Joram growled but continued eating, and the men rushed upstairs behind the old servant, staying close together.

CHAPTER SIXTEEN

"ALL ENEMIES, in this world and the other, are unwelcome here. We give this space, and the hours we will fulfill here, to a mighty God. We give no permission for darkness to enter, nor its servant, the serpent who crawls on its belly and seeks to exalt itself over the world of men. We surround our sister Jehoshebeth with light and goodness and beg God to complete what He has begun." The midwives prayed together, holding hands in a circle around Jehoshebeth. This home was unlike any in the city; it had no stalls for livestock and no loft. It was built from baked mud bricks over an earth floor, beaten smooth and free of dust. There was no furniture either, except for a birthing stool and a table that held a basin of water and folded linen cloths. The room had been swept and beaten and swept again in preparation for Jehoshebeth. Flour dusted the floor at the doors and windows so that nothing could enter undetected.

Jehoshebeth sat in the center of the room, comfortable on a birthing stool made from smooth rocks before the next wave of pain. The women lit lamps and began singing the songs of the midwives.

"Breathe with the music," one encouraged. Jehoshebeth closed her eyes as a younger girl rubbed her back and shoulders and concentrated on air flowing in and out as the song rose and fell. Their voices caressed her and the child inside.

You created the mother in Your great love and compassion,
You created the child in her womb,
Everything in each is good and blessed.
We praise You, our God, who does not abandon us
At the moment of birth
We are blessed because we are Yours,
We are blessed because our wombs have seen the work of God,
You have done in darkness what we cannot understand in the light
We will bless this child
Arriving so new from Your hand
We will draw the child safely out
From the seas that separate man from God.

Jehoshebeth sighed, then held her breath as another contraction hit.

The old woman Sebia, who had dressed her on her wedding day, stepped forward and the midwives moved aside for a moment. "Breathe deeply," Sebia crooned. The women sang louder. Jehoshebeth tried to exhale, but the air fought to stay inside and press against her womb.

"Breathe with us as we sing," Sebia repeated.

Jehoshebeth nodded, then groaned again, and the midwives checked her progress and pushed gently on her abdomen. She was stripped naked, but thin linen sheets that had been beaten with stones in a river until they were soft like the skin of a lamb were draped across her shoulders to keep her warm. The midwives consulted and nodded. Jehoshebeth rested her head against Sebia's stomach as the matriarch stood over her and stroked her hair. Then Sebia motioned, and a younger girl handed her a red string. Sebia reached down for Jehoshebeth's wrist, tying the string loosely around it.

Jehoshebeth looked up, not understanding. "Why tie this to me?"

"We wrap the red cord seven times around the tomb of Rachel, the beloved mother, who in her pain delivered our father Joseph, who saved us from the great famine. The red string is tied to the wrists of our mothers, who in their pain seek to deliver goodness into the world, for in the darkness of the womb, God seals the scrolls of our history."

Jehoshebeth looked at the bracelet made of a coarse dyed twine. She touched it.

Sebia resumed stroking her hair. "Let it remind you that in the fear and pain of life, God is near."

Jehoshebeth nodded, then groaned again.

"She is entering into the great pains," one murmured to the women gathered round her. "It is time."

Silently, the women watched Jehoshebeth, who strained between contractions to understand what was happening. The midwives soothed and sang to her, and she gripped their hands tightly until her groans turned to screams. Tears came down her face, and the women sang.

Lord, answer her in her distress
May the Name of the God of Jacob protect her
Give to her now the fulfillment of her desire

We will shout for joy when she is victorious
And we will lift up our banners
In the name of the God Most High.

She pushed, and cried out, and brought forth a child.

AHAZIAH SLEPT fitfully, his mind perceiving sound in silence and a shuffling movement when all was plainly still. He cursed himself for having drunk any wine after a day of such hard riding. The dawn had not yet broken, but he made his way downstairs and into the great dining hall, where he found King Joram already dressed and waiting.

"Let us talk now of our fathers and our kingdoms," Joram said. His eyes were rimmed in red and Ahaziah knew he had not slept either. Ahaziah was preparing to sit when a scout burst into the room.

"There is news, good king! A rider approaches from the battle! He is with a company of men and seeks your face!"

Joram nodded. "Send a rider to meet him and find out if the news be good or ill for us, for I am not a man of patience," he commanded, but the boy spoke again.

"This your sentinels have already done, my king, and the messenger fell in behind them without giving us a sign, and now both ride to the palace to deliver the news."

Joram and Ahaziah exchanged a glance, and both stood. Joram went up the stairs, and up yet another set spiraling toward a narrow crevice in the palace wall. As they climbed, Ahaziah thought he spied a woman, her burnished image reflecting from a brass mirror hung in the hallway just beyond the staircase. Her dark hair crawled over her shoulders and slithered down her back, not concealing her bare form as attendants moved through her chamber and little fat things scurried near her on the floor. He saw her thick red lips part into a smile and she reached out for him. Ahaziah shook himself, and the image was gone.

At the top floor now, where a wide window gave view of the horizon, Joram was looking toward the riders and pointed out the captain to Ahaziah.

"Who is it?" Ahaziah asked.

Joram clapped him on the back, rushing back down the stairs. Ahaziah followed.

"We will ride out to meet him, though he is yet a long way off. By the driving, I am guessing it is Jehu, the captain of my armies, known for his fierce sword in battle and terrible skill with a chariot." He laughed, bounding for the stables. "He would not break away from the battle unless the news was very good!"

The dawn broke open before them and did not betray the intentions of the day.

THE WOMEN sang and clapped their hands as the infant girl cried.

"She asks to be adopted by a mother of earth. Who will claim this child?" Sebia asked.

"God has given me this daughter, and I claim her," Jehoshebeth replied.

The women wiped the tears from their eyes and finished attending to the child. Her cord had been severed, and she was rubbed with salt and wrapped in a blue blanket. The blanket made official her adoption into the world of the living; its color identified her as the honored daughter of Jehoiada. The midwives, having completed the work of securing her into this family, handed her back to Jehoshebeth, who cradled her with weak arms and let her tears fall again as the baby rooted and nursed. She winced and the other women giggled. One moved behind her, propping her up a bit, and another woman helped the child latch on. She also moved Jehoshebeth's arms, adjusting them so she would see how to cradle the child as she ate. She nursed only a minute, to Jehoshebeth's great relief, and closed her eyes for sleep.

"She is perfect," Jehoshebeth said, entranced by the delicate curves of her face. All of Athaliah's sorcerers could not mimic the deep magic of a child at peace. "Her name will be Ayla, my tree. From a tree I first saw my future, and in her face I see it again."

Sebia bent, smiling, as Jehoshebeth lightly stroked the indentation above Ayla's pursed lips.

"Do you know what those two little ridges between the lips and nose are?" Sebia asked.

Jehoshebeth shook her head.

"She has been so close to God and has heard such indescribable secrets that just before she is born, God must press His finger against her mouth to seal it, so that the baby will not share what she has seen with her mother."

Jehoshebeth stared at the woman, and then the two laughed out loud.

Sebia took the sleeping child to her bosom, cradling her close, and walked outside to present her to Jehoiada. The midwives continued to rub and push on Jehoshebeth's abdomen, sharing small, nervous glances with each other.

They could hear Jehoiada outside weeping and praising God. Jehoshebeth heard him, but she was so tired. The elation of birth was overshadowed by her craving for sleep, long, deep sleep, and she felt her eyelids dropping.

She motioned for one of the midwives.

"Jehoiada must go now for his time of service at the Temple. Give him my love. Tell him his family will be waiting when he returns," she murmured. The women did not stop their efforts, consulting in fast whispers, but they allowed the youngest one to send the message. Then, they told her, run as quickly as you can for the village healer, the man who grows the herbs and knows something of surgery.

THE RIDER dismounted and walked toward the palace but would not enter. Athaliah, watching from her chamber window, felt fear, not the welcome familiar kind, but the kind from her childhood, like little black flies that droned through her veins and picked at her from the inside.

The rider delivered his message to a guard, who met him as the horse approached. The guard listened silently to the report and Athaliah could hear the rider screaming at him. He was young, she realized. His scream sounded so like her own.

She sat, closing her eyes. These were the last moments before fear closed the distance between suspicion and certainty, before grief washed over everything, staining everything with the black mold of regret that would only grow in the darkness of memory.

Athaliah did not jump when the knock came. The door swung, its hinges the only announcement that the boy had ascended to her at last. He entered the room, clinging to a wall, his face white.

She began braiding her long hair herself, though her people had always worn it long and in curls. She watched him without comment, weaving the strands, her hands working smoothly in their rhythm. She removed a pin from her dress and wound the braid tightly into a knot against the back of her head, then pinned it into place. The pin dug into her scalp but she did not flinch. The boy watched in horror as a drop of blood ran down her neck. She drew a long breath and looked at the boy. He tried to speak but glanced back at the door. Finally, he fell to his knees and sobbed.

"I do not wish to die!" he cried. "I did not ask to bring you this message!"

Athaliah wet her lips and waited. The whimpering boy lifted his head just enough to see her.

"There is no man in this palace with courage enough to come into your chamber and tell you what has happened," he accused. He drew one last, great breath, and spat out the words that would end his life. "God has declared an end to the house of your father Ahab. Jehu, the captain of the armies of Israel, is made king of Israel by God's own hand. He slaughtered your brother King Joram and your son King Ahaziah, and God's vengeance is made complete by the death of your mother Jezebel. All who bore the name of Ahab and Jezebel are dead, save you, and you are now stripped of all power. You are a dried twig cut from this tree uprooted. You are no longer queen, nor mother or wife. May you die in the streets like your mother!"

At this, he ran through the chamber and flung himself out the window. She heard the dull smack that followed. She stood and sighed and only then wiped away the blood on her neck. She stared at her fingers before licking them clean.

But one thing she had never dared. The voices of the

dark waters who called her urged her to many times. Yet Something louder than they spoke too, and somehow this voice she feared. She had stayed at the water's edge. But the relentless tide was strong, stronger than her will, and she felt herself being pulled away.

This tide swept her to the border of a forbidden land, the land of the supernatural that hemmed humanity in at all sides. She could be wrenched and dragged across a border, such as at the moment of death, but few ever crossed into the shadowlands willingly, and none returned fully human. These were the boundaries, the dark territories no human was meant to trespass. Black breathing spirits begged her to step over. *Kill,* they whispered. *Kill the children. Join your mother.*

She lifted her foot, only a small motion at the knee, and in her mind she heard the battle scream of victory. Darkness fed upon itself, writhing with the promise of fresh blood.

She called a guard into her chamber. She could hear them arguing about which one should obey. Finally, one entered and bowed before her.

"Give me your sword," she commanded.

JEHOSHEBETH FOUND it hard to wake. She was so sore, so sleepy. The midwives shook her again and again until she pulled open her eyes and tried to take them all in. They had been crying.

"What is it?" Jehoshebeth asked. "What has happened? Where is Ayla? Is she all right?"

"Yes," they replied. "You have lost much blood and are weak. We do not want you to sleep, lest you not wake again."

"Why then the tears?" Jehoshebeth murmured, smiling in relief to see her daughter sleeping in a girl's arms nearby.

Sebia entered and snapped at the girls. "We will not burden her with such news!" Jehoshebeth looked at her, but she would not meet Jehoshebeth's eye.

"What is it? What has happened?" Jehoshebeth asked, but the woman busied herself and did not reply.

"I command you to speak, woman!" Jehoshebeth said as loudly as she could. The woman snorted a little laugh and turned.

"Didn't God once promise," Sebia asked, "that an heir of David would always sit on the throne in Judah? We lived in peace knowing we were secure. But your father brought a curse to our land."

Jehoshebeth frowned, her head too heavy to rise and face the accusation. "Yes, I know of whom you speak. But I am the wife of Jehoiada now and cast away from that house," she said.

Sebia came near her bed and looked down on her. "You do not speak the truth."

Jehoshebeth tried to focus her eyes on Sebia, but the room seemed to be spinning, growing fainter and farther away.

"Why do you say this, Sebia?" she asked.

Sebia looked at the other midwives, watching them.

"King Ahaziah has always loved you, and you were loyal to his name. But your brother is dead. God has set Himself against your house."

Jehoshebeth gasped. She tried to sit up, but hot little pinpoints of light forced her head back to the pillow. She couldn't see for the sudden rush of tears, but she felt for Sebia's hand and clutched it hard.

"What you say, is it true?"

"And more," Sebia replied. "For at this moment, Athaliah

is slaughtering all the babies in the palace, the very children of her son Ahaziah. She will cut us off from God forever. The mothers have hidden the children as best they could, but what child doesn't cry in the dark? Athaliah is moving through her palace, killing every baby hidden and every child crouching in fear at this very moment! By sundown, there will not be a male child of the house of David left alive, and our time as God's chosen people will end. A curse on your name, Jehoshebeth! A curse on your father and his house!" Spit flew from her lips and rage made her face tremble.

Jehoshebeth gripped the hand of the woman sponging her face with water. "Bring me Gabriel," she called hoarsely. The woman frowned.

"Now!" She tried to sit up. The faces in the room swirled and she sank back, retching from the dizziness. She gasped and sat up with force, breathing unsteadily. She swung her legs off the mat, and then the women moved to her, supporting her as she stood. A rush of fresh blood ran down her legs.

"You have not the strength," Sebia said. "We were unable to stop your bleeding for a very long time. You cannot do this."

"I can do nothing but this," Jehoshebeth said.

Sweat popped on her forehead and then ran down her face. She moved toward the door and saw that the light was dimming. She heard the approach of hooves. But the blood would not stop and her gown grew heavy and sticky. She grasped the edge of the door and her stomach heaved. Nothing came and she fought for the breath back.

"What can we do?" a young midwife asked.

"Pray," Jehoshebeth said as the women struggled to lift her to Gabriel's back.

"Perhaps there is something of David in you," Sebia said. "It grieves me that you will die for your father's sins."

Jehoshebeth tried to focus, but she couldn't find the reins to grasp them. A woman followed her fumbling movements and placed the reins in her hands. Then the woman slapped Gabriel's flank and he burst away. Jehoshebeth slumped over, her face resting against his neck as he tore off.

A crack of thunder made her start, and she felt the stinging first drops of rain.

CHAPTER SEVENTEEN

THE RAIN struck Jehoshebeth as Gabriel ran, and she struggled to keep her eyes open.

"Help me," she whispered, but the rain stole even her whisper from her. The noise from the rain hitting the trees and rocks was deafening, and lightning cracked overhead, making her grip Gabriel's neck more tightly. She felt her life draining and longed to feel the power of God, of a right cause, pouring into her dying flesh, but Yahweh did not rescue her as the storm grew in anger and power around her. Ahaziah's face stayed in her mind but his death seemed too large a thing to grasp. He could not be gone. She saw Athaliah's hands holding a dagger, swinging down, and winced. With the children dead, Ahaziah dead, what would be left of her? Jehoshebeth would be a cursed woman, waiting in life only for death. This perhaps God would withhold to punish her for her father's sin.

Gabriel slipped once in the mud made thick and slick by the force of the driving rain. She gasped as she grabbed his mane and struggled to stay on. A sharp pain ripped through her belly and she screamed, but no sound came from her mouth as she opened it wide.

Steam poured from Gabriel's nostrils as he climbed the path, the palace above them. Lights flickered in all the windows, and she heard a mother's shrill scream of despair. Jehoshebeth looked up to see a woman throwing herself from the palace window, her hair flying above her as she fell to her death. Jehoshebeth's mouth would not close, her fear constricting every muscle in her body. She saw she could do nothing. She was not armed, and she was known by all the guards, who would surely kill her as an enemy of the throne as soon as they saw her. Death encircled her; swift death if she entered the palace, where she would die with her house and the slow death of a scorned life if she returned now to the village. She chose.

This was to be the end of her life, then, she knew: to die along with the children and the mothers and the house of her father, to offer herself as the last inadequate shield from the terror loosed by his hand.

White limestone jutted up everywhere along the path. The earth was marking its own forgotten dead, and their voices moaned through the storm, bidding her to hurry, her punishment to see the little souls cut from this life so cruelly.

Gabriel raced, dashing between the stones as he got closer, the palace gates within sight. His body braced and she could feel his anger at being assaulted by the rain and wind, the lightning striking closer to him with every blow. He raised his head toward the storm and screamed back at it, then surged with a last great effort toward the summit.

His hooves slipped. Gabriel's front legs crumpled underneath him. Jehoshebeth's chest cracked against the ground, expelling all the air left in her body, stunning her. Gabriel lay motionless across her body, crushing her.

Another mother screamed from the palace and begged for her child, offering her life in exchange. Her screams turned to something else, a wailing from the depths of spirit as Jehoshebeth had never heard, she knew it was too late for the child. Jehoshebeth struggled to move, still pinned under Gabriel, and she sobbed as the screams seared her mind, but she could not move her hands to stop up her ears.

Gabriel was still. Jehoshebeth tried to nudge him with her face. He did not respond.

"No. No. God!" Jehoshebeth prayed, her agony of soul and body indistinguishable. She wrenched a hand free and pounded on Gabriel. She tried to turn her head as the rain punched at her eyes, and she saw his leg, the bone ghostly white in the moonlight, snapped clean through.

Gabriel opened his eyes, the light fading from them as the rain stole away his blood, carrying it down the path. He laid his head back to the earth, mud seeping into his nostrils now, and closed his eyes.

"Gabriel!" she screamed as a roar of thunder cloaked her cries. The storm became a monster tearing at them both.

Her loss of blood, and the fever that had been brewing hotter and higher since childbirth, finished its work. Jehoshebeth's body gave way completely. She felt herself sinking into the earth under Gabriel's jerking body.

"I have seen the end," she mouthed. With the infants in the palace murdered, there would never again be a king of David's line. The great promise of God was broken. The world was lost.

Her eyes closed, and she exhaled, willing her spirit to leave her now.

The voice of God came then, a quiet note between the stings of rain and fists of thunder, a note she remembered from her tender dreams in childhood, in the gentle sway of hope she had felt when she was with child. She did not hear the words, for they were not spoken with a tongue of man. They were words from the other world, in a voice she remembered from long ago, from before she had memory, a voice from the nurture of the womb that spoke the mother tongue of all peoples. God bent to her, and this voice whispered:

I am near

A brilliant light peeled away the blackness and she felt warmth filling her, moving through her veins, replacing the blood she had lost. The sensation began in her feet and climbed through her body until she felt she was floating beside Gabriel, no longer pinned under him but buoyed in a thick sea of gold and honey. When the warmth reached her head, she passed out.

A hand on her shoulder shook her awake. Thunder cracked overhead in a terrible roar, like a lion having caught a glimpse of his enemy. She opened her eyes and blinked rapidly, and with one hand wiped the mud and rain from her face. She was standing. She no longer bled. Her heart slammed against her chest. Gabriel stood next to her, snorting and pawing the ground. She searched his legs but there was no break. Her own legs began shaking, and she braced against him as she searched for the one who had awakened her. Only the trees stood witness to what had happened. "Oh, God." She wept and threw her arms around Gabriel in thanksgiving.

A new scream from the palace snapped her attention back to the dying children. The power that had touched her had not yet departed, and she felt a boiling white anger raising itself against the palace. She leaped onto Gabriel's back even as he lunged toward the Horse Gate. It would not be well guarded tonight.

With his muscles surging and his hooves chewing the ground beneath him, Gabriel conquered the last stretch in an instant. In the courtyard, Jehoshebeth slid off Gabriel and concealed him in a dark corner. She saw a guard, very young and covered in blood, retching in a far corner. This young man saw Jehoshebeth too, and his eyes searched hers with the agony of his heart. He said nothing and did not move, except to turn his face away.

"Thank you," she gasped. She ran inside the palace entrance toward the children's quarters. Two children had been left dead in the hall. She covered her mouth to conceal her scream and could not look at them. Jehoshebeth pressed her body against the opposite wall and tried to keep her gaze elsewhere as she crept quietly along. Blood made her passage treacherous by the dim light of the torches.

Jehoshebeth put her belt in her mouth, biting down to keep from screaming at the horrors. She felt her stomach roiling and concentrated all her power on breathing. If she vomited, if she screamed, she would be discovered.

She silently blessed God for the days of her childhood spent stealing through these halls undetected. Just as she neared the back passageway to the nurseries, someone reached out, grabbing her from behind with one hand over her mouth, dragging her into a storeroom. She thrashed wildly but was no match for his strength. He kept his hand over her mouth, pinning her against the wall until she saw sharp pinpricks of light dancing in her vision, and her arms went limp. Then, only then, did he release her and turn her to face him.

Midian.

He pressed his sweating face to hers and kissed her on her cheeks as she revived. "I knew you would come," he cried. "They're waiting for you, too, and will kill you as soon as they know you are here. No child from the house of David is meant to survive this night."

Jehoshebeth, the blood returning painfully to her head now, shook free of him and moved toward the door. "I have to try, Midian," she said.

"No," Midian said, blocking her. Then he smiled and a tear rolled down his face.

"All your life, haven't I stood just outside your door, anticipating every move, every need? I had only those deeds to tell you how I felt, never words, but when I die, tell the people I was a good and faithful servant who loved you to the end."

Jehoshebeth shook her head in confusion. She reached again for the door, but Midian grabbed her hands, spinning her around. He lifted a woven cover from a stock of supplies. A young girl crouched, clutching a sleeping infant to her chest. Jehoshebeth gasped and Midian covered her mouth. He nodded to the girl, who moved the baby gently, rolling him a bit so that his whole face was visible. It was Joash, the son of her brother.

"His face is unmistakable," Midian said. "Just like yours. He is of the house of David."

Jehoshebeth wept and reached out for the baby, just as a noise above made them all freeze in fear. Midian motioned for them to remain still. He edged toward his sword, which was lying on the floor next to the door. The heavy steps above them moved on, and they heard a distant laughter. Midian stopped.

"What of his mother?" Jehoshebeth asked.

Midian shook his head. He drew close and whispered. "Take the nurse and the child, and flee now. Hide them in the Temple, for Athaliah will not enter there. She fears your God. Go now and I will help you as I can tonight."

"But there are others," Jehoshebeth argued.

Midian shook his head. "All dead," he replied. "Twenty children and their mothers."

Jehoshebeth shook her head, "No, this cannot be."

"Yes. All lie murdered above us, even nursemaids," he replied. "Now take Joash and run for your lives."

Midian opened the door, edging his face into the hallway and looking at both ends. He reached back in and motioned for them to run. Jehoshebeth grabbed the nursemaid's sleeve and pulled her to the door. They stepped out, careful to make no noise, just behind Midian. They made five good strides down the hall when Jagur came down the stairs from the passage above, wiping a stained dagger across his robe. He saw them.

Midian froze. He turned to Jehoshebeth, fear stretched across his face.

"Run!" he yelled.

He charged into Jagur, knocking him off balance and onto his back on the stairs, grabbing the dagger where it fell. Jehoshebeth and the nursemaid ran, jumping over the men's tangled legs. Midian landed a blow with the dagger but not before Jagur had wrapped his hands around Midian's neck. Jehoshebeth glanced back to see each man struggling to die last and she fled as terror choked her. They flew to Gabriel unnoticed. The stallion took both women on his back and sped from the palace gates, his iron legs pounding the path like a blacksmith's hammer, each strike shaping the future stolen from the flames.

THE MIDWIVES had fled the birthing home long before the storm reached its fury. Each woman, huddled in her home now, passed a sleepless night. Toward dawn its rage was spent, and the streets were too thick with mud to venture far beyond their court-yards. They pushed their faces out into the drizzle and glanced round. There seemed to be no one, and nothing, stirring. Each woman retreated inside again, some hanging iron bowls over a fire for soup, some grinding the breakfast meal. All had their thoughts on Jehoshebeth, who rode last night to her death.

The oldest priest, Eli, was leaving the Temple. His gait was slow and he gripped a walking stick as he crept through the gates. It kept sinking deep into the mud, and he would sigh and wrestle with it each time, pulling it free before he took another step. No one was about at this hour to help him. Even if people had been present, Eli wasn't sure they would assist. Athaliah had poisoned the union of God with His people. The covenant of love was no longer valued. Wrestling the sinking stick once more, he caught a glimpse of the Temple rising behind him as he left its narrow street.

"David dreamed you, Solomon built you, and I have loved you," he said as if it were a favored child. "Would that you were full of life once more and had the heart of the people." The sad sound of rain met his ears. "Ah, but this is only the prayer of an old man who needs a warm fire and a long sleep."

Just as he was about to plunge his stick into the mud for another step, the sound of a horse's hooves caught him. He saw a glistening horse approaching carefully through the mud and rain. A woman walked beside him, holding his reins. Another woman rode him, one arm wrapped around a bundle partially hidden in her robes. The old man shielded his eyes from the rain and looked again. Yes, the bundle was a baby. When the woman carrying it saw the priest, she bit her lips to keep from crying and tried to spur Gabriel to walk faster through the mud. Gabriel caught her relief and pressed forward with new resolve. The man opened his arms wide to receive them. The woman leading the horse bowed before him and took his hand, kissing it over and over.

"My child, what has happened? Is this not Gabriel, the horse belonging to Jehoiada the high priest?" Eli asked.

She fell in his arms, weeping and trembling, but did not answer. In a moment she righted herself and wiped the mud from her face, letting her robe fall away from her head entirely.

Eli cried out when he recognized the high priest's wife. The baby stirred and the old man's mind raced.

"What has happened, child?" Neither Jehoshebeth nor the nursemaid on Gabriel could reply. Her eyes were wide and glazed, and she did not open her robe to nurse the baby, though it began to cry and squirm against her. She only stared and clung to the animal. Jehoshebeth begged, "Hide them. Hide them well, and tell no one what you have seen. When I have finished my time in the birthing room, bring them to my home."

CHAPTER EIGHTEEN

WHEN THE morning sun had burned off the last of the storm, the midwives ran through the streets and found Jehoshebeth in her bedroom in the birthing home. She would be unclean for two weeks after delivering her girl. She would rest here until she was strong enough to return home but even then would not participate in any public activity until her purification time had passed.

Enormous bruises crossed her body, even her ribs, as if something heavy had struck her. Her hands shook when they gave her soup, and she could not find the will to eat. They pressed her for details, but she would not say much.

"The storm was so great. I could do nothing in my own power."

The women nodded. The news had reached everyone in the village, and then the city, that all the sons of David who might have sat on the throne were dead. Mourning poured from every home into the streets, and when the funeral pyres were lit beyond the palace, great sobs echoed off the stone pavement. Then a messenger told them Athaliah had burned the bodies and forbidden burials for the royal babies and their mothers. The line of David was gone from the earth. Evil would reign.

In their homes father after father looked upon Athaliah's trinkets, the figures of folklore once a welcome distraction from Yahweh's jealous purity, and found these things detestable. Idols were broken and tossed into the cooking fires. Women and children cried and smeared the ashes across their faces and tore their robes. The death of God's promise was unbearable.

AS THE IDOLS split and burned, the smoke pushed through the streets just ahead of the gossip. Sebia sighed and rubbed her tired legs just above the knee as she stood near the stove in her own courtyard. All the midwives knew Jehoshebeth had made a run for the palace, but she had been near death, unable to make the journey. Yet, she returned in remarkable health. Many of the midwives suspected sorcery, the kind that Athaliah's ashipu were known for. Perhaps, they whispered to Sebia, Jehoshebeth could not forget the entitlements of her crown and had ridden not for the children of the house of David but for herself. And yet the palace had not held her but spit her back out into the common streets. It was not good, they urged her. Jehoshebeth was hiding something from them all, and it could bring disaster to their houses. She must denounce the woman, they cried, and forget the day she helped birth that child. Sebia decided, as she turned her flat cakes over on the hot stones, that Jehoshebeth's name would never be spoken again. All women in the city would live as if Jehoshebeth were not among them, if they wanted a midwife alive to attend to their family.

Jehoshebeth finished her time in the birthing room, then returned with her daughter to her home. Jehoiada would be finishing his duty at the Temple, and he would find his family had been greatly expanded. She wondered what he knew of that dark hour. However much it was, he did not know everything. Jehoshebeth hid a secret, two of them, in fact and flesh.

JEHOIADA ENTERED his home in a heavy silence. His time of service at the Temple was completed, and Jehoshebeth would be home by now too, her time of ritual uncleanliness being finished. Grief had seared long lines across his forehead, and his hair had turned a dull gray from the shock of the last month. He entered with just enough strength to lie down on his bed. Jehoshebeth was nursing their daughter in a chair across from the bed. A baby's cry that would not stop made Jehoiada roll over and look at his daughter.

"It is a sound that should bless me," he said. "But I am dead in my heart, Jehoshebeth." Tears fell from him and he covered his face. The baby continued to cry. Ayla was nursing contentedly.

Jehoiada looked up, confusion registering. Jehoshebeth called, "Noemi, all is safe and well."

A girl emerged from the bedroom chamber. She was holding an infant.

"Look, husband, I have brought you the heir of David, the rightful king of Judah. It is Joash, son of my brother."

Jehoiada stood and stared without breathing. He reached out to steady himself against something, but found nothing, and sat back on the bed.

Royal trumpets sounded in the streets below and Jehoiada's heart missed another beat.

"Athaliah," Jehoiada said, glancing toward the noise, the color gone from his face. He walked to the baby, and his legs shook with his steps. "She has picked the new heir to the throne and will make him king now," he said.

"But there is none of David's line left, except this boy," she said.

Jehoiada stared at the baby squirming in Noemi's arms. He held out his hands. The tremors shook them too as he cradled Joash. Jehoiada saw himself in his mind, pale and weak and trembling, holding an orphaned son, red and wailing, thrashing with life. He willed himself to find his strength.

"She would not let this child anywhere near the throne," he told the women. "If she knew he was alive, she would kill us all."

"But . . ." Jehoshebeth argued, her voice rising before she caught herself, breathing hard and forcing her words through clenched teeth, "only he can be king!"

"He is an infant, Jehoshebeth," he replied. "Even with the blessing of Athaliah, he could not take the throne until his seventh birthday."

Noemi looked frightened and took Joash back, trying to make him stop crying.

"Who will reign in Judah?" Noemi asked.

Jehoshebeth looked at Jehoiada. "Go!" she said, "Go and find out what you can. We will stay hidden."

The frost of shock was still on his face, but he left again.

A PRIEST'S WIFE saw him leaving and complained as he passed. "Your child cries so much. I don't think she ever eats or sleeps."

Jehoiada ran into the streets to join the crowd converging and pressing toward the palace. Trumpeters played the call to coronation, and everyone looked around in confusion.

"There are no male children left, neither from her own people, nor from the house of David. Who is made king?" the people murmured.

"The palace does not recognize the Temple's authority," one woman stated. "The king will be crowned without the blessing of God."

"There is no one left of the covenant," a man scolded her. "The Temple and the palace no longer rule together."

The crowd parted as guards moved through them to the center of the city near the open market. The crown of David was carried out. Everyone craned their necks to get a glimpse of who walked in behind Athaliah.

But no one did. Athaliah approached alone and sat. A guard placed the crown of David on her head, and the crowd recoiled in gasps.

Athaliah called out to the people. "See here today that a woman rules in Judah. By design of nature, women give life to all. By design of reason, she is fit to rule all as well. Listen now, mothers of Judah: The children of David are dead. A new covenant must be made in Judah, a covenant among mothers, not between men and their God. My child Ahaziah is dead by Yahweh's sword, as is my brother, my husband, and my mother. Who here has lost more than I?"

Tears streamed down her cheeks and her chin trembled as she spoke.

"Who here, then, is more fit to rule?" she called out. "When a God bids us destroy each other, we must destroy such a God. I will offer a new life to those who see the wisdom of change, just as I will surely kill any who oppose me."

She rose. "Hear me, mothers of Judah: We have all lost so much. There can never again be war in Judah, for when men draw swords for their God, it is our children who die."

Jehoiada watched from behind a market stall, seeing Athaliah shadowed by the palace and the Temple above her. Either looked ready to topple and crush her if pushed only a bit more. But Athaliah parted the crowd with a last kiss of peace. He wept.

THE PEOPLE bowed before her as she exited. Ornat stayed close to her.

"The children of David are not dead, my queen. A daughter remains."

She brushed him back. "A daughter is of no consequence. I would almost be content to let her live out her days in fear, but she may give birth to a son. I have been distracted, securing the kingdom that was lashed by strong winds of change. It is time to end Jehoshebeth, to be free forever of her name and womb. Send men by night to the chamber of Jehoiada and kill them all. Tell my men" — Athaliah began to smile, her first smile of the day, broad and bright — "tell them I want Jehoshebeth to be the last to die."

JEHOSHEBETH HAD both babies wrapped and sleeping. She was waiting, watching the light soften through the tiny openings along the tops of the walls. Nightfall was coming but she did not feel the peace of a day well-ended. Every hour that passed softened the shock of the palace terrors but made the complications plain. Panic would rise in her throat, and she would let it stay there, crowding the breaths that she tried to take, until she let it push her almost to wish she had never rescued this child. Then she would force herself to see Ahaziah's face and let the shame of being so weak strangle the fear.

Noemi had fallen asleep on a rug near Joash, who lay on the bed. There was one cradle and the babies had to take turns in it. Jehoshebeth bit her lip as the fear rose again. There was no way to care for two babies without risking death to them all. Jehoshebeth saw Noemi's half-eaten bread and worried for her. In an unexpected instant, the horror of what she must have seen, of what Jehoshebeth did see, burst through the fear and Jehoshebeth gasped, covering her mouth with her hands and running to the door. Tears were raining down her cheeks and she clenched her eyes so tightly it felt as if the skin was bruising, but she could not shake herself free of the images. She knocked her head against the wall, but the images kept stabbing at her eyes.

She felt her knees getting weak, fear working its way through her body, until she slid down the wall. She lay there, unable to even raise an arm and wipe her face, until she at last heard salvation.

Jehoiada came quietly into the house. Jehoshebeth rose, unable to meet his eyes, unable to think. Somehow the familiar called to her and seemed right, so in its strength she poured water over his hands, wiping them dry, and then washed his feet. She motioned for him to sit. There was no emotion left for her voice, and she felt ashamed that she could give voice to the unspeakable without trembling, but she did. She told him everything. Together they sat and talked in low voices in the last hour between sunset and darkness.

"The nursemaid cannot stay here," Jehoiada said. "We will be discovered."

"No," Jehoshebeth countered. "She is too young to trust with this secret. We do not know how that night has affected her. By now, her own mother must think she is dead, killed with the mothers that night. She will not return to the palace, and she cannot return home."

Jehoiada sighed and looked at the sleeping girl.

"Who is she?"

"A girl from the village, her family poor. A boy was to marry her and she became pregnant, though she told no one. He collapsed working in the fields one afternoon a few weeks later. They tried to cut his skull, she said, to release the evil spirits that were tormenting him, but it was no use. He died."

Jehoiada shook his head.

"When his family discovered the pregnancy," Jehoshebeth continued, "they wanted the child if it was male. She did give birth to a son, but he did not live. She was sent to Athaliah's palace to be a nursemaid there." Jehoshebeth rubbed her face with her palms, trying to stay awake. "She has nowhere to go, Jehoiada."

A knock at the door interrupted them. It was the old priest Eli. He gave a weak smile and stepped inside, his heavy stick bearing him up with every step.

"I have brought a gift for your daughter, and for the infant king," he said. Jehoiada smiled at Eli, who clearly bore nothing for either baby. Eli had long been regarded as the poorest among the priests, and yet he made many public shows of denying even his rightful pay. They indulged him in everything because of his age and service.

"That is unnecessary, Eli," he began, but Eli cut him off with a wave of the hand. He motioned for both to draw closer, and they did.

"Haven't I always lived in a separate home from the priests, nearest the Temple, the dwelling regarded as the least desirable?" Eli asked. "It is low and plain, an outcast building that many wished was torn down. But I have no family who should make me desire better. My only regret is that you may not think so well of me once you discover that I am not the man you think, the one so content to live in poverty," he said. Jehoiada motioned for him to continue and patted his knee. Then Eli leaned in.

"My home has a secret that no man has known save me and my father before me," he wheezed.

"On a summer's day, many years ago, when the earth still had the scent and seed of Solomon's gardens, my father was but a boy lingering as his mother cooked the evening meal. He was a fine boy but curious and impatient, and in the mother's exasperation she sent him to find firewood. He was wandering near the Temple, where the great trees meet the path, when he tried to lift an old log, and he fell through. He fell through the earth!" Jehoiada raised his eyebrows, and the old man laughed.

"My father had discovered the secret treasury of David, where the swords and shields of David and his mighty men were stored, along with many riches of David's kingdom. It was said that the greatest of pieces were smuggled away, that David never stored his sword in the Temple treasury; some believed the tunnels never existed. But there was so much gold that even the meager light breaking through the earth set all the dark passageways ablaze in golden rays! My father returned to the spot where he fell and made sure it was well hidden, until the day he was ready to establish his own home. Everyone thought him so humble, requesting the least desirable portion of land covered in thorns and rocks. Yes, but that was him also, for he had pulled every good plant that tried to grow and scattered there every rock he had found!" Eli laughed and wheezed until Jehoiada had to pound him on the back.

"It is the place you must live now," he continued. "Even today the tunnels are undiscovered, and no one knows of the secret entrance. You can hide a child and his maid within a moment if trouble ever threatens your home. And who knows that in time you will not have use for the swords as well, for the will of God is not always an easy thing."

Jehoiada frowned. "Even if all this is as you say, we can't move in with you, my friend," he said. "We would burden you, and no explanation would satisfy the gossips," he reasoned.

"Oh, don't worry about that. I am too old to serve in the Temple anymore, everyone knows that." He patted his thin legs where the muscles twisted unnaturally across the pale flesh. "Bless these bad legs! I will go to live with my great niece, for she is a wonderful cook with many small children who will read to me at night while I wait for God's patience with my infirmities to wear thin," he laughed and coughed, waving his hands in front of his face as if to clear his throat.

"What may we send with you, Father, for this kindness?" Jehoshebeth asked. The word *Father* stuck in her throat. It hurt to say the word even in courtesy.

"Ah, well," the priest said, gesturing as if his meaning would be understood without embarrassing words.

It was. Jehoshebeth embraced him, kissing him on the cheek.

"I have loved him well, but he will serve you better now." Jehoshebeth looked at Jehoiada. "Let Gabriel be readied for the journey."

The priest stood to leave, raising one finger to introduce his last thought.

"It would be best if you moved at night, lest someone see how your family has grown," Eli said. "I leave tonight. May God bless your days in the house, as He has blessed mine."

Jehoiada held Eli in a hug as Jehoshebeth kissed him again.

"Thank you," she said.

Eli peered at her through his watery eyes. "Now you will learn what it is to pray. If Athaliah ever learns of this child, you will all die."

JEHOIADA AND his family prepared their few belongings and walked to Eli's home within the hour. The air was moist and had the sharp sweet scent of deep earth. The home was sparse but clean with a main room at the entry, a partition for a separate room at the back, and a ladder to a cramped bedchamber above. From Jehoshebeth's vantage point, the bedchamber did not seem tall enough for a man to stand in it, even a man as old and bent as Eli. There was a table to recline at and take meals, and it sat in the center of the main space. Jehoshebeth realized this was all there was to see and sighed heavily. She had hoped this new place would somehow carry with it a bit of Eli's comfort. She did not know whether the many prayers and songs sung here could linger somehow.

She watched as Jehoiada did not rest until he found the secret doorway to the world beneath; it was well hidden by the man's straw bed mat behind the partition. Now a rug was across the hidden door and their eating table on top of that, so that now they would eat in the back of the house, and a sleeping chamber would be near the door. Jehoiada seemed pleased with his design and said he would sleep near the door for their protection. Noemi and Joash could sleep above, and the partition could be set against the wall beneath them to make a bedchamber for Jehoshebeth and Ayla.

They opened the secret door only once, to know what was there. Stone stairs disappeared into darkness stale and damp, like secrets bottled and forgotten. The stillness was punctuated by the sound of dripping water and the scratching of creatures that moved unseen. The women scrambled back to the room with relief.

"If Athaliah's men come in search of the child, Noemi must take Joash beneath. Take no light with you, for if they come at night the men will see a hint of it from under the table. You will stay there until I call you up."

The women shuddered to think of hiding there in the darkness, of the things that crawled away from their lamps. Noemi begin to tremble, and Jehoshebeth put her arm around the nurse.

"What if you don't call for me?" she asked.

Jehoiada and Jehoshebeth looked at each other, but neither spoke.

"We're all going to die!" Noemi cried.

Jehoshebeth tried to soothe her. "You have seen too much death for your age," she said.

Noemi glared at her. "It is not my age that makes this hard to bear. You should have left me to die at the palace! It would have been finished. Now I must live as a prisoner here, wondering every day when it is I will die!"

Jehoshebeth tried to hold her, but Noemi shoved her away.

"Noemi, please do not be afraid!"

"I am afraid! It is the only thing left I feel!"

They did not talk of Athaliah's men again, or of the secret beneath them.

THREE WARRIORS stood in the center of Jehoiada's home. Two of the men held their hands over the bed and along the table where food would have been served.

"Still warm," one murmured.

"But where would they have gone?"

"Someone has betrayed us."

"Athaliah will kill us. Our families too."

One man rubbed his cheek with the fingers of one hand while he looked at the other two. "We'll tell her we killed them. We can take a goat from the priests' livestock and smear the blood and hair across our arms and swords."

"It won't work," one of the men protested.

"What else can we do? Jehoiada and his family have fled. Athaliah doesn't walk through the streets or visit Yahweh's Temple; she'll never hear gossip about where they went."

The men glanced at each other uneasily. The one who named the plan made more confident strides through his logic. "We're already sentenced to die. If we tell her we failed, we die tonight. If we lie and the plan fails, we die later, that's all. But if we keep this secret from her, we keep our families and our lives."

"Someone knows where they went. Someone will talk."

The third man shook his head and silenced him. "No one would bring this news to Athaliah. Who would risk her anger over being betrayed? She has earned her reputation for killing even her allies."

It was decided, and the sleeping priests did not hear a goat bleating as it was lifted from the pen.

THE HOME was actually much larger inside than it appeared from the street; the old man had carried on his father's tradition of feigned poverty quite well. For on the outside, the place was uninviting and troublesome pebbles littered the path to the low door, where bits of moss creeped around the indentations left by a worker's knife. Repairs to crumbling limestone had been made with mud and straw bricks, earning it further disdain.

But inside, the women were able to move freely and establish a bedroom for Noemi in the loft of the home. Joash would sleep with her for now. They never ventured into the hidden space beneath them, and never spoke of it. The women tried to focus on keeping the babies quiet and fed. Noemi was a capable nursemaid, but her heart was beyond mending, and Jehoshebeth felt a sadness watching her care for Joash. Perhaps she would have been a good mother. That life was sealed off forever now, but a thousand daily reminders showed Noemi her dead dreams.

As do all babies, Joash and Ayla grew quickly, their bodies taking the milk and the bits of soaked and softened bread, transforming the sleepy babes quickly into children. The women stood in awe many nights watching them sleep, measuring the length of their bodies with their hands and shaking their heads in wonder. The children flourished in secret, amazing the women who suffered. Time had found the hidden children and spurred them through long days, past unnoticed weeks, and delivered them at last through fleeting years.

Only once did the children question the strange wooden square resting under a rug, tucked under the table where they ate. Their mothers warned them of monsters, of terrible biting things and a darkness that light could not penetrate, and the children avoided the board. Joash's eyes narrowed a bit as they told of the dark place beneath them and its danger, but he asked no more questions.

Jehoshebeth discreetly provided the food and drink the family consumed. She had memorized the days and times each vendor worked the market and knew how to stagger her shopping so that no one knew what quantities she bought in whole. From the rations provided the priests — the grains and meats — she took only what would have been hers as Jehoiada's wife and the mother of one. It was in her dealings in the market that she made up the difference.

She stumbled some days walking to market, exhaustion setting on her at unexpected moments. The women had never fully received her again. She heard their whispers as she picked through their goods. They never called her by name.

"She was dying, had lost much blood, yet when she returned the color was back in her cheeks. It is sorcery, mark me."

"Her home is poor, and I hear it is wildly unkempt, for she will not even entertain visitors from the Temple. She has violated our law of hospitality."

The vendor who sold oranges often spoke directly to her, crossly. Jehoshebeth gave the booth wide berth, but one afternoon, on her second shopping trip of the day, the vendor called out, "What say you about the wife of your father?"

Jehoshebeth shook and crushed her lips together to keep from crying or returning this idle challenge.

She received no better treatment from the wives of the priests. There was a courtyard in the center of the priest's quarters where the women baked the bread every morning in a fire pit oven they shared. Jehoshebeth, hiding her basket, was the first there and the first to leave, working in secret, and the other women named it arrogance.

She listened to their laughter as she scurried away one morning and felt a sharp pain in her ribs. It felt like a fresh grief, though her body was worn from so many others. She paused at her threshold moments later and pressed a hand to her side. It was the grief of loneliness, she decided, Adam's pain. But there was nothing to do with it today, except to allow it to nettle and steal her thoughts away as she served bread, the same bread she had served the day before and would serve tomorrow. Every day was the same now. There was always a light breakfast, some fruit and a flatbread. Lunch was a stew or bowl of parched grain and figs with honey. Dinner was curds or cheese, more bread, roasted lamb or fowl sometimes, and more grains. The days were marked only by the meals, and the women marked the hour by which room was heated by the sun. When it was too much for Noemi, she would cover her face in her hands and weep quietly.

"I would rather die than live this way," she cried. "Yet if I leave, we all will."

Jehoshebeth never had the words to comfort her. She could only pat her hand and try to give her the finest portion of the evening meal. She tried to keep resentment far away from her heart. Noemi did not know what a blessing it was to be unknown in a world of women who hated and spat the name of your father. Noemi suffered only from her own thoughts and isolation. Jehoshebeth suffered her own but also the stinging barbs of other women. That was the mystery of age, she decided, that her wounds hurt no less, and yet she must spend her time comforting another.

Noemi was never let from the house. She stayed prisoner in the rooms, and the low house had no windows except for thin slits in the top bricks to allow air to circulate.

"Opportunity tempts thieves and lovers." Noemi sighed, tracing her fingers along a wall where a window might have been.

"Do you dream of him?" Jehoshebeth asked as she set the table for breakfast.

Noemi blushed.

"No," she said. "I dream of finding another."

Jehoshebeth was not prepared for this answer. It made her sick, like the breath of a stranger on her neck.

CHAPTER NINETEEN

"I RULE NOW, and there is no authority above mine," Athaliah repeated to the landowners who had gathered to hear her in the king's court, where she sat upon his throne. "Yes, you have heard of my battles with those who worship Yahweh, and it is true I will not honor that God nor go near His Temple. No one who serves me can support that strange religion. But the matter before you today is wealth, not worship."

The men listened, but she could not read their faces. Without an heir, there was only one way to secure her crown: greed. Greed could do the work of a thousand allies.

"No longer are you required to bring the first fruits of your harvest and flocks to the Temple of Yahweh. But do not think to enrich yourselves yet when there is so much to be done in our land. Bring these offerings to me. We must use them to pursue trade as well as peace, for both have been neglected. The old kings would not deal with all nations, and we must make amends."

The men nodded and accepted her plan. And so it was the seed broke ground, and the sprout sprang to life, promising the hidden glory of the bloom. Six dreamless years passed as the people watched this new wealth unfolding in their land. The beauty of the thing blinded them so they did not see the children still dying around her.

THE OLD healer shook her head and pleaded with the father. "You must take the girl to the priest Jehoiada. There is nothing more I can do," she begged.

The girl screamed, "I will not submit myself to his judgment!"

The father wrung his hands and looked from healer to daughter, each piercing him with her gaze, trying to sway the uncertain man to her side.

"We will go," he eventually replied. His daughter pulled out a clump of her hair as she rocked on her mat.

Jehoiada met them at the entrance to the Temple grounds. He listened and nodded. The fathers had been coming to him, only a few at first, but more now, and the first meeting was always the worst.

"You must tell the other fathers," Jehoiada warned. "Give no thought to the reputation of your house, for others will die if you keep silent. Her priests spread this sickness when the girls are brought to offer their bodies to Asherah. Warn the fathers to keep guard over their houses, to give their daughters reason to follow the old ways, even if they do not follow our God. It is the only hope for those not yet infected."

The father sighed and watched his daughter, who was lying on her mat, a fever making her skin flushed and lovely as she approached death. The slick little blisters that had sprung up around her groin now made their way across her body, and the father moved the blanket to hide them.

Jehoiada caught his eye. "I do not wish this upon you, friend. I grieve with you. But I charge you to save a life for the one you have lost."

The father nodded, and carried away his girl with some effort. She still clutched the clay god she had bought in the market, although her grip was looser now. Jehoiada felt a sadness that was new to him. He had felt anger many times as a priest, but this woe was new, and he realized it was only since he had held his own daughter that it had dwelled within his heart. He grieved that death did not come all at once for anyone, but ate away at all, slowly, day by day. Often it was the children who fed it willingly. They were too young to understand and too proud to agree.

The chaos of many gods saved them from blaming themselves. Jehoiada knew that was why he was the last to see a child before death. The children, the young ones, the innocents who had not lived long enough to earn caution — these were the ones who suffered from freedom. The tragedy broke him, making a wound he could not mend. He had a father's heart at last and wondered why this love showed him so much sorrow.

The days were long for Jehoiada. He sacrificed and prayed alone, attended only by a handful of faltering priests who had nowhere else to go. A few people of the city remained constant, but even they made sacrifices and petitions under the cover of dawn or dusk. Athaliah permitted the worship of Yahweh, but she held no favor for those who did. Disfavor often strained a house until it broke.

Jehoiada sat outside the gates of the Temple and would call out to those who passed by, offering prayers of healing and reconciliation. Each day became a day like most others and no one in Jerusalem marked its passing. The week slipped away into the next, and then the month, for time herself had learned to creep by undetected as the people ate, and slept, and birthed. And if the air over Jerusalem had once been thick with the breath of God, now it had the stale smell of guilt, like a rain that stayed too long and made all things damp and gray.

Jehoshebeth watched the children playing and remembered through them her own days of childhood, the pleasant hours spent idly with Ahaziah. Joash reminded her so much of her half brother, and she loved the child as fiercely as if he were her own son. Everything about the pair brought her joy: the gaps in their teeth, their unruly hair, the way they became fascinated with a bug that foolishly made its way into their home only to be trapped underneath a pot for their unending amusement. Sometimes, it seemed to her, life with them was so dear that she must have only imagined the great evil that dwelt in the same world with these children.

Jehoiada spent his days in service to the Temple, empty though it was. His nights were given to teaching the children. He told them the stories of faith, of laws and mercy. He told them of the house of David, of how God called a king from the most unlikely of places. As it had been for that gentle shepherd, He would call another boy out from the shadows to rule a nation. Ayla gobbled the stories up, even the ones too large to be believed in one sitting. Joash, however, would sigh and squint at Jehoiada, trying to discern if it was all real. If he were to be the king, why did they live in fear, he asked? Why would such a powerful God hide Himself too, and for so long? There were never enough answers for the boy, though he learned the laws by heart and readied himself for a day he said would probably never come.

By Athaliah's cold rule, the fires of war were extinguished, and boys who had once served her returned from the fronts as men. The people lived in the shadow of the palace and began to sense the poison of their easy freedom. Enemies with swords and arrows were easily marked for destruction, but this compromise of faith made their own flesh the enemy and the price of victory nothing less than themselves. To return her freedom was to kill what they had birthed: their lives without God, without Law, without glory. Slowly, the people began to hate the shadow, and the dark queen who ruled within it. They began to talk again of the past. The courage of memory filled the void of the present and summoned hope in the future.

ON AN UNREMARKABLE evening, the moon stole out from fits of clouds that tried to cover it as the children ran through the house. Noemi was asleep, taking her turn getting a nap in between caring for the children. Jehoshebeth had been grinding meal for tomorrow's breakfast. She had so many cakes to make each day that she could only be first to the oven if she worked the night before. As she worked tonight, however, she fell asleep, slumped over the bowl in her lap, her mouth open as she took long breaths.

Joash stopped short and Ayla crashed into him from behind.

"Do you hear that?" Joash murmured.

"No."

"It is quiet. We can try it now." Joash pulled Ayla's hand.

"No!" Ayla murmured. "It is dangerous!"

Joash pushed the table aside, careful to lift it on the corners so it would make little noise.

"Come on! Are we not six years old? What should we fear?"

He took a lamp and crept down the stairs cut from the rocks below.

JEHOSHEBETH AWOKE with a start. The children were gone. The wooden door gaped. She woke Noemi up in a panic. Noemi held the oil lamp as Jehoshebeth stood atop the ancient steps. There was no light below, no noise or indication of where they had gone. She tried calling them, but was afraid to raise her voice beyond a low call. She looked at Noemi, who began trembling.

"No, I will not go under there!" she whined.

Jehoshebeth snapped at her. "I didn't ask you to. I'm going. Hand me the lamp once I am down."

Jehoshebeth lifted her robe and stepped down. Her legs dipped into the dark air and she felt goose bumps lifting all over. She took another step, and another, descending quickly into the darkness. When she was several steps down, she lifted her hand back to Noemi to reach for the lamp.

"I'm sorry," was all Noemi said as she shut the door over Jehoshebeth.

BENEATH THE house, light broke through in places, and the walls shimmered as water slid down and into the river below that fed the underground springs. The children saw tunnels stretching before them in every direction. The earth made a crunching sound beneath their feet, and they saw that it was littered with bits of rock that had been hewn away by the ones who had made this place.

"It's beautiful," Ayla whispered.

Joash punched her on the shoulder. "You don't have to whisper. No one can hear us."

They picked a tunnel, and began walking. The air was cool and moist. They ran their hands along the walls and reached up to see how high the ceiling was. As they turned a dark corner, a man stood before them. Ayla cried out, but Joash covered her mouth with his hands, and they pressed themselves against the wall to stay out of the light. They watched him standing in the shadows, waiting for them to move. They didn't. Only their breath stirred in the passage between them. Joash bent, keeping his eyes on the man, and picked up a small stone. He tossed it across the passageway, hitting the tunnel across from them with perfect aim. The man did not move. This time, Ayla picked a stone and threw it. The man was still.

They ran to him, their hearts still crashing in their chests, and saw the shield and boots and helmet were strung up against a wall.

"This is no man!" Joash laughed.

Ayla had gone white and pointed beyond Joash. "This is the treasury of David and the fabled Mighty Men. How many stories have we heard at night about them?"

Joash replied under his breath, "I did not believe half of them."

They peered into the darkness and lifted their lamp. Suits of bronze armor, inscribed swords, rotted cloaks and heavy knives were stacked into the small opening before them. Their mouths fell open and they entered the storeroom, touching each piece with the awe of a child meeting a bedtime legend. Joash tried to raise a sword above him but staggered, tipping a shield into another and making such a noise that both children froze.

Nothing happened. No sound came back save their own breathing, so they slowly resumed.

They were so enthralled that they paid no attention to the lamp they carried, now wearying of its labor and drawing short. It burned out as Joash spied a belt woven from gold and tried to strap it round his own waist. The darkness was sudden and complete.

Both gasped. They felt through the blackness until they touched hands, then stumbled in small starts toward where the light had once been. Creeping along, pressing themselves against the walls and praying they did not fall into a watery crevice below, they wandered in fear, watching for a patch of light. When they found one, their steps became more sure and swift, and they laughed quietly at their great fear.

A woman's voice, not their mother's or Noemi's, echoed back and bid them come to breakfast. They followed the sound. A boy, his voice tired and ill-mannered, shot across the tunnel.

"Do not wake me! I was having a pleasant dream! Keep yourself quiet!"

The children continued creeping and found the source of the noise, a small crack in the wall made by the shifting of the earth over time. Joash wiggled his eyebrows at Ayla and pressed his hands around his mouth as he shouted in a strange, high voice into the crevice.

"Little boys make tasty meals for evil spirits!"

They heard a scream of terror, then they doubled over in muffled giggles.

Another full hour passed before the haphazard spotting of light led them back to the tunnel beneath their home. Joash stopped and held Ayla back with his hand. A woman's crying could be heard, though it was soft. And it was not above them. It was in their tunnel, just ahead.

CHAPTER TWENTY

A BOY SPRINTED through the city gates, holding his side as he doubled over finally for a breath. The guards posted there pulled him aside and waited for him to speak.

"Our enemy Jehu has made peace with Shalmaneser!" the boy gasped. "He has sent a great tribute to the king who has spat on our name for so long!"

The guards shrugged at each other and one moved to lead the boy to the palace.

The boy recounted his story for Athaliah. He kept wrapping his arms around himself as if he were cold, even after so long a run.

Athaliah watched him from the shadows in the council room just outside the throne room, as she reclined alone in a chair near the window. A thick drape did not move when the wind, soured by the dead garden below, blew in.

"Jehu has proven himself a traitor again, paying tribute to a king we could have defeated had he not taken the crown as he did," she said. "But it was wise to build an alliance with another, lest I seek war with him alone. I will not fight both Jehu and Shalmaneser."

The men in her chamber stood silent.

Athaliah began laughing.

"How have I ruled Judah? Is it not by appealing to the mothers, that no more of our children should die?" No one replied, but a few nodded.

"Jehu would expect a king of Judah to respond to his threat with men and horses. Perhaps he assumes because I rule as king that I think as a man."

She rose now and came out of the shadows to face them. The weak light transformed her smile into something malformed, her glistening teeth setting everyone on edge. "Yes, may my will be unveiled before the world now, for I will break the back of the north and unite us again as we were under Solomon. Solomon's weakness split the twelve tribes of Israel. By the strength of a woman, we shall again be one. But for this moment I was born, for this moment that I have lived."

She motioned the boy to step forward.

"How many children are in the palace of the king of Israel, dear?" she asked.

The boy cleared his throat. "I would not know numbers, my king," he replied, then glanced at the guards to see if this was how he was to address her.

"But if you had to guess, child?" she asked.

The boy shrugged as he thought. "Well, I saw a group of about eight playing in their courtyard, and there were many more in the palace itself, because I heard them calling down to their friends. I was only a messenger, but this is what I saw and heard."

"Well done, and so to be well rewarded," Athaliah said and dismissed him.

The guards escorted him out. Only her advisers were left in

the room now. Ornat escorted her back to her chair and bowed with a flourish of his hands. He had not stopped smiling since she had spoken of conquering the north. The other men came near to listen.

Athaliah sighed and settled back into the darkness.

"Israel tore itself away from Jerusalem in a fit that was rash and unwise. Israel will rejoin us now, or we will destroy her," she said. "We will begin by sending our best warriors, just two or three of them, to raid the palace of Jehu. They will kill as many children as they can until they themselves are killed."

She motioned for an adviser to write. "Write a letter to this Jehu, and say,

'Thus shall every child in Israel be, unless you pay tribute to Judah and swear to serve her with all loyalty for your reign. For if we seek war with you, we will never strike your men, or treasuries, or even lay claim to your trade routes. We will creep quietly through the night and kill a child, until every child in the kingdom is dead, unless you make peace now and forever. Do not test me in this, for I am sure my reputation has secured for me your fear.

I am, in all respects,
Athaliah,
Daughter of Jezebel.'"

THE BOY who had delivered his report to Athaliah ate a hearty meal of curds and seasoned lamb and asked for his money, which was handed over. He stretched and loosened his neck and shoulders, then ran from the palace, his feet, thick with

calluses, carrying him like a mountain cat up the rocky path. His ran without stopping until he was at the Temple, then he ducked into a market booth and watched. The streets were busy today, and no one seemed to notice him. The coins in his pocket were a distraction and he patted them as if to quiet them down. When he was sure that no one paid him any mind, he stepped out and walked deliberately toward the Temple.

The Temple was quiet, and the boy patted his coins again as he walked through the main entrance. A priest greeted him.

"I want to see the high priest," the boy said flatly. The priest frowned but the boy stared at him. The priest exited.

Jehoiada returned moments later.

The boy eyed him. "You are the high priest?" he asked. Jehoiada nodded.

"Do you have much gold?" the boy asked.

Jehoiada frowned. "Athaliah has removed all our gold already for her own temples. What business does a boy have asking after it?"

The boy inched closer. "I gave my heart to a girl once, but I still held a little piece back in case one better came along."

Jehoiada's frown deepened. "What is it you say to me? What do you want?"

The boy inched closer again and murmured. "I am sure you have a little gold somewhere that Athaliah knows nothing about. And today is the day you need it, my Father. For I have news of a plot that stirs itself together in the palace, a plot that a man such as yourself would sell his soul to hear. So you see, it is not such a bold thing to ask for just a few coins."

Jehoiada glanced at the priest standing nearby, who was straining to hear any of the words. Jehoiada took the boy by the ear and dragged him to a corner. The boy shouted out in pain and swung his arms at Jehoiada but could not strike him.

Alone in a corner, Jehoiada released the boy, who rubbed his ears and glared at the high priest. Jehoiada rested one heavy hand on the boy's shoulder and with the other patted the coins that had made such noise as the boy was dragged.

"You sold information to Athaliah," Jehoiada surmised.

The boy stuck out his chest and drew a deep breath, smoothing his hair with one hand. "I will sell that information to you as well. In fact, I will freely give it to you when you pay me for the other. You will get twice what she got for the same price."

Jehoiada looked at the boy with compassion. "So young," he said, "so young to be out fending for yourself, selling scraps of news where you can. Are you providing for your mother, or family elsewhere?"

The boy stared at the ground before replying. "No, there is no one but me that I must care for."

Jehoiada grabbed him by both ears and dragged him out of the corner. "Good," Jehoiada said, "then no one will starve when you are killed for double-crossing the queen. And I will get a handsome reward myself for having turned you in."

The boy cried out. "Please, no! Let me go! Do not betray me to her!"

Jehoiada spoke slowly to the boy squirming in his pinch. "You will tell me everything."

The boy nodded vigorously.

"And you will make a nice donation to the Temple before you leave," Jehoiada added. The boy opened his mouth to protest and Jehoiada began dragging him again.

"Yes!" the boy cried out. "I will, only let me down!"

Jehoiada stopped and released one ear.

"Tell me what you know."

JEHOIADA'S MIND raced between thoughts as he walked home. He had planned what to do when the proper day came, but this news forced the urgency. He could not spend much time winning the confidence of the other men. They would either be with him or turn him over at once as a traitor. He marveled that Athaliah had never killed him or Jehoshebeth. It was a strange mercy she had shown in letting them live. Perhaps their withdrawal had appeased her.

He saw the door to his home ajar.

"Jehoshebeth!" he yelled and sprinted to the door, tearing inside. The house was empty and entirely undisturbed. Except for the table. The rug had been cast aside. He walked cautiously toward the door, circling it, trying to understand what message this might be when he heard the voices. He kneeled and lifted the door. The children and Jehoshebeth jerked their faces away from the sudden bright light. Jehoshebeth shielded her face with her hand and called up to him.

"Noemi's gone!"

SHE WANDERED through the streets, breathing the air that tasted so clean and fresh and feeling rapture at the sight of stars. The night wind was her forgotten sister, whose fingers brushed the hair back from her face. Only a few drunks were out at this hour, but closer to the city gates and the palace there would be guards. Here, in the inner streets of the city, in between the palace and the gates, she was safe. She ran her hands along the limestone walls as she walked, grateful for stone under her hands at last instead of baked bricks. Everything begged to be touched, and she could not stop staring at the sky. It was so black, but not the black of terrible dreamless nights. It was rich and tender, and every star burst across the darkness to comfort her. She walked until her legs grew tired, and then she sat down in the doorway of a quiet home, watching the changes of night as the moon traded its place in the sky for another. She smiled again as she dozed off. She had no idea what would happen tomorrow. She didn't need tomorrow. Tonight was an extravagant gift she had afforded herself. Tomorrow could bring nothing better than what she had now and nothing worse than what she had suffered for years.

"WE WILL NEVER Agree to it," a commander of the army, Elishaphat, declared.

Jehoiada shook his head. "You don't have to agree to it. She will find a few who are willing, and she will carry out her plan," he said.

"It will invoke the wrath of God," Elishaphat said. The other four commanders nodded in the lamplight. Each of them commanded a regiment of one hundred soldiers and reported directly to the chief of Athaliah's guards. Each of them had been summoned this night by Jehoiada's careful request.

Jehoiada peered at them. "I thought you did not believe in God."

Elishaphat smirked. "You have served us well, Jehoiada, caring for my men when the sickness of Asherah struck their families. You have proven to be a faithful servant, even though you know we do not worship here. But this thing you say, it is so vile, it cannot be believed."

Jehoiada stood and faced the commanders. "It has already begun. Every day, do we not walk past the graves of the children she has murdered here? This thing is coming to pass, and our nations will be at war, a war never seen before, where even our women take up arms, sister against sister, and we will not fight for gold but for the blood of the next generation. This thing is already in motion."

"What does a priest know of war?" one man asked. "Why do you bring this to us?"

"I guard a secret that will cause such awe and wonder as to change the world forever," Jehoiada replied. "Every man you know to be loyal, send him to me. They must make sin offerings and be restored to God. Only then will I unveil what is to be done."

Elishaphat shook his head. "We talk of war, and you bring us round to God."

Another man laughed too. "He is a priest."

"You are men of war," Jehoiada said, "but we are not so different. For when you dream, do you not think on the tales your mothers told you growing up? Do you not remember the stories of David and his Mighty Men, the promise between an invisible God who drew near and promised that a lamp of David's house would always shine before Him? Do you not, when your children burn with fever and your women cradle them without hope, do you not remember the promise that God's favor would forever rest on the house of David? We have not lost His favor, men, and He has not abandoned us." He leaned in and lowered his voice. "If you are men with the courage to believe twice, give me your hand."

Elishaphat was the first to offer his hand. Without words, each man laid his own hand on top of his, until they were all joined in the oath.

"Go now," Jehoiada said. "Go to the head of every family, and bring the men here. Be very fast, for time is against us."

NOEMI WOKE when a daughter of the house opened the door carrying a jar on her head. She must have been going to fetch water for breakfast and washing, because she held it lightly and nearly stumbled across Noemi's legs. She cried out in alarm and Noemi, awake at once, begged forgiveness and scuttled away. Her heart was pounding as she watched the girl casting mean backward glances at her over her shoulder, and Noemi couldn't help but laugh. It felt so good to feel anything in the open air, even fright. Noemi joined more women walking to the water well nearby. She could smell fires burning in the courtyards of homes, and knew the women must be baking their bread. Her stomach was aching, she realized. It was the first sensation that did not feel good. The more she thought on her stomach, the emptier it seemed. She wanted a drink of water, and curds, and a large hot flatbread. She could smell them and it made the hunger worse.

But she had no money. A market was opening up at the end of one street, and she wandered past it to amuse herself. Sashes for robes, jewelry, clay gods and shrines, incense were all sold. Some vendors sold food too, but she kept her eyes away from these tables.

She noticed a man studying her movements. He had a kind face, with a nose too broad to consider him handsome, and eyes with heavy folds of skin above and below. He nodded to her when she caught him staring. Noemi smiled. He rose and approached her, and Noemi held her breath. She had spoken to no one except Jehoshebeth and her family for six years. What would it be to speak to a stranger? He looked so gentle.

"You wander as if you would buy something, but you have no purse for coins." Noemi tried to think of a reply — how many times had she imagined such conversations? — and now she was struck dumb.

He patted her arm and walked alongside her.

"I have daughters," he said. "Daughters sometimes make rash decisions and leave their homes."

Noemi nodded. "Yes," she mumbled. The many words she had imagined when confined to the secret home evaporated, and she felt foolish.

"It is not safe for a girl to wander like this," he said. Concern made the wrinkles around his eyes grow deeper. "How long have you been away from home?"

Noemi cleared her throat and glanced around. "Not long."

"Your family will not be looking for you?"

"No," she replied. "I will not return, either."

He pursed his lips and clucked.

"You must be hungry. Come with me to my home and allow us to feed you. Then we will discuss what you should do next. You cannot wander the streets with no money, no shelter."

She followed him, because she did not know what else to do and he spoke truth to her, facts she could not argue with. The thrill of freedom began slipping away from her and she felt stung that it was not hers to keep.

The gate to his courtyard was beautiful, a large wooden door with iron handles that curved and were fashioned like swimming women. The courtyard was clean, its stone oven in the middle still radiating heat from the breakfast fires, swept clear and ready for its next use. Several small homes were connected, each facing out into this courtyard. He led her to the biggest of the three, and when she entered, she felt at ease right away. The lower level was just like her parents' home, with stalls on each side of the main room for livestock, and a set of stairs to the upper living quarters. He called out for his daughters, who appeared immediately upstairs.

Noemi thought for a moment it was odd that they looked so dissimilar, but the sight of a table above filled with food dismissed all other thoughts. She followed the man to the upper level, and when he urged her to eat, she did. The girls watched her in silence until the man motioned them away. Noemi saw them moving to a back chamber, draping beautiful scarves across their shoulders, adorning themselves with gold earrings and necklaces. They were painting their eyes when Noemi slowed her eating and asked her host why they dressed this way, at this hour.

He did not take his gentle eyes off her face.

"They are sacred prostitutes. They are paid to give their bodies in service to Baal and Asherah."

Noemi recoiled and realized she was still holding a bowl of milk. She set it down, spilling some. The food in her stomach began to spoil as she understood.

"No," she murmured. "No, I could not do this."

His face turned sour like her breakfast, and he jabbed a finger at her.

"Don't be stupid. It's this or dying. No girl can take care of herself without assistance. And you have eaten my food and sought shelter in my home. You will repay me or be arrested."

"No!" Noemi cried and the girls paused to stare at her, their expressions lifeless. "No, I will never do this!" She jumped up to run, but he caught her by the hand. He snapped at a girl, who yelled down from a window near where she dressed. The man was still holding Noemi by the arm, his thick fingers bruising her, when a guard appeared in the doorway below.

He forced Noemi down the stairs, and her legs trembled as the guard came to her.

"Arrest this thief," the man called down. "If by tomorrow she repents and wishes me to claim her, I will. But I will only extend my generosity for one day, and then she can die in debtor's prison for all I care."

The guard grabbed Noemi, and his grip was worse than the man's. He shoved her out the door, back through the courtyard.

"Please," Noemi pleaded. "Please do not take me to this prison. I have a secret, one that the queen would pay any soldier dearly for bringing to her. I could make you rich if you take me to her instead. Please!"

He shook his head and dragged her away.

AT DUSK on the next day, Jehoshebeth rose from her sewing to prepare the beds for each one. They had not played today, but had clung to her legs and whined. Breakfast gave way to fights that lasted until lunch. Jehoshebeth could no more control their fighting than she could her thoughts that stole away, too, to the city. Noemi had opened the door for them all, and fear drove the children back, deeper inside the home, so that they hid themselves in Jehoshebeth's robes between squabbles.

Jehoshebeth stopped for a moment and looked around the walls of the home. Tears filled her eyes, and she wrapped both of the children in a tight embrace that made them squirm and fight for a bit of dignity as she showered them with kisses. Then Jehoshebeth led Ayla to her bed first.

Joash moved to sit near Jehoiada. Jehoiada had been restless since he arrived home a few hours ago, checking the light coming from the slits above, listening for sounds from the street. He was distracted and answered no question with more than two words.

"It is time, isn't it?" Joash asked. "I know now all your stories are real, even this one about me."

Jehoiada turned his thoughts out from their hiding place, and looked at Joash carefully.

"Yes, it is," Jehoiada replied.

"Will I go to live in the palace, then?" Joash asked.

Jehoiada nodded. "That is the home of the king. All your fathers before you lived and ruled there."

Joash bit his lip and tried to stop his chin from quivering.

"And none of you can live there with me," he said. "You must stay and serve the Temple."

Jehoiada reached out and drew the boy into an embrace.

"You will never be alone. You can call Jehoshebeth and Ayla to you whenever you'd like. I will always be near you, to help you rule as you should, to walk with you according to laws of the covenant. You must not fear the future, though it seems now a terrible thing bearing down on you."

Joash nodded. He opened his mouth to say something, but Jehoiada held up his hand.

"Let us say no more tonight. You must sleep if you can."

Joash nodded and took heavy steps toward his bed.

"IT IS TOO FANTASTIC to be believed," the guard said, his tone sharp.

"But what if it is true?" the younger man asked.

The guard stared out from his post at the city gates. All of Jerusalem was quiet, homes lighting as oil lamps were filled and trimmed and all returned from their business of living. A few had been beyond the city, tending to fields and herds. They came last, just outpacing the final rays of the sunset, and the guards prepared to close the gates for the night.

The older guard picked his teeth with a long fingernail and sighed.

"It is late. The city sleeps, and the queen surely does too. It would be wisest to bring this to her attention in the morning. If you disturb her rest, she might kill you for the inconvenience. No, go back to your post and wait for me. At dawn we'll collect her and take her to Athaliah. If the child has hid for six years, one more night won't make any difference."

CHAPTER TWENTY-ONE

AT DAWN, the commanders of each division of the army came to Jehoiada, and they brought with them the appointed men from each family. The men fell silent as they walked through the Temple gates and into the courtyard. Jehoiada was waiting, alone. The other priests were assigned duties elsewhere, and the dark sky bore heavy witness that the day herself was not ready for the pending events, and the men felt her unease. No one had been told what the urgency was, only that the fate of all depended on their loyalty at this moment.

The men numbered well over one hundred, and they stood in small groups, whispering. All studied the Temple with intense interest, scouring for clues of what great thing would unfold. Many men had not been in the Temple courts for the six years of Athaliah's reign. They saw the place now, David's dream, bereft of her gold and jewels, and they cast their eyes to the ground.

Jehoiada led a bull to the altar and slit its throat, keeping his eyes on the men as his hands stretched to the heavens. Then he hacked away the animal's limbs, separating entrails and fat, and placed the offering on the altar to burn. The dripping, bloody refuse he carried away to its assigned place. A man in front wept silently, and as the fire snapped and bit at the burning bull, the men's hearts gave way. Some clenched their eyes and steadied themselves by making tight fists, others fell to their knees, shaking their heads. Jehoiada saw their repentance and blessed them. Peace slipped in among them, like a song from a forgotten dream, and the men took their first full breaths since entering the courts. Only then did Jehoiada turn his back on them. He walked toward the massive columns of the Temple itself, heaved open the ornate doors, then backed away, his back still to the men. They strained for a glimpse of what would be revealed. As Jehoiada backed down the steps, they saw.

A boy. A king's robes were draped around him, and he held a sword as tall as the length of his body. The boy moved down the stairs, holding the sword between him and the crowd so they could not see his face. The men glanced at each other and waited as he drew closer. Finally, he stood before them. Elishaphat was the first to read the markings of the sword and cried, "It is the sword of David!"

The boy lowered the sword and revealed himself. He met their shocked gaze with a steady stare of his own and waited for them to understand. A man from the family of Levites dropped to his knees, but Joash raised a finger to his lips.

"Praise God!" the man yelled. "Long live the king!"

The other men understood at different moments, and as the whispers ran among them, saying "A son of David!" they too fell to their knees.

Jehoiada laid a hand on Joash's shoulder.

"Let me tell you of a night that ran red with the blood of the house of David. Let me tell you how this child alone was spared. As a woman began each of our days, a woman must begin our story, and her courage shall be our measure. We will meet courage with action and place the rightful king on his throne. The days of Athaliah are over."

ATHALIAH AWOKE and was pleased to see that Mattan was gone, crept back to his temple. She hated the sun for exposing her shame but she needed an heir and there was no time for a marriage. She rolled away from the light, burying her face in her blankets.

A knock at the door, so slight that she was not sure she'd heard it, made her sit up.

"Someone desires entrance?" she called.

The door opened and her guard bowed, keeping his eyes on the floor, never looking on his queen before she was adorned.

"My queen, there is a guard below from the debtor's prison. He tells a tale, a strange tale, and says you must hear it. He says you have been betrayed, and your enemies are still alive, but he will say no more until he sees you. I think he wants money."

Athaliah frowned. Everyone wanted money for secrets, and most secrets were of no value to her.

"I will dress. Send the guard to me while I eat my breakfast, and I will hear his tale. But warn him: if this is a fool's errand, he will pay."

BACK INSIDE the temple, Joash was pale and trembling and kept locking his knees and taking gulps of air. Jehoiada embraced him.

"I am sorry that I could protect you no longer from this," Jehoiada said.

"I understand why I must be called out," Joash replied, staring straight ahead.

"When it is over, I will return to your side." Jehoiada brushed the back of his hands against his eyes and walked out, shutting Joash within the safety of the great doors.

Outside in the courtyard, Jehoiada realized he could hear no birds, no sounds of life, and felt his palms growing wet. All was in motion except his heart, which seemed to freeze.

A regiment of guards moved past the Temple, on their circuit around the palace. The commander Elishaphat glanced at the Temple and took his men on a final lap of patrol. Another regiment entered the courtyard as if to worship. A third regiment came near and stood guard at the Temple gates as men from the pledged families also entered.

A woman in the street noticed the number of men entering the courtyard and ran to tell her neighbors.

Jehoiada motioned to the priest who held the heavy drum, and he began a slow cadence. Jehoiada threw more sacrifices on the altar, one for every family, and the flames grew higher. The villagers came in numbers, more and more, pressing into the courtyard, wondering what festival or day they had forgotten.

Hearing the deep call of the drum even as the scent of the burning animals caught him, Elishaphat brought his men away from the palace and moved toward the Temple.

AT HER BREAKFAST, Athaliah heard the strange sounds coming from the Temple as her guards escorted a dirty young woman into her presence. The drums grew louder, and her stomach clenched.

"Tell me this secret," she commanded, and the girl fell to her knees to begin the story.

A PRIEST LIFTED the trumpet. His chin trembled as he drew a deep breath. Men around him lifted their swords high above their heads.

The trumpet rang clear in the silence, and the villagers were blinded by the flashing raised swords. The doors to the Temple gates slowly opened. The creaks and pops of the old bolts ricocheted across the crowd.

Joash emerged, wearing the robe of the house of David and carrying a sword inscribed with his ancient father's name. An old man who had known the grandfathers and great-grandfathers of those present, understood first and cried out. Joash stepped into the center of the Temple courtyard as the guards flanked him and the trumpet heralded the return of the true king.

ATHALIAH GLARED at her attendants, who were frozen in shock and confusion.

"No, no!" she screamed, the blood gone from her face, her eyes white and wide. The girl had not finished her tale and was still trying to explain how it had come to pass, but Athaliah's screams ended her efforts.

Athaliah tore down the main staircase and out the grand entrance, through the dead gardens and up the path to the

Temple. She did not summon a litter or stop to saddle an animal. The guards were trying to catch up, heaving great breaths as they carried their swords and armor. But she was swift, swifter than any creature in her stables, for the mighty sisters of terror and rage carried her quickly over the uneven paths. She saw the crowd, even her own guards. Elishaphat saw her first and met her eyes as he commanded the men to part.

Athaliah slowed and stumbled as she came face to face with the image of King David's line brought to life. He looked so much like his father.

"Treason!" Athaliah screamed, her hands clenched to kill him, held in front of her, shaking.

Jehoiada yelled, trying to stop Jehoshebeth, who moved from the crowd to face Athaliah. She had hidden her face with her shawl but lowered it slowly now, peeling away the dread she had always felt of this moment.

Athaliah paled. "They told me you were dead," she whispered. She screamed it now. "They told me you were dead!" She whipped around to grab her guards as she screamed, but she saw their backs, the men slipping from her fury and running now.

"Treason!" She turned and swallowed, and a flicker of life passed through her mouth, warming into a smile.

"Jehoshebeth! My daughter!" she cried. "They told me you were dead! They have betrayed us both! You must save me!" She held out her hands but Jehoshebeth took a step back.

"You lived a life of secrets. How rich that the last secrets, the greatest secrets, are kept from you alone," Jehoshebeth replied. She removed a necklace from her robes, showing it to Athaliah. "My mother once wore this, before you murdered her. There are so many questions I saved for you, Athaliah, but there is no time. Some secrets will die with you today."

Athaliah slapped the necklace out of her hands, and Elishaphat's men jumped into the gap between the women. Seeing she was abandoned by her guards and cut off from her enemy, Athaliah screamed, raking her fingernails across her own face, bringing blood to the surface. Her lips flared away from her teeth as if she would devour them all. Elishaphat's men grabbed her by the arms and no one tried to prevent them.

Jehoiada raised his arms for silence. "Athaliah, you once swam in the blood of children — now by a child's command you will drown in your own."

Joash gave his first command as king.

"Finish it."

Elishaphat moved toward her with an ax drawn.

Jehoiada's voice rose above Athaliah's curses.

"Take her outside the Temple gates to do this!" Jehoiada commanded.

The men had Athaliah by the arms, and she kicked at them with her feet, wrenching her body in every direction, biting and spitting and cursing. More men rushed in and grabbed her feet. One slapped her, drawing blood from a torn lip as she shrieked. They had her outside the Temple gates in a moment and dragged her like an animal caught on a hunt back down the path to the palace she had stolen. There, at the entrance of the stable, they dropped her onto a dung heap. The crowd of men was still around her, so the people of the village did not see the moment of her death, marked only by an ax swinging high and then a moan like a lost winter wind. The ax swung high again, and she was silenced forever.

Elishaphat commanded his men to move now to the worship places of Asherah.

"Let all who will leave freely live, but kill Mattan," he ordered.

A group of guards dispersed and ran to erase the last of her reign. The main temple of Baal and Asherah was no more than a group of altars and offering places set on a high hill. The men kicked the altars down, smashing the heads of the clay gods with the butt of their swords and crushing clay bowls underfoot. Mattan was found hidden beneath a great stone altar, and his death commanded no more dignity than Athaliah's. He did not stop crying out for mercy until the sword met its mark.

Joash walked from the courtyard toward the palace, alone, as the guards followed. The people fell to their knees as he passed, some remembering to cheer, "Long live the king!" Sebia stood in the crowd, other midwives having come with her. Jehoshebeth caught her eye and the women stared at each other as the midwives whispered without taking their gaze off Joash. Sebia fell to her knees and blessed the new king, tears on her cheeks that were lifted as she smiled broadly at Jehoshebeth. The midwives did the same, and Jehoshebeth pulled free the sharp blade that had pierced her soul.

The palace was before Joash now, its gates open, ready to receive its son. Jehoshebeth walked behind him through the open gates. A fresh wind swept past them and she inhaled a long, free breath. Had the palace ever seen such a morning? It had been a place of many dark memories and voices, but it stood clean and warm now, and they entered its gates with singing.

JOASH WAS LED to the Throne Hall. Scenes of his fathers in battle were carved in ivory and inlaid along the walls, and he saw the painting of the Red Sea parted as his people crossed into a new life. Joash felt the stillness of the room as if it were a burial ground, the dead remembered not as they were but as they could have been. A Presence drew near to him. It had swept back greater enemies than water to see him take these first steps into a new world.

JEHOSHEBETH WANDERED the halls alone. The palace had emptied immediately when Athaliah was executed; no wise servant would stay and await a new king until his goodwill was certain. Joash came today to join his fathers, but she had come to say good-bye to them at last. So she climbed the wooden steps to the hall that led her first to the bedrooms of the royal children. Lamps were burning on tables outside a few chambers, although no children had lived in these rooms for years now. She saw that the floors and walls had been well cleaned; she was the only surviving witness to what had happened here. She dropped to her knees and pressed her cheek against the floor where a child had once laid, dead. She closed her eyes and whispered the name of Yahweh.

Her father's chamber was directly above her, but she knew she would not enter it. She did not want to relive his death, or remember him in it, alone. She recalled the days he had walked the halls and been received with giggles and tugs of his robe. She tried to remember what joy the sound of his footsteps had brought in those short days. She would not return to her own chamber, either. Perhaps she would feel Midian again and sense him there still. She could disturb his memory no more. He had given her too much, she thought, in life. In his death she hoped he was free of her and this place. She rose and walked to a room off the end of the hall, a room she had seen many times as a girl but never entered. Its odor had always frightened her, the odor of incense and fluids and sweat.

She pushed the heavy door open, an olivewood door polished and made smooth. The room was sparse but not foreboding, and she smiled to think of herself as a child, grimacing with her half sisters at the births that went on here. She saw the birthing stool, still in the center of the room. There was also a bed and a table, dusty from neglect. No royal had given birth in this room for many years.

She sat on the bed and let her heart speak to her and show her the faces of those who were so loved and taken too early. She let those tears fall unminded. If this was once a place to birth new life, it was the best place to grieve that life lost. She honored the dead with her tears and felt no shame, and no shadow that should make her hold them back. But the settling sigh that always came after hard tears did not come and she wondered why.

"Why do I not rest?' she asked. "Whom have I forgotten?"

And at once, she recognized the face she had never known. "Mother."

So many had been lost, so many had been taken, but her mother had been the first. She brought forth life in this room, where it was stolen from her as well. How her mother must have suffered and wept to know her child would never be her own. Jehoshebeth's eyes burned as new tears stung her, regret that her mother was a stranger to her, forever lost in this room.

Something stirred around her and she held her breath.

He bent to her again, His powerful hand lifting the veil to the other world, and a voice, singing the song of the mother, reached from the unseen to soothe her, and a gentle kiss floated through the earth's breath to land on her cheek. His peace had found her, even here.

Jehoshebeth closed her eyes in the rapture, smiling.

The sound of a child's laughter from another part of the palace broke the spell. She opened her eyes, sighing, and saw Jehoiada standing in the doorway. He gave her his hand, and she took it. Together they walked to join the new king and witness the promise of God, true and triumphant.

From out of David's descendants God produced a
Savior for Israel, Jesus, exactly as he promised.

Acts 13:23, The Message

EPILOGUE

AND THE LAST sound that will be heard in the age of man will be the sound of a trumpet, signaling the end of our long winter's wait for justice, and the return of our own true King. But our revolution round the sun is not yet complete, and winter has not released us from her mighty grip. And so we wait, under the dim light of a Serpent Moon. . . .

A U T H O R ' S   N O T E S

A HISTORICAL NOVELIST is an archaeologist at heart. We sift through the ruins of time and try to sweep free the humanity beneath. It was a formidable task for me in *Dark Hour* to balance setting, history, and humanity.

I faced some profound problems trying to recreate this story, the first being abandoning my Western mindset so that I could fully enter the story. In Jehoshebeth's day, there was no Messiah and no hope of salvation as we think of it today. There were legions of competing gods and goddesses; women especially partook in the cults because they could set up altars within the home and worship as they went about their daily activities. When *Yahweh* declared He was the great I Am and that no other god must be worshiped but Him, it upset the balance of a society that was used to letting everyone worship as they pleased.

Another problem was hiding Joash for six years. Hiding in the Temple complex poses all sorts of obstacles, including issues of ritual uncleanness which would have prevented Joash from entering the Temple. Because he was hidden with his nurse-maid and women have more times of ritual uncleanness, the problem is compounded. For my novel, I chose to keep them in the priest's living quarters, but these quarters may have been offices of sorts and not actual living spaces. No one will ever be sure how Jehoshebeth and Jehoiada pulled off this feat, but I admire them for what was surely amazing resourcefulness.

Some other questions, too, I answered with speculation. The most frequently asked question I get when working on histori-cal novels is, "Did that really happen?" Readers especially want to know if the characters existed. You can read the portion of the Bible this story is drawn from (2 Chronicles 21–23 and 2 Kings 10–11) to get an idea of the "real" characters. I assure you that Jezebel, Ahab, Athaliah, Jehoiada, Jehoshebeth, and Joash were indeed actual people in history. Ahab and Jezebel have been well documented in extrabiblical sources. In fact, Jezebel's grandniece founded the ancient city of Carthage. (Carthage's historians are embroiled in debate over whether her people practiced mass child sacrifice there. It's a subject of much interest to me as I work on my next novel, *Midnight Throne*. If you're curious to know more, read the *Wall Street Journal*'s article by Andrew Higgins "Carthage Expert Battles to Clear Its Baby-killing Reputation," May 27, 2005.)

If you read the biblical accounts of this story, you'll notice *Jehoshebeth* is also spelled *Jehosheba*. I decided to keep her name as Jehoshebeth to honor a friend, Beth, who struggled against breast cancer while trying to save her young son from a termi-nal illness. God intervened in her story, too, and her son is alive today, but Beth went home to be with the Lord. Her bravery and fierce courage inspired much of the strength Jehoshebeth had.

The next question is one you won't solve, but I'd like to bring it to your attention anyway. (No sense in me being the only one to have a sleepless night.) Was Athaliah Jezebel's biological daughter or her stepdaughter? Scholars are undecided. The Bible refers to her as "Ahab's daughter," and of course Ahab was married to Jezebel. Ultimately, however, I decided it didn't matter. "Daughters become their mothers" seems to be a timeless axiom that is dependent on proximity, not biology. My mother never killed anything in cold blood, except for a hairy caterpillar that bit my brother. I watched as she bludgeoned it to death with a shovel. Poor Athaliah — she probably witnessed much worse. We'll cover that territory, and Jezebel's story, in *Midnight Throne.*

Another question which stumped your humble author for a while was the question of Christ's lineage: If God saved the line of David through Joash, why isn't Joash listed in the genealogy of Christ, such as given in Matthew? The answer is deceptively simple: Matthew skipped generations, assuming his readers would understand his pattern. He left out Ahaziah and Joash, but they are certainly in the line. Theoretically, other heirs of the house of David might have been alive to continue the bloodline. But God used Joash. It's startling to think that the future of Christianity, of the person of Jesus Christ, was held in the hands of one terrified woman defying an evil queen. It's a story we should read from Scripture to our daughters often.

For details on setting and culture, I relied heavily on the thoughtful work of the Biblical Archaeology Society archives, plus Lawrence E. Stager's and Philip J. King's book, *Life in Biblical Israel,* as well as the expert advice of renowned professor Dr. John Walton of Wheaton College, a respected authority of the First Temple period. Dr. Walton read the early manuscript and made incredibly detailed, comprehensive suggestions. It was a humbling education for me, having already combed through dozens of research texts. Most of the insights I have into the culture and the emotional connections to the cults of the time came from him. Dr. Walton also answered detailed questions about structures, chronology, and rituals. He was the one to bring to my attention the seeming impossibility of hiding a child in the Temple bedrooms for so long. I admire Dr. Walton tremendously for his ability to balance rigorous scholarship with sincere faith.

There were, however, a few key points from Dr. Walton that I did ignore for dramatic purposes. As an example, Jehoshebeth would not have had a horse, as the royals rode donkeys and spared their horses for battle. But a donkey charging up to the palace in a storm to save the children lacks a certain flair. I also had to condense time to fit the story into one novel. (You'll get a fuller understanding of the length of time the story spans by reading the biblical accounts, and you may be interested to read about the life and rule of Joash after he becomes king.) So please blame me for details or dialogue that may be inconsistent with scholarly understanding of this period.

Minor issues like these can trip up a writer, or can provide interesting food for thought. Did any of you wonder about the name of Jonah, the boy who anointed Jehu? Some scholars believe this Jonah is the same Jonah who will later get swallowed by a whale. Dr. Walton kindly created a timeline for me, showing me that Jonah would most likely not have been born quite yet, or at least be far too young to undertake this assignment. But I loved contemplating the two meeting.

The red string tied around Jehoshebeth's wrist during the birth of Ayla was another point for contemplation. Red string is wound around the tomb of Rachel seven times and then is cut to make bracelets that are worn to protect a woman during childbirth or to guard against envy or the "evil eye." No one is sure when the bracelets became part of Jewish tradition, although red string is mentioned in the Old Testament when Tamar gave birth. This old Jewish custom was newly popularized when Madonna began wearing one after studying Kabbalah. Unfortunately, it has become more an object of superstition than a reminder of the matriarchs of our faith.

Finally, a trivial question: Why aren't my novels dedicated to anyone? (My dad especially would like a book dedicated to him, for all the brilliant ideas he's fed me, quality plots like time-traveling squirrels.) THE SERPENT MOON TRILOGY will focus on the most evil women in Scripture; how could I dedicate the books to anyone? (A few candidates have come to mind, but that's where those names will stay.)

For those of you, like me, who once believed the lie that the Bible is a tale of repressed women mastered by men and submitting through force, coming to the tale of Athaliah and Jehoshebeth is a shock. Athaliah did what no woman had ever done, ruling as sole monarch in Judah. Jehoshebeth was a formidable enemy and ultimately proved to be her undoing. I read the Bible now and am impressed with the role of women in the story: We were spies, allies, mediators, murderers, advocates, heroines, and lovers. We inspired greatness, lured others to destruction, and saved nations. We birthed and buried the Christ, and were the first to witness the new age of humanity when He rose from the dead.

I believe God has written boldly of good and evil and encourages us to draw the right conclusions about the men and women recorded in His pages. Similarly, I hope you will investigate the passages of the Bible from which this story is drawn and reach your own conclusions about its meaning. And I hope you will join me in the summer of 2007 for the next release of the Serpent Moon Trilogy, *Midnight Throne*. Until then, my friend, remember: *He is near.*

Ginger Garrett, January 2006

www.gingergarrett.com

READER'S GUIDE

1. Why was Athaliah so threatened by people who recognized and worshiped only one God? Are monotheists more difficult to rule than agnostics? When a country is divided over religion, what role does the government have in promoting peace?

2. Compare the romantic love Jehoshebeth felt for Midian with the self-sacrificing love she chose with Jehoiada.

3. Late in the novel, it seems as if God has allowed the line of David to end, nullifying His promise to the people. Have there been times in your own life when it felt as if God had let you down? How did it shape your faith?

4. What other children in biblical stories had to be hidden from evil rulers? What role did these children play in setting their people free? What is the greatest threat to children in the world today?

5. Throughout the novel, innocent people die so that Athaliah can secure her reign. Why does God seem to allow evil to prosper? Why do we allow it?

6. Consider the many supernatural elements of the story. Was the supernatural or spiritual world more evident or believable in biblical times?

7. In this story there was no hope yet of heaven and an afterlife with the Messiah. Without this hope, how did people feel about worship, sacrifice, and a love of God?

8. By the end of the novel, Athaliah has succumbed to evil and Jehoshebeth has clung to faith. What is the price each woman paid for her decision?

ACKNOWLEDGMENTS

I WANT TO thank some key people who have enriched this book and encouraged me as an author.

Dr. John Walton, professor of Old Testament at Wheaton College and Graduate School. He was recommended to me by several sources as the absolute best in his field, and I was not disappointed. His passion for understanding the Old Testament in its cultural context is inspiring.

Erin Healy, the editor who taught me that POV isn't a lane on the highway. Erin showed me how to write the book I envisioned. She was relentless and I am forever indebted.

The team at NavPress: Jeff Gerke, Andrea Christian, Jessica Chappell, Melanie Knox, Terry Behimer, Dan Rich, Kent Wilson, Darla Hightower, Kris Wallen, and the sales team: Toby Lorenc, Sheila Dean, Heather Hebert, Sean Mitchell, Brent Klassen, Candis Pflueger, Eric Helus, Michele McGuire, and Pamela Mendoza. I said it at dinner with the staff a few years ago, and I'll echo it again here: I feel sorry for any writer who hasn't had a chance to publish with NavPress. Nav invests in writers, not just books.

Lee Hough, my fourth agent, and the first not to quit the business after representing me. Lee is a great agent, a fine Texan, and a man of wisdom and patience.

Ann Fisher, for breaking me of my love of commas and cheering me on. Ann has a skilled eye for knowing when to push you to explore a subject, and when to give up.

My writer friends: Siri Mitchell, Jay Forman, Rob Eager, Sue Lang, Lisa Crayton, Jenn Doucette, and Mary DeMuth. Each of you has made me laugh and encouraged me to push through every obstacle.

I also have some special friends that I must mention:

Penny, Robin, Betsy, Tammy, and Peggy at First Christian. Everyone at First Christian creates an atmosphere of down-home Southern family, where strangers are welcome at the table and Christ is always present.

To Pamela Holliday, Carolynn James, Gidget Nichols, Ashley Clark, and Louise and Jim Reinoehl at Northpoint Community Church, Sherrill McCracken, plus the three best girlfriends I could ever ask for, Stephanie Linnabary, Courtney Doss, and Riki Craze. I admire each of you *so very much*. Each of you gives me courage, and Jim keeps me humble.

To Mom and Dad and Martin and Elaine, thanks for your constant support and always thinking I'm special. My grand-mother Eloise keeps me in her prayers every day, which is important when my brain goes numb and I hate myself for signing a book contract. For Priss and Craig, Genessa and Zack, Chris and Andrea, Wes and Stephanie, and Steve and Stephanie, another thanks. My sister-in-law Andrea has allowed her house to be ransacked by my kids so that I could write when a deadline was tight, plus her passion is gourmet cooking, and she frequently feeds me.

And finally, my husband, Mitch. What can you say about a man who spends his Saturdays taking the kids to the park so I can write, and does the laundry too? I am eternally thankful my dog had the good sense to pick him out from the crowd thirteen years ago and to bite my next date.

Excerpt from

MIDNIGHT THRONE

Coming in June 2007

HE SAW the spirit only briefly, a glimpse of its dark hair and slight body moving silently through the forest. He had known it was there before he saw it. The hair on his arms had raised and he held up a hand to the men following him, who all drew their horses to a quick, noisy stop. Birds called above them and squirrels fled from lower branches to the higher perches. The silence returned.

A roar shook the men. They held their breath until they could hear the lion's steps cracking the undergrowth. He was moving away.

When the lion's steps grew faster and fainter, Ahab knew the spirit was near. The men, ignorant, mumbled and urged to keep their horses still. Ahab saw the spirit in that moment, her bow drawn tight against the gutstring, sliding between the trees in front of him. She lifted her head to draw the scent from the wind and let her arrow fly. The lion screamed. Then she ran.

He jumped from his horse and followed. The forest was nothing like his arid home, and he tripped and fell as vines caught his ankles and branches slapped his face. He tried to move faster and leap higher, but the forest had broken many rash men and she prevailed again. Panting, he leaned against a tree.

He had heard that this land of the north worshiped a great goddess, a fearsome woman who was not of man, but he had never imagined she would seduce so perfectly with a glance. Her magic wove its way into his flesh, biting and burrowing, devouring weaker promises and memories of love. He held up his hand and looked at it as the leaves above parted with a breeze to allow the sun a view.

His skin was pristine. He looked unchanged.

"Our bodies lie until age forces them to tell the truth." He sighed. "Keep then my secret from my men so that I will not be made a fool."

He staggered back to his men, torn and bleeding, and resumed the journey north.

THAT NIGHT he slept close to the fire, and the forest fog stole around the party as they made camp, blanketing them in the way of the wild, that bitter mother, who welcomes and warns in the same caress. Darkness was alive here. Eyes blinked from behind the trees. Throats opened and sang. Footsteps broke through vines and dead wood as creatures drew closer to smell the men and horses. The horses snorted and circled.

A thick brew was passed around, an elixir they called saddle cure because of its powerful magic that could put a trail-weary explorer to sleep in minutes and soothe sore muscles. The next morning they would feel worse for drinking it, but no man on the trail thinks of tomorrow. The lions crawling through the underbrush nearby reminded them there may be no need.

So Ahab drew nearest the fire and let the other men take the outer edges of camp to sleep. He felt a few sparks land too near and brushed them away. He would rather suffer a small singe than a bigger bite. Life as a king meant weighing which pain should get preference. Ahab had grown up watching his father get devoured by the needling little wars of politics even as he crushed armies. King Omri had been dead for two weeks, and Ahab knew the world was changed. The wars for new land were over; now men would die for gold and gold alone. He would make his first bold move as the warrior king of Israel tomorrow, when he claimed a bride he did not want.

He had gone on many such journeys with his father to claim lands and peoples. It was a simple matter: He who struck first and hardest won. The sword was impartial to temperaments and whims. Politics and war were alike in that neither gave room for desire; all was won and weighed by leverage. So it was with this expedition. A princess would be given as a treaty between the kingdoms, and the kingdoms would unite against the savage Assyrians growing in power along the borders, who would go to war for the trade routes in the heartland.

Ahab was not pleased to take a wife. He had a harem of women he could call on to serve him in silence. A wife was a burden he was ill equipped to handle, for what arguments could be solved with the sword? He lived for blood, not women. But this woman was a necessary cost. Ahab spat into the fire thinking of it. The fire didn't blink, and his gesture was lost. Ahab sighed and turned over.

Deep in the night, a spark singed him along his arms. The touch was so slight that Ahab only acknowledged it in his mind and did not even wake. The heat from the fire had kept the night bugs away but made him too warm to sleep in his clothes, so he slept naked, covering only the essentials with his blanket. Then the sparks came more numerous, spitting on and poking into his exposed skin along the thick part of his arms and chest. Finally he sat up in disgust, determined to move away from the fire's reach.

But the fire was only glowing embers. There were no sparks.

He heard a soft laugh catch in a throat, and he reached for his sword. A hand shot from the darkness and caught his. The creature, on all fours, edged closer and smiled. Ahab froze. Her eyes were large black hollows. Her lips were dark and sharp-edged, though full through the middle. And she was beautiful. The moonlight made her pale olive skin look like polished marble, and he wondered if she would return to stone by morning. The goddess crawled across the dust and dead sparks, holding him firmly. She dropped the arrow she had used to rouse him.

He drew back, holding his breath, using his other hand to arrange the blanket where it was suddenly needed. Her long fingers moved across his face and she closed her eyes when she touched his mouth. She breathed deeply, then looked at him. Ahab felt cold though he was so near the fire pit; his mouth seemed numb and he found no strength to resist as her arm moved to her belt and brought up a knife fashioned as a serpent. She held it to his face, her beautiful mouth occupying all of his mind and will so that he could not move as he watched it.

No man in the camp made any sound beyond snoring and turning. She released his hand and crawled closer so that her knees were against his hip. She lifted a section of his hair and cut it loose, returning the knife to her belt and the hair to a pouch next to it. She looked at him again now and waited. She did not blink.

Then Ahab remembered a dream he had once, when he had been a boy, of falling. In this dream, he fell from a very safe place into a deep, cold well where no one could hear him. He remembered how every revolution, every stone that passed by as he fell into the darkness, marked the bitter descent. When he awoke that morning, he saw he had only fallen from the bed as he slept, but he cried anyway, then wiped his tears with vigor so that his servant Obadiah would have nothing to report to his harsh father at breakfast.

But now he fell and did not dream. He moved his hands to the small of her back and felt her small frame, moving his hands up her back to the shoulders and drawing her face to his now. The lines of her mouth split into a smile, and he kissed her. He held her there as she released a soft breath into his mouth. Swallowing, he kissed her again and reached to pull her on top of him. She slipped from his grasp and stole back into the darkness, like a little bird that only needed a moment's distraction to make its escape.

He laid back on the earth and cried.

ABOUT THE AUTHOR

GINGER GARRETT is a novelist with a passion for exploring the lives of biblical women and understanding how their ancient stories impact our lives today. Ginger also enjoys writing nonfiction for women and teens. Beyond writing, her interests include supporting The For Pete's Sake Foundation, a nonprofit that raises awareness and funds for children with Wiskott-Aldrich Syndrome.

You can learn more about Ginger's books, including her newest NavPress novels, by visiting her at her website: www.gingergarrett.com.

EXCITING NEW FICTION FROM NAVPRESS.

Murder, Mayhem, and a Fine Man
Claudia Mair Burney   1-57683-978-8
For Amanda Bell Brown, turning forty is murder! How's a
woman supposed to grapple with her faith when she finds
herself in the middle of mysteries—and not the God kind?

Chosen
Ginger Garrett   1-57683-651-7
She came to conquer a king but discovered a man and, in
the end, saved a nation. What really happened in Xerxes'
palace? Queen Esther's secret diaries tell all.

Chateau of Echoes
Siri L. Mitchell   1-57683-914-1
Suddenly widowed in a foreign country, Frederique Farmer
did what any girl would do: She bought a castle. She just
never imagined that its history would bring her back to life.

Stealing Adda
Tamara Leigh   1-57683-925-7
Just because a girl writes best-selling romances doesn't mean
she gets to live one.

Watching the Tree Limbs
Mary E. DeMuth   1-57683-926-5
At age nine, Mara knows many things (how to do laundry,
for instance), but there are lots of things she doesn't know—
like her mother, or her father, or even God.

Visit your local Christian bookstore,
call NavPress at 1-800-366-7788, or log on to www.navpress.com
to purchase.
To locate a Christian bookstore near you,
call 1-800-991-7747.

NAVPRESS
BRINGING TRUTH TO LIFE
www.navpress.com